A DAN CONNOR MYSTERY

PALE MIST
Drifting

R. J. McMillen

Shogun Press
shogunpress@rjmcmillen.com

LIBRARY AND ARCHIVES CANADA CATALOGUING
IN PUBLICATION
MCMILLEN, R.J., 1945—AUTHOR
Pale Mist drifting / R.J. McMillen.

(A Dan Connor mystery)
Issued in print and electronic formats.
ISBN: 978-1-7752002-2-2

I Title. II. Series: McMillen, R.J., 1945—. Dan Connor mystery

Editor: Linda Rich
Proofreader: Monika Hope
Design: Jim Barnes & Luis Mancera McCormick

PALE MIST DRIFTING

Prologue

Samantha Chauvet heard the girls long before she saw them.
There were three of them down on the beach below the cliff
where she was walking, their laughter echoing off the rocks as
they sat on the warm sand.

It was a beautiful day, the sunlight sparkling on the
water and a blue sky reflecting off the surface, and there
weren't many like that on Porcher Island. It was located only a
hundred miles or so south of Alaska, and while there was
seldom snow, on most days there was rain. It was why she had
come here. Not that she liked the rain. She didn't, but most of
the other people in the group she had so carefully cultivated
had problems with their health, among them an allergy to the
sun's rays. They needed the clouds to protect their skin and
Samantha needed the people. It had taken time for her to
recognize and acknowledge that fact and it hadn't been easy.
At first all she had known was that they needed her. After all,
none of them came from families like hers, families with pure
bloodlines that could trace their ancestry back for generations.
None of them had the same superior genes. None of them had
her intelligence, or her looks, or her money. If only . . .

If only the accident that had taken her leg hadn't
happened. But it had, and she needed these people even if they
came from families she would not usually associate with. If
she was going to be able to use the masks and the totems and

1

the other things she had asked Martin to bring her in order to punish the people who had teased and bullied her because of her leg, she needed them all.

The accident hadn't been her fault of course—she had only been three at the time—and it certainly hadn't been the fault of anyone in her family. Some ignorant peasant had been driving the truck that crashed into the car she and her nanny had been riding in and her leg had been crushed. Her parents had told her she was lucky to have survived, and her father made sure the peasant would never hurt anyone again, but even with all their money and position they hadn't been able to save her leg.

***

The leader of the group of girls she was watching had two legs, both of them long and smooth and attached to a sleek, lithe body. Samantha guessed she had either come off a visiting yacht or was on a tour and had rented the boat in Prince Rupert. Other than the people living in Samantha's small community there were less than thirty people living on Porcher, and all but one of them lived in Oona River, on the east coast and made their living from fishing. None of them looked anything like this.

When the girl turned to smooth more sun tan oil or her body, gold glistened on her neck, one of her wrists, and an ankle. In fact everything about her looked golden: her skin, her hair, even her bikini. The surge of jealousy Samantha felt was familiar and she didn't fight it. She welcomed it. She even encouraged it. It was what drove her. What she used to focus her energy.

That's how I was meant to be, she thought. *I was supposed to look like that. If only the accident hadn't happened* . . .

There might be nothing she could do about the accident, but she had decided several years ago there were things she could do to those who had tormented her as she was growing up and the thought of those things made her smile.

***

"Hey, Suze! Need a hand?"

The question came from one of the girls and something about the way it was said told Samantha there was more to it than just the words. It sounded odd. Sarcastic maybe. Said with a sneer. And it was followed by a chorus of snickers.

The cruel tone was so familiar that for a moment Samantha thought they were talking to her, but that was impossible. They were looking in the opposite direction and hadn't seen her where she stood in the shadow of the trees far above them. She turned to follow their gaze and saw there was someone still aboard the boat they had arrived in, which lay at anchor in the lagoon. It was another girl and she was moving awkwardly along the deck, leaning against the cabin to support herself as she trailed an arm that ended above the elbow. Her hunched shoulders and bent head said she was used to being left out. Used to being taunted, just as Samantha had so often been taunted.

Samantha turned her attention back to the girls on the beach and mentally added them to the list she had been working on for years. She didn't know who they were, and didn't care. It wasn't necessary to have names and addresses. Those were only for people who lacked her abilities and her resources. People who didn't have access to the power she was soon going to wield. All she had to do was wait for Martin to bring her the last of the talismans and jujus she had asked for and she would be ready. She almost laughed aloud at the thought.

Chapter 1

A shrill scream pierced the night air and brought Dan Connor racing out onto the deck. The evening had been quiet, he and his partner, Claire, enjoying their last hours together before she left to take up a three month research contract in northern Australia. This intrusion into their serenity was, to say the least, unwelcome.

"What on earth was that?" Claire asked as she joined him. "It sounded like a banshee!"

He smiled and put his arm around her shoulders although his eyes continued to scan the marina and the shore beyond.

"I think it was a false alarm." His gaze drifted up to the mast above the cabin. "I've heard something similar a couple of times before, but I thought I had it fixed."

He pointed to the wires leading up to the array of antennae fixed to the masthead. "Every now and then the wind hits at just the right angle to create some kind of vibration between those wires and the mast. I've tried adding straps to tighten them up, but I guess I still need more." He turned her gently towards the cabin door. "At least this time it wasn't in the middle of the night. Scared the hell out of me last time it happened. It was two o'clock in the morning and I was sound asleep—dreaming of you no doubt." He kissed the top of her head. "Not the best time for a banshee to come calling!"

She laughed. "Is there ever a good time to hear a banshee?"

***

Before the interruption they had been in the wheelhouse of Dan's boat, standing in front of the computer looking at a map of the north coast of Australia where Claire would be heading the following day. In their absence, the screen had gone dark, but a quick flick of Claire's finger brought it back to life. Dan leaned down and peered over Claire's shoulder at the image that appeared.

"It looks empty," he said. "Are there any towns there?"

She laughed and moved the mouse to reveal more of the coastline.

"There's at least one," she said. "But it isn't very big." She expanded the view. "There it is. It's called Maningrida."

"Does it at least have a store?" Dan asked. "How will you get supplies?"

"They've promised the boat will be fully stocked when I arrive," she replied, "but they said there's two or three small stores there where I can pick up anything else I need."

"How about a doctor? I don't see anything that looks like a hospital." Dan put his hands on her shoulders and rested his chin on her head. "What if you get hurt?"

Claire leaned back and looked up at the man she had shared her life with for the past five years. A few strands of gray had crept into his dark hair, and the scar that ran high across his cheekbone had been joined by a few lines around his eyes, some courtesy of the weather but most due to his job. They both had their own careers, she as a marine biologist and he as a detective with the Royal Canadian Mounted Police, but while they had often been apart for days, and occasionally weeks at a time, they had always stayed in close contact. This trip was different. They would be a long way apart for over three months and because of the difference in time, staying in touch was not going to be easy.

"I'll be fine," she said, reaching up to touch his cheek. "The dugongs live in the inlet where the water's shallow. I won't be out on the open ocean." She pointed to the screen where a scattering of roads and houses had appeared. "There's even an airport and it's only an hour or so to fly from Darwin. You could come and visit me."

Dan laughed. "Yeah, sure. Somehow I don't think my boss would agree, and even if he did, it's what? Seventeen hours? Seventeen hours locked in a sardine can flying over the Pacific? And that only gets me to Sydney. How many hours after that to get up to Darwin? We're talking close to a week just to get there and back. Australia's a damn big country— and you know how I feel about flying."

She did know how he felt about flying. It was one of the few things he was afraid of. It was something he had admitted to her early on in their relationship when she had asked him why they didn't simply take the plane down to Vancouver instead of taking his boat. After all the plane would only take an hour while *Dreamspeaker* would take almost three days.

"I like being on the water," he had said, shrugging off her question. "I like going slow. It lets me relax. I can watch the coast slide by, see the bears and otters on the beaches and the eagles in the trees. If I'm lucky I'll see orcas, and humpbacks, and maybe dolphins. I would miss all of that if I flew down on a plane."

"Surely you can see otters and orcas here at the marina. Isn't that enough?"

"Nope. Not even close," he had answered, but his response had been too quick, too easy, and she had seen the evasion behind it.

When she had raised her eyebrows and continued to look at him, he had given her a sheepish look and told her the truth. "Flying's just something I don't like to do. It scares the hell out of me. It's . . . unnatural. Those things have no right getting up into the air let alone staying there."

Listening to him now, she could hear the worry beneath the disparaging humour and she stood up and wrapped her arms around him. "Do you really mind my going? It's only twelve weeks. I'll be back before you know it."

He snorted and pulled her close. "Yeah right. Only twelve weeks. More if you add in travel time. I'll barely have time to miss you—although come to think of it, I did see this good-looking woman walking around town the other day . . ."

He doubled over as Claire poked her fist into his stomach.

"Don't even think of it," she said. "If you want something to do you can fix that winch up front so it actually works properly, and those doors in the stateroom need some work too."

"Yes ma'am," Dan said, pulling her back into his arms. "And no, I really don't mind. In fact I'm happy for you. Yes, I'm going to miss you, and yes, I'll probably worry about you, but I know you'll be careful and it's too good an opportunity to miss. I'll be fine. Now tell me about these things you'll be studying." He pointed to the odd-looking creature that had appeared on the screen.

"Dugongs," she said, sitting back down in front of the computer. "I've been reading up on them and they really are quite amazing. They're related to manatees." She pointed to the image of a large, gray creature with a short trunk-like nose and tusks.

"Not quite as cute as a sea otter," he said, "but probably better looking than a banshee."

She sighed and shook her head. She would miss this easy bantering. "I don't think they have any banshees over there—although I'm sure they have their own spirit creatures." Her face turned serious. "Do you believe in them—spirit creatures?"

"You mean like the ones Walker sometimes talks about?"

She nodded.

He took a long time to answer and when he did he didn't dismiss the idea outright as she had expected.

"Not really, but I know he believes in them, and he's one of the most sensible and grounded people I know so I can't completely dismiss the possibility. Hell, you and I have both seen the kind of strength he can find when he calls on them, but whether it's really spirits or simply the strength of his belief that works for him, I don't know."

He glanced at the beautifully carved paddle that was attached to the wall of the wheelhouse. It had been a gift from Joel, a young Haida man he had helped a couple of years before.

"If you had asked me that question a few years ago, I would have had a completely different answer," he said. "Now . . ." He shook his head.

Claire watched him for a few moments then shrugged, picked up the cup she had been drinking out of and took it to the sink.

"Well, no spirit, even a well-intentioned one, is going to help me pack for this trip, so I had better get to it." She turned to look at him. "Will you come to the airport and see me off?"

"Depends on which airport," he answered with a smile. "Port Hardy is an easy drive. Vancouver on the other hand . . ."

She laughed. "Knowing how you feel about flying I wouldn't drag you to Vancouver. Port Hardy will be fine, thank you."

They moved to the master stateroom and Dan sat and watched as Claire sorted through her clothes. Like everything else she did, she was quietly efficient, quickly discarding anything she didn't think would be necessary. She was almost finished when Dan's cellphone rang.

"Claire left yet?" It was Markleson, his boss, whose unmistakeable voice rasped liked crushed gravel. Although the man swore almost daily he was going to quit smoking and get in shape, he had never succeeded in doing either. Instead he seemed to gain weight and smoke more every year.

"Her plane leaves Port Hardy early in the morning. Why? What's up?" Dan knew Markleson was fond of Claire, but he wasn't the kind to call simply to say good-bye.

"I've got a job for you. Come in and see me first thing." Markleson ended the call before Dan could answer.

"Right. Aye-aye sir," Dan said as he stared at the now silent phone he held in his hand. When he wasn't out on the water investigating a case, he spent his time working out of the local RCMP station. Markleson, who as North Island Commander had his office there, was well aware that Dan would be at his desk in the morning just as he was every morning when he was in town, so why had he gone to the trouble of calling?

"Problems?" Claire asked.

"Maybe," he answered. "Something's bothering Markleson and that usually means he's got some unpleasant job he wants me to do."

"Well at least if you're on a job you won't have time to worry about me," she said. "And that's a good thing."

He laughed. "I'll worry about you anyway, but yes, it's probably better that I have something to keep me occupied. I just hope it doesn't mean heading up north. You might be heading into summer down-under, but it's already well into fall here and the winds up in those channels make for some very uncomfortable seas."

She snapped the lid of her suitcase closed and put her arms around him. "So it sounds like it's me who should be worried about you, not the other way round." He pulled her into a bear-hug. "No," he said. "We'll both be fine."

Chapter 2

It was cool out on deck when Dan stepped outside. The scent of mist hung in the air, a promise of rain to come, and he pushed his hands deep into the pockets of his jacket. He hadn't slept well since Claire left and the memory of her stepping onto the plane in Port Hardy two days ago was constantly in his mind, repeating itself over and over again in an unending series of goodbyes.

If he had it figured correctly, she would be somewhere between Sydney and Darwin, staring down at some vast desert shimmering under the rays of a hot sun while here in Port McNeill he was looking out over a dark sea lit only by distant stars. Maybe once she had landed and he was able to talk to her he would be able to relax, get some sleep and focus on the job Markleson had given him, but so far, he was getting nowhere.

He moved to the stern where the lights of the marina were blocked by the roof of the wheelhouse. Beyond the breakwater, starlight danced on the restless surface of the water and a glowing line of surf marked the far shore of the bay. Above him the sky had the bottomless depth of infinity and it echoed his loneliness.

Loneliness, at least loneliness like this, was something new to him and he didn't like it. Seven years ago, when his wife, Susan, had been murdered, he had at first been too shocked to feel anything but horror and disbelief, and then grief and guilt had taken over, a combination that had driven him to alcohol and ultimately to quitting the RCMP.

He had renamed the old fish-packer he had converted *Dreamspeaker*, a name he and Susan had planned to give the boat they had dreamed about getting, and tried to lose himself in the maze of islands off the west coast of Canada. For almost two years he had been alone—but he hadn't been lonely. He had spent his time huddled over his pain, holding it close, immersing himself in the memory of Susan's torn, blood-stained body, trying to convince himself that it had not been his fault.

The memory still brought sadness and regret, but it was more distant now, blurred by time and newer, happier memories of his time with Claire.

He shook his head and breathed in the clean, damp air. He needed to focus on the present, not linger in the past. Somewhere out there in the darkness a thief was at work, and Markleson had assigned Dan the job of finding him.

On the surface the case should be straightforward. Dan had spent most of his working life tracking down thieves and solving robberies. He had done it so many times over the past years it was almost routine: talk to neighbours, interview people on the street, check for security cameras, visit the pawnshops. But this case was unique. There *were* no streets, no cameras, no pawnshops. Only a handful of people living in tiny, remote communities.

According to the reports he had been given these were very different kinds of robberies performed by a very different kind of thief. Thieves usually operated in cities or towns and stole from the wealthy or the careless. They stole goods that had commercial value and were easy to dispose of—jewels or silver or art. Maybe electronics. Sometimes cash.

This thief had done none of that. The only things missing were ancient artifacts: masks and rattles and cedar robes that had been hidden away for years in tiny villages, never seen by anyone but the people who lived there—and that didn't make sense.

These villages were too small to even be on the map let alone to attract a thief. Too far up narrow, winding inlets for fishermen to bother with. Too deep in long fjords for tourists to venture.

And that left only the people who lived there—but Dan knew that none of them would even think of taking something so important, so intrinsic to their way of life. Something that would be almost impossible to sell because no museum or art gallery would accept it. And that meant it would have to be for a collector.

And unlike museums and galleries or even second-hand stores and pawnshops, collectors who traded in forbidden goods didn't advertise their collections and generally kept a very low profile, which made them hard to find.

***

There had been four thefts reported so far, each from a different village, each located deep in a different inlet, and each separated from the others by many miles of ocean. The list of stolen items included a Thunderbird transformation mask, a wool cape woven in what was described as ravenstail, a chilkat apron, a cedar robe, a bentwood box, several rattles and a chief's staff. All were very old and according to the statements Dan had read, each told in brief, halting language that spoke volumes about the depth of the loss, they had been in the respective families for many generations. There were no photographs to go with the descriptions—these were sacred

14

items, cherished by the members of the community they belonged to and seen only by them—and that was going to make them almost impossible to properly identify even if they were found.

Dan knew why Markleson had assigned him the case. Not only was he the designated "lone wolf," intimately familiar with the coast after his many years travelling up and down its shore, he was also one of the few people able to visit those villages, some of which would not normally welcome outsiders, and certainly not a white police officer. But then there weren't many white police officers who wore a cedar bracelet given to him by a grateful village family, or that had a button-blanket hanging in their stateroom and a carved canoe paddle in the wheelhouse.

The day he had received those gifts was still vividly imprinted in his memory: the crowd of people clustered on the shore to celebrate the return of one their own and thank the man who had found him. The tables groaning under the plates of venison, halibut, smoked salmon, prawns, and crab. Bannock cooking over the fire. Handshakes and laughter. Walker sitting on a log on the beach, relaxed and happy.

Walker. Dan smiled as he thought of the man who had become his friend. He could still picture him as he had seen him that day, bare shoulders rippling with muscle, long braids hanging down his back, his canoe pulled high up onto the beach by willing hands to ensure he wouldn't have far to walk on his crippled legs.

Ten, even eight years ago, Dan would never have put 'friend' and 'Walker' into the same sentence. Then, Walker had simply been yet another criminal convicted of robbing a bank, a criminal Dan himself had arrested following a chase that had led up onto the roof of the building and that had resulted in Walker falling onto the street below.

It was that fall that had put him into his canoe when after months of hospitalization followed by two years of jail time he had been unable to walk more than a few feet. Now that Dan thought about it, it was also what had, in the odd and convoluted way that everything related to Walker seemed to happen, led to the start of their friendship.

A dog barked somewhere up in the town and pulled Dan's thoughts back to the present. Now was not the time for daydreaming. What he needed was to find a place to start his search. A plan for how to go about it. And most of all more knowledge about what had been stolen.

He knew next to nothing about traditional regalia, and while he had seen and admired many totem poles and carvings in the communities he had visited, he had no knowledge of their significance or of how to interpret them. Perhaps if he researched that he would be better able to understand exactly what it was he was looking for, but doing so would take more time than he wanted to spend. He preferred action. Looking at a screen or studying the pages of a book or a document was too slow. Too far removed from what was happening. Even worse, it would give the thief more time to move the items, making tracing them more difficult.

***

Dan stood by the rail and stared out across the water, searching the darkness for inspiration. To the east a scattering of lights identified the streets and houses of Sointula on Malcolm Island, and beyond that the snow-capped peaks of the coastal mountains glowed with a ghostly radiance. It had been a night just like this when Walker had last visited him and Dan wished he would return. Talking to Walker would be by far the fastest way to learn what he needed to learn.

Like the people in the communities where the thefts had occurred, Walker was indigenous. He had relatives spread up and down the coast and had probably visited all of them over the past few years, many in the last few months. He would know exactly what it was that Dan was looking for.

And there was something else. Walker had once made his living as a thief and he could well have some ideas about how a thief might operate in these remote areas. It was even possible he knew where these kinds of traditional items could be sold.

Dan smiled. Yes, if Walker would go with him to talk to the villagers, maybe together they could get a better idea of not only what these items looked like, but also who might have taken them and where they were likely to end up.

He dismissed the idea almost as soon as he came up with it. It was impossible. He had no idea where Walker was or how to find him. He hadn't seen him for months and he had no way of contacting him. Walker didn't use a radio and usually spent his days out on the water in his canoe and his nights in some rough shack or lean-to he had built in a remote cove. Going out to look for him would be pointless. Even a brief glance at a chart of the area showed hundreds of miles of shoreline stretching along a multitude of inlets, islands, bays and estuaries. It would be like looking for the proverbial needle in a haystack.

Dan straightened up, and drew in a deep breath. He needed to do something to get his mind and body working. He had spent his life searching for that first loose thread, the one that would start unravelling a crime that at first appeared to be perfectly woven. There was always an opening. A flaw in the illusion. He just had to find it. It was a challenge he enjoyed.

Pulling open the cabin door he slipped off his sneakers and took off his jacket. He shivered as the night air brushed his skin, but he continued to remove his shirt and added it to the pile. He would start by doing his katas. Not only did they help him think, but they kept him in shape, and he had been neglecting them the last week or so, wanting to spend his time with Claire.

An hour later, breathing hard and covered with a fine sheen of sweat, he headed for the shower. He knew where he was going to start.

Chapter 3

The ferry to Alert Bay was almost empty, as was the U'Mista museum when Dan arrived there. As he waited for the young man at the reception desk to find someone who could show him what he needed to see, Dan stared up at the artwork adorning the walls of the lobby. It wasn't hard to understand why someone would want to collect it. Beautifully executed carvings, the ovoid shapes painted in rich, bright colours. Graceful paddles, some with the blades smooth and perfect, others deeply etched with powerful designs. Two felted wool robes, one in the familiar red and black, the other in dramatic black and white. Gleaming black argillite sculptures and pendants. Copper bracelets. It was all superb and it was all made to be sold. None of it was what he was looking for.

"Dan Connor?"

The voice was soft and feminine and Dan turned to see a petite woman with iron-grey hair dressed in black pants and a pale blue cotton shirt.

"I'm Vivien," she said as she held out her hand. "I've heard a lot about you. It's a pleasure to meet you."

Dan's much larger hand engulfed hers. "You've heard about me?"

She smiled at his look of puzzlement.

"I'm Billy's aunt," she said, watching his face as understanding dawned. Billy was the man whose cedar bracelet he wore. The man whose body he had found the previous year and whose murderer he had arrested.

"Ah," he said, fingering the bracelet. "I'm truly sorry I didn't find him sooner, but I'm not here about Billy. I'm hoping you can help me with another case. Maybe help me solve this one a little quicker."

Her smile disappeared. "Another murder?" she asked.

"No, not a murder," he said. "A theft. But to the people who were robbed, I think it's probably almost as bad."

He explained what had happened and what he was looking for. She listened carefully then led him through a darkened room where the insistent beat of drums surrounded them, into another space where a large box sat on a platform enclosed by glass.

"You said one of the stolen items was a bentwood box?" Vivien nodded towards the display. "Do you know what size it was?"

"No," he said. "That's part of the problem. The information we've been given is vague. There isn't much detail."

He leaned forward to study the intricate carving on the front of the box. "I've never seen one before, but I always imagined they were much smaller than this."

Vivien had moved ahead but now she came back and stood beside him.

"They come in all sizes," she said. "Some were small and were used to hold rattles or whistles, but the ones made to store eulachan oil could hold up to fifty gallons. With those it sometimes took two men just to lift the box out of the canoe!"

"And they're made from just a single piece of wood!" Dan's voice echoed the admiration on his face. "Would this one have been used for food? It's really beautiful."

Vivien shook her head. "No. This one was to store regalia. The ones to store food were smaller and had less decoration—often none at all. For regalia storage, or if they were for burying the dead, they were decorated with representations of our spirit ancestors." She pointed. "This is the front of the box and that's the chief of the undersea world. You can see he has both fins and human hands and there are double eyes—two salmon heads joined at the nose."

She beckoned him around to the other side of the glass display.

"This is the back. Like the front it was first carved and then painted, and that killer whale crest represents the clan the owner belonged to." She pointed to the side. "The sides always had much simpler decoration and they were only painted."

She watched Dan as he moved around the display, angling his head to see a particular feature better. "You seem very interested in the details. Is that just because of your job or are you an artist?" she asked. "Do you work with wood?"

He looked up at her in surprise. "An artist? Oh no. Not even close. But I do love to work with wood—usually driftwood—when I have the time." His gave a rueful grin. "Not that I seem to have had too much of that lately."

He realized as he said the words that it was something he would like to get back to. The twisted wood, smoothed and contorted by years in the ocean, spoke to him somehow. Soothed him. Connected him to both the earth and the sea.

They moved on and stepped down into yet another room, this one redolent with the scent of cedar. A wide, raised platform ran along three sides, each one displaying a series of masks of various shapes and sizes. As Dan let his eyes roam over them he felt an inexplicable sense of . . . what?

Connection? Communion? The room was completely silent, but the air seemed to hold the silent whispers of ancient stories. In some way he couldn't quite understand he felt as if he had entered a sacred space.

Vivian stopped about halfway down the platform.

"You said one of the things stolen was a transformation mask?"

Dan nodded. Her words had brought him back to the present.

"Yes," he said, pulling a piece of folded paper out of his pocket. "A Thunderbird transformation mask, but there are other things too." He passed the list to her and watched while she read it. She took a long time. Finally she looked up.

"This is a long list. These have all been stolen?"

Dan nodded. "Yes. At least this is everything that's been reported so far. There may be more."

She handed the list back to him. The vibrancy he had seen on her face when he first met her had been replaced by a look of sadness.

"It never ends." Her voice, always quiet, had fallen to a whisper and Dan wasn't sure if he had heard her correctly.

"I'm sorry?" he asked. "Are you saying this has happened before?"

"What?" She jerked her gaze up to his face. "Oh, no. No. At least not recently that I know of. But in the past the government stole hundreds of items, mostly during the potlatch ban. Others were stolen by people visiting abandoned villages, or were bartered by smallpox survivors for food and medicine. Many ended up in museums or private collections."

She gave a bark of bitter laughter. "Talk about irony! Here I am talking to you about traditional items stolen from our villages, and I'm flying to New York this afternoon to pick up a mask the American Museum of Natural History has finally agreed to return after months of negotiation. I spend my life tracking down our history and bringing it home, and now someone is out there stealing it again."

***

It was almost five hours later when Dan left the museum and headed back to the ferry terminal, his shoulder weighed down by a woven bag holding several books and a stack of photocopies, his mind reeling with the information and stories he had been given. All were gifts Vivian had given him before a car had arrived to drive her down to the harbour where she would catch a seaplane to Vancouver.

He looked at the village with new eyes as he walked back along the road, past the tiny hospital and the plain, clapboard houses. Past the dilapidated net lofts perched on ancient creosoted pilings. Past a tiny gift shop selling sophisticated clothing and specialty coffee. Past a simple restaurant with cracked Formica tables that would have looked at home in a 1940's movie.

Vivian had talked about the recent thefts being ironic. A contradiction. But in many ways this whole community was a contradiction.

A culture that stretched back more than ten thousand years but that had built a museum as modern as any glass and metal-framed edifice in Toronto or London.

A woman who casually flew to places like New York and Amsterdam and yet who was completely at home attending potlatches and talking about mythical, spiritual beings.

A group of people largely isolated from the rest of society who practiced their ancient traditions even as they were negotiating with some of the largest and most sophisticated organizations in the world.

Dan had gotten the information he came for. He had not only seen several transformation masks including a thunderbird mask with a bill that could be made to snap open and shut with the toss of the dancer's head, but he had also been shown how they all worked. He had seen bentwood boxes of all sizes, plus rattles, clubs, staffs and paddles. He had seen a ravenstail robe in the process of being woven on a loom, and a chilkat robe hanging on a stand. He had seen totems and mortuary poles and burial boxes and been shown how to identify the various symbols or crests on them. He had even been shown how to recognize a good fake—sadly becoming more common as native art rose in popularity. And while he hadn't learned what the stolen items looked like— that was an impossibility—he now at least knew some of the questions to ask when he arrived in the villages that had suffered the thefts.

He sat on the Alert Bay wharf looking over the water towards Vancouver Island as he waited for the ferry to arrive. A fine rain had started to fall, blurring the distant shore, and Dan's thoughts blurred along with it. What would it be like, he wondered, to dance a mask like the transformation masks he had been shown. To know that your father, and grandfather, and great-grandfather, and all the generations before that had worn it. Had danced the same dance. Had told the same story. To feel all of your ancestors dancing beside you.

The thought made him feel somehow lonely. He had never known any of his grandparents. His father had left Nova

Scotia when he had been barely seventeen and had worked his way across the country until he arrived on the west coast and got a job as a deckhand on a seiner. For eight years he had saved every penny he possibly could until he had enough money to buy his own boat, and as far as Dan knew, he had never gone back home.

His mother, who had died when Dan was only ten years old, had immigrated from Ireland, and although she had often spoken of taking him there for a visit, had never done so.

Once, when he was feeling adrift after Susan's death and was desperately searching for some way to anchor himself, he had gone to see the house he had grown up in. He hadn't been there for years, but he could still remember the old wood stove, and the scent of the lemon oil his mother had used on the furniture. He remembered the sunshine that sometimes poured in through the west-facing windows and illuminated the dust-motes that floated in the air. He could even remember the floral chintz curtains that fluttered in the kitchen window.

It had taken him two days to find it. The city had grown up around it, and when the house finally appeared in front of him he barely recognized it. It had been old even when he was a child and the years had not been kind. Where once there had been life and laughter and the warm smell of bread baking in the oven, now it stood empty and silent, and the leaning 'For Sale' sign, almost hidden by weeds, only emphasized its abandonment. Death, he remembered thinking as he stood out on the sidewalk looking at the sagging roof and the peeling paint, erases all traces, all memories of the lives that once existed.

But he had been wrong. It was only now, after talking with Vivian, that he realized that for those who belonged to a culture different than his, death was simply a transformation. The dead lived on in their stories, their dances, and their hearts.

And most of all, they lived on in their traditional regalia, and that made these thefts much more than simple robberies. They were a form of murder.

Chapter 4

Two hundred and fifty miles away, in a tiny village towards the end of Dean Channel, a thin crescent moon was already slipping below the horizon and only the diamond glint of stars pierced the blackness above Charlie Jack's head as he left the Big House to collect his regalia. The night was cold and as he started down the path and crested the rise, he pulled his jacket, a gift he had just received from his uncle, tighter around his body. The wind was stronger here, coming straight off the ocean where it was rattling the rigging of the fishboats tied to the wharf, and he was glad for the warmth it provided.

Behind him, he could hear the rhythmic beat of the drums, and cedar smoke drifted in the air, a sweet incense carried on the night wind from the fire that burned in the centre of the floor in the building he had just left. Once, long ago, that fire would have warmed the four families who shared the space, one to each corner, but tonight it warmed the entire community. They had all come to participate in the potlatch his uncle was holding, the first in over a year and an event they had all been looking forward to for many months.

Charlie considered himself to be a lucky man. He had been born the same year the residential school in Ya'lis, the village the white man called Alert Bay, had closed and the zeal of the Canadian government to 'civilize' his people had faded. That simple stroke of luck had allowed him to escape the horrors both his mother and father had suffered, but not the effects those horrors had caused.

His grandparents had left the village after their daughter had been stolen, determined to continue to live traditionally on a small island hidden deep in one of the many inlets that pierced the coast. When his mother had finally found her way there two years after having been released from her imprisonment, she had been married, pregnant with his sister, Brenda, and already an alcoholic. Her parents had done all they could to help her, but the scars were too severe, the memories too overwhelming. A year later she returned to the city leaving both him and Brenda behind. Three years after that they heard she had died from a drug overdose. They had no idea what had happened to their father. They couldn't even remember his name.

Not many people would consider that story a lucky one, but Charlie knew of others who had suffered the same fate as his mother, and whose children had not had grandparents to bring them up. Children who had not been taught the stories of their people, who had not learned the traditions, who didn't know the dances. Children—now men and women the same age as he was — who were as lost as his mother had been.

He reached the old arbutus tree whose branches had been bent and twisted into strange, contorted shapes by years of exposure to the wind, and turned onto a much narrower path that led to the small shed where he kept his regalia. Built by his grandfather many years ago, the shed had withstood the test of time and sat deep within the forest, its weathered wood almost indistinguishable from the ancient trees that surrounded it.

It was even darker under those heavy branches, but Charlie didn't need light to find his way. He had trodden this same path many times and knew every turn, every dip, every root and bramble along the way. Despite the treasures the shed held, for most of those years he had never bothered to lock the door. Why would he? Nobody locked their doors here. Few outside the village even knew the shed existed, but a couple of months ago he had heard of a theft from another village further up the coast and although he still found it hard to believe, he had added a padlock. He wanted to be cautious. Regalia like the robe and the mask he was about to don for tonight's ceremony, could never be replaced. It had belonged to his family for countless generations with each generation passing it on to the next until finally the honour had been passed to him.

He still remembered the winter t *'seka* ceremony several years ago when he had been given the right to wear it. He had danced it for the first time that night and at every ceremony since. It was who he was. When he was wearing the robe and mask and felt the beat of the drum join the beat of his heart, he took on the spirit of his ancestors. Became one with them. A part of their transformation. He couldn't imagine not having it and the responsibility to keep it safe was something he took very seriously.

The padlock was not an addition he was happy about. Not only was it something from another world, an intrusion into a place he had always felt was itself somehow sacred, it was a nuisance. It meant that every time he visited the shed at night he had to carry a flashlight so he could see well enough to unlock it. Several times he had forgotten and was forced to go back to get one, cursing all the way, but still he kept the shed locked. If his *'na'mina,* his clan, had managed to keep the family crests and regalia safe through the long, bitter years of the potlatch ban with the threat of imprisonment hanging over them, then locking a door was the least he could do.

The ancient wood that formed the walls of the shed, and the now-faded outline of the raven his grandfather had painted on the door had, like the treasures inside and the dances and the stories that came with them, also become a part of his family's tradition. They too held the history of his people. His own history.

He reached the dip in the path where he had dug a few rough boards into the earth to bridge the pool of water that collected there every time it rained, and pushed aside the thick blackberry canes he had neglected to trim on his visit earlier that week. Even though the rain had eased a couple of hours before, the canes still felt wet and slippery. This deep in the forest it was always damp and he could hear the sound of raindrops dripping off the leaves.

He felt in his pockets for something to wipe his hands on, but he hadn't thought to bring a kerchief or a rag so he reluctantly used the sleeve of his new jacket. It wasn't that he was fastidious about his clothes—most were stained with berry juice and fish scales—but this jacket was special, a potlatch gift from his uncle. Still, he needed dry fingers to turn the key because even with the frequent application of grease, metal corroded quickly in this climate and the lock was already getting hard to open. Besides, a little rainwater wouldn't harm this coat. It was waterproof. Made for the rain. The nicest coat he had ever owned.

The shed appeared in front of him, looming out of the deep shadows surrounding it, its regular shape setting it apart from the random lines drawn by nature. Only when he was close enough to touch the door did he turn on the flashlight, not wanting its light to blind him to the night. The narrow beam slid over the faded outline of the old raven and he reached for the padlock, but his hand froze halfway there. The hasp was open, the padlock missing. Instinctively Charlie shone the flashlight onto the ground below and there it caught a glint of metal. The padlock, partly covered in mud.

Damn that Jimmie Alfred!

Charlie had given his nephew, Jimmie, the spare key earlier that day and told him to check the mask to make sure it was in proper working order, that the strings that opened and closed the beak were still strong, and that no spiders had taken up residence in the cedar robe. The young man would himself inherit the regalia in a few years and he needed to become familiar with it and learn how to care for it. Charlie had thought he was ready for that kind of responsibility, but it seemed he still had a long way to go.

Charlie pushed open the door and his flashlight lit the wall ahead of him. The uneven texture of the old boards created a familiar pattern and shadows formed and disappeared as the beam moved across them. It sought out the two cedar hats and the headdresses, each hanging on its own wooden peg. It illuminated the two canoe paddles that stood, one on each side of the north corner. It found and caressed the contours of the carved staff whose intricate shapes told the story of his family, each crest emerging from the gnarled wood just as his ancestors had once emerged from the sea and shed their animal forms.

Past another corner and the light slid over the cedar robe he would wear later that night when he danced the transformation mask. Like the mask it was heavy, and it hung on a special hanger he had carved himself, its form echoing the powerful rounded shoulders of the creature it represented. Even after all the years and all the dances, the cedar strips were still supple and held the scent of the forest they had come from.

He turned yet again and now stood facing the door. It was a routine he had developed, a part of the ritual he performed every time he entered the shed, a way to show respect: he always looked at the mask last. It was his most treasured possession, leading back past all the ancestors who had gone before, holding within it their stories and their spirits. Every time he looked at it he could feel their presence and hear their voices. Every time he danced it, he joined them, shared their lives, absorbed their history.

It took several seconds for his mind to catch up with what his eyes were showing him. There on the wall was a pale outline to show where the mask had once rested, but the mask itself was no longer there.

Charlie blinked, his heart racing even as his breath stopped. It made no sense. Only he and Jimmie ever went into the shed, and Jimmie only when he was asked and given the key. Jimmie might have forgotten to lock the shed, but he would never have removed the mask. It was sacred and no one else from the village would think of even touching it, let alone taking it. It was as important to them as it was to Charlie himself.

A moan escaped from his throat and he sank to the floor, his legs no longer capable of supporting his weight. His mind too refused to function, unwilling to acknowledge the message his eyes were sending and unable to comprehend the enormity of all it represented. His hands grasped his head, holding in the memory of what had been lost as he rocked back and forth.

Dawn found him still sitting there, staring at the space where the mask had been, willing it to reappear even as the hollow ache of loss ate into every cell of his being.

Chapter 5

It was Charlie's uncle who found him early the next morning, still sitting on the floor of the shed staring at the empty wall. He had been missed at the potlatch, but Jimmie Alfred had not shown up either and Jimmie was known to go on a bender every now and then, usually after a few days out fishing that ended with a visit to the floating store down in Rivers Inlet. Charlie used to do the same, but he had been sober the last few years.

Still, people were known to fall off the wagon and Jimmie had only been home from one of his fishing trips for a couple of days so it was likely he had a sizable stash left—at least enough to tempt Charlie into joining him. Besides, the night had been cold, the fire in the Big House was warm, the food was plentiful and good, and the dancing and drumming had everyone involved. Charlie would turn up when he was ready.

The weather had steadily worsened overnight bringing heavy rain and strong winds, and when everyone had gone home and Charlie still hadn't made an appearance, his uncle went up to check the shed. He returned minutes later to ask for help getting his nephew home and shortly after that the entire community gathered once again.

Soon the path through the forest was solidly packed with people, their feet churning the wet ground into mud, their shoulders brushing the wet tips of the cedar branches and their hands pushing back the thorny blackberry canes in their rush to reach the shed. Those at the head of the line pushed their way inside to stare at the empty wall and the empty man sitting in front of it.

Charlie's uncle finally got the crowd moved back outside and kind hands lifted Charlie and guided him back down the path, steadying him when he stumbled. As he passed, the shocked whispers turned to silence, only to be replaced by murmured comments when his sister pointed out the dark stain on his jacket.

"He's hurt," she shouted. "Let him though. His arm is bleeding."

"That's old blood," someone else said. "Probably came from a fish."

But Charlie's grandmother, almost ninety years old and a respected elder in the community, disagreed. She had grown up hearing the stories of how her people had come into the world, the rituals and ceremonies that preserved their history, and the dances that brought it all to life. While the celebration the previous night had been a potlatch and not the big winter *t'seka* ceremony, she knew the spirits of the *Hamatsa* were out there in the forest, waiting.

That wasn't old blood on his sleeve.

"It was Man-eater," she said, her voice firm with conviction, and several heads around her nodded their agreement.

A few people checked the shed and news of the theft quickly spread until soon everyone had heard of it, but it was too momentous to take in. How could it have happened? With no answer, they busied themselves bringing strips of smoked salmon and bowls of halibut stew and baskets of freshly picked blackberries to Charlie's house. Fires were lit, bannock was made and children sent out to scour the shoreline for wild asparagus. What else could they do? No one went out fishing. No one worked. No one slept. The loss of the mask was too great a loss to take in. It was unimaginable. Impossible to believe.

A few of the elders whispered that perhaps it had been Raven, the Trickster himself. Others said it was the evil *Sisiutl* twin. Grandmother remained unmoved and stood firm in her conviction. It was Man-Eater.

In time, most started reluctantly running through a list of their neighbours. Almost everyone in the village was related in some way, but who else could it have been? There had been no strangers at the potlatch. No guests from outside.

Charlie himself did nothing but sit staring into the fire. Someone had removed his jacket and draped a blanket around his shoulders, but the offerings of food and the jugs of wild ginger tea sat unnoticed at his side.

It was a long time later, when the rains had stopped and the winds had eased, that anyone remembered the shriek they had heard, and the stories a couple of the kids had told them about seeing *Bak'wus* out in the forest.

Leaving Charlie in the care of his mother and grandmother, his uncle gathered a group of men and headed out to search for Jimmie Alfred. Jimmie was still missing and considering what had happened, they needed to find him. Some of them went down to the wharf to check his boat—he had been known to sleep off a hangover there—while others headed back to the shed. Charlie was known to be teaching Jimmie the family stories and dances, and care of the regalia was an important part of that, so perhaps Jimmie had been there with him.

It took them over an hour to find him. He had been wearing black jeans and a dark green jacket and it was hard to see him where he lay, deep in the salal in the dark shadows of the cedar trees. At first they thought he must have just fallen asleep there, too drunk to even notice the weather, but once they had fought their way in through the thick tangle of stems, pushing aside the drooping branches of wet cedar and the thorny blackberry canes, they could see how his body was twisted. How it lay where it had been thrown. Discarded like an old rag.

It wasn't until they lifted him out that they saw the blood, and it wasn't until they carried him back to the house and laid him out on a blanket on the floor of the kitchen that they discovered the wounds, deep slashes on his chest and belly that had to have been made by a sharp knife.

* * *

"We have to call the police."

Charlie's uncle had sent one of the kids to get the chief and he in turn had gathered a few of the elders together. They had each gone into the house to pay their respects to Jimmie's mother who, with the help of two of her sisters was gently removing Jimmie's clothing and washing his body, and then they had gone back outside to gather in the woodshed.

"Think that blood on Charlie's sleeve came from Jimmie?"

"Nah. Not enough of it and it was too high up his sleeve."

"Maybe came off those blackberry canes where we found Jimmie. Looked kinda like it was scratched on. Easy enough to check it out."

"Yeah, but the rain would've washed it off by now."

The men talked back and forth until finally one of them left to check the blackberry bushes.

"Looks like it was Jimmie's blood," he said as he returned to the group and held up his hand to show a red smear on his fingers. "Guess it was left on the leaves when he was thrown into the salal. Ain't much left, but you can still see it under some of the leaves. I figure Charlie must have brushed against it when he went to the shed."

"Police ain't gonna believe that. They'll say Charlie got that blood on his sleeve when he killed him."

"Even the police can't be that stupid, but they won't like it that Jimmie was treated properly—washed and dressed in his regalia."

The group fell silent, their heads nodding as they took in all that had been said.

"Nothing those white man's police can do 'cept get in the way." The eldest of the group turned and spat on the ground. He could still remember the police raiding the village when he was a kid and had no desire to invite them back now. "We should just bury him here. Bury him our way. Be better for everyone."

Another agreed. "The police will take him away," he said. "Probably keep him over there in some damn refrigerator for weeks. Cut him up even more than he is now. Heard they did that with a guy from Compton Island."

Chief Manuel had remained quiet but now he spoke again. "They will, but I don't think we have a choice. Jimmie was murdered. If we don't report it and they find out, they'll come here anyway and dig up his body." He removed his glasses and pinched the bridge of his nose. "And they'll probably arrest a bunch of us at the same time."

They sat quietly, staring out into the dim light of early morning. The rain had started up again, gentle now, falling softly on the earth.

It was the youngest of them that broke the silence.

"Maybe Walker could ask that friend of his to come. The one who found Billie Jules last year. I heard he made sure everything was done right."

"Yes," another answered. "And he brought Harold home too."

Chief Manuel didn't answer immediately. He wasn't one to make quick decisions and he took his time considering the suggestion as he let his eyes roam across the other faces surrounding him, looking for signs of disagreement. He didn't see any.

"Does anyone know where Walker is?" he finally asked. "He hasn't been here for a while."

"Manny said he saw him last week when he was out fishing." It was the youngest speaking again. "Said he was up there near Tsatsquot."

"That's a long way away. Take a long time to reach him."

They talked back and forth for a while until someone came up with a solution, and then they stood and headed down to the wharf. All the boats had VHF radios, and while there was no way those radios could reach as far as Tsatsquot, they *could* relay messages to other boats who in turn could pass the message on to anyone fishing up near the end of Dean Channel close to the old village of Kimsquit. It was a popular place to fish for chinook, and it would be easy for any of the people up there to contact Walker.

***

Back in Jimmie's house, the mingled scents of sweetgrass and sage drifted in the air and Jimmie lay peacefully on the kitchen table, resting on a bed of cedar boughs, dressed in his button blanket and wearing a cedar headdress. He was surrounded by the women of the community. The men had all left to go to the cemetery. There was a grave to be dug.

As the elders made their way back through the village, each heading for the familiar comfort of their own house, the clouds parted and for just a moment a ray of sunlight escaped and lit the windows of the house where Jimmie lay.

Chapter 6

It was late by the time Dan returned to his boat. He had spent a couple of hours wandering the streets of Alert Bay and studying the mortuary poles at the cemetery before getting back on the ferry. Then, once he arrived in Port McNeill, he had stopped in at a restaurant for a meal of fish and chips. The light was starting to fade as he headed down the float.

Many of the boats that had filled the harbour earlier in the summer had left, and most of those remaining were dark and quiet, locked up for the season. The sharp scrape of metal on metal and a muttered oath drew his attention to one of the few that were still occupied.

"Need a hand Willie?"

No one knew just how old Willie Pete was, but both he and his boat looked to be in the same state of disrepair.

"Wouldn't say no." The old man was leaning over the side tugging on a piece of string.

"Goddamn thing's caught on somethin'. Prob'ly some piece of shit those damn tourists dumped overboard."

Tourists, as Willie liked to call anyone he didn't know, took the blame for any problem he had—and he had many.

Dan smiled and moved down the finger float to stand beside the ancient boat. It appeared to be listing to starboard even more than usual although he couldn't hear the sound of the old pump working so perhaps it was just his imagination.

He took the string from Willie's gnarled fingers. "Maybe it'll come lose if I pull it from down here," he said. "Different angle."

"Don't pull too damn hard. Got a big one on it. Maybe two. Don't want to lose them."

Willie appeared to survive almost exclusively on the crabs he caught on his homemade hook. Made out of a piece of string tied to a bent wire coat-hanger and baited with whatever fish head had been discarded up at the cleaning tables, it provided him with a seemingly endless supply of the Dungeness that grew large on the offal thrown into the water by fishermen.

It took some time, but with a bit of gentle nudging and a few careful tugs this way and that, the hook finally came free and Dan pulled it up the way Willie had shown him, slow and steady so as not to dislodge any crabs that might be clinging to it.

"Damn, would you look at that!" Willie's face broke into a toothless grin as two large Dungeness dropped onto the float by Dan's feet. "Told you they was big."

He picked up an old bucket and handed it to Dan.

"Throw that smaller one in there. You can have the big one."

"Thanks Willie." Dan put both the crabs into the bucket and lifted it over the rail. "You keep them. I'm fine. I grabbed something in town on the way down and I've got to get the boat ready to leave in the morning."

"Heading out?" The old man stared at him for a minute then looked up at the sky. "Gonna blow tomorrow. Be some rain too. Hope you're heading north."

Dan nodded. "Yeah, I am. Nice to know the weather's going to cooperate."

It was standard knowledge along this part of the west coast that if you wanted to head north, you hoped for bad weather. Bad weather brought winds from the southeast, and with the current ebbing in the morning both wind and sea would be pushing the boat from behind.

He waved goodbye and heard a cackle of laughter as he started back along the float.

"Watch out for *Bak'wus*! He likes it wet!"

Dan froze. *Bak'wus* was a name he had now seen in two reports. He had asked Vivian, and she had shown him a *Bak'wus* mask, but there had been no suggestion that any mask like that had been stolen, only that something or someone called *Bak'wus* had been seen in the area.

"*Bak'wus*?" he asked as he turned back to look at Willie Pete. "Who's *Bak'wus*?"

"Ghost," said Willie, rolling his eyes and waving his arms in the air. "Wild man of the forest. Don't eat nothing he offers you or he'll turn you into a ghost too!"

Dan chuckled, shook his head and waved again. Willie had a habit of coming up with crazy stories. He had spent his youth in residential school and had only a superficial knowledge of the myths and traditions of his people, gained from infrequent visits to various coastal villages. Like a child brought up on fairy-tales who saw a firefly for the first time and thought it was a fairy, he clung to his own interpretations.

Dan had grave doubts about ghosts, didn't think it likely that he would run into any on his travels, and certainly none that would offer him food. He did however want to check *Bak'wus* out a little more. Maybe it was a nickname for somebody local who spent a lot of time out in the forest. Perhaps someone with a complexion light enough to make him seem ghostlike. If that was the case and the people in the village thought they had seen him, then he would be someone Dan wanted very much to talk to.

***

Back on board, Dan took a beer out of the fridge and sat down to sort through the police reports, matching them to the information Vivien had given him. There was no discernable order that he could see, at least in terms of location. The first theft had occurred mid-coast, at the end of a narrow channel leading off one of the smaller inlets. The second was further south in a long fiord leading off Seymour Inlet, not far from where he was now but on the mainland side, while both the third and fourth had occurred up north, in two different waterways leading deep into the Kitlope.

He turned on the computer and plotted each site on the navigation system, looking for coves and bays inside the entrances to the various inlets that would provide protection from the winds. Although the coast of British Columbia was only about a thousand kilometers from north to south as the crow flies, due to its many long fjords and over forty thousand islands, the total length he patrolled was over twenty thousand kilometers, and he would have to travel a good number of them to get to where he needed to go.

Each of the four villages lay hidden far up a different, narrow, twisting channel. He would have to use the Zodiac to reach each one and that meant finding a safe place to leave his boat. Even with several hundred feet of chain, anchoring in the inlets themselves was not an option. These waterways had been carved by glaciers thousands of years ago and their depth made anchoring impossible while their steep sides prevented tying up to shore.

He also knew the people in the communities themselves would not welcome a boat like *Dreamspeaker*. She had the scarred wooden hull of the fish-packer she had once been, but she looked like what she was: a white man's boat.

She was equipped with hydraulic winches, stainless-steel stays and bronze portlights, with polished brass lamps on port and starboard. A forest of antennae sprouted from the cabin roof with more on the masthead. Teak railings gleamed from constant attention and a custom-made cradle held the big rigid-hull Zodiac with its twin Mercury engines. The people in these tiny villages lived their lives much the way their ancestors had. Even arriving in the Zodiac with its fibreglass hull and PVC tubes would guarantee a cool welcome—something he never experienced when he arrived with Walker in his canoe.

Walker. He kept coming back to Walker. It would be so much easier if the man came with him, but it was impossible. Walker was simply out of reach. Dan shook his head to bring himself back to reality, saved the course he had plotted, and turned on the weather channel to check the forecast for the following day. Willie Pete had been right—rain and winds from the south-east. Lousy conditions for a holiday, but perfect for a trip north and it sounded like it would hold for a few days. As if in confirmation a sudden gust of wind blew into the harbour and rattled the rigging.

He moved to the chart table and pulled out a chart that gave him a full picture of the coast from the north end of Vancouver Island all the way up to Prince Rupert. It wasn't that he didn't trust the state-of-the-art electronic navigation system he had installed a few years back. He did. But he wasn't about to give up his stash of paper charts. He had grown up using the paper version on his father's fishboat and he still found they helped to give him the big picture of where he was headed. Not only that, but he often used them to plot the location of the crimes he was investigating, marking each one with a coloured pin. More than once that had helped him see a pattern he hadn't noticed before.

As he spread the sheet out on the chart table he felt a familiar vibration start to throb beneath his feet and he looked up at the clock. 9:30 p.m. The last ferry from Alert Bay was a few minutes late. He made a quick calculation and realized it was around 2:00 in the afternoon in Darwin. Claire would have landed less than an hour ago. Right now she was probably on her way to her hotel and a dinner meeting with the people who had hired her. By the time that was over it would be late. She would be exhausted and he would be asleep. There was no way he would be talking to her tonight.

He pushed aside the pang of regret and went back to planning his trip. If he made an early start, and if the forecast was correct and the winds held, he would take advantage of the weather and head for the two northernmost villages first. That should put him somewhere around Namu the following night. It was a usually a good place to anchor, but this late in the year the winds that gave Whirlwind Bay its name might have started. It would probably be safer to anchor off Hakai Pass.

Thinking of Hakai made him think of Annie, the woman he had first met almost five years ago when he and Walker had been searching for Claire. Annie was both reclusive and cantankerous. She lived alone far from the nearest village and much like Walker, seemed to survive on the fish she caught and the plants she collected. She discouraged visitors by pointing a shotgun at them and her one vice seemed to be the chocolate chip cookies she bought on her occasional visits to the floating store at Dawson's Landing.

But no matter how rough her surface, Dan had soon come to realize that underneath it all she had a quick mind and a soft heart. It was partly thanks to her that the search for Claire had been successful and he would be forever grateful to her for that—plus he had to admit he liked her. He hadn't seen her for a couple of years, but this could be a good time to pay her a visit. She not only knew Walker, but it was possible she knew where he was. More importantly, she was observant. While she might not welcome visitors to the tiny cove where she had anchored her rusty old boat, she always knew they were there. She took note of everything that happened, from the arrival of a new family of sea otters, to a visiting Humpback whale, to a lone kayaker. She would certainly know whether there had been any unusual activity in the area.

He taped the chart to the top of the chart table, then used his brightly-coloured pushpins to identify each of the villages, hoping it might trigger some new idea or give him an insight he might not otherwise have seen. It didn't help. They were each so far apart, so far up narrow waterways, that whoever had stolen these things had to have gone in by boat or seaplane—yet no one had mentioned hearing or seeing either of those.

As he had thought earlier, that pointed to someone local, but that in turn would mean the thefts had been committed by four different people, one in each village, and that was so far-fetched as to be ridiculous. So he was back to an invisible stranger—and that too seemed impossible.

Another gust of wind threw a scattering of raindrops on the windscreen. The storm was on its way and if he wanted to get away early it was time to turn in for the night. Briefly he considered using the bunk he had built behind the chart table in order to give himself a place to snatch a few hours of sleep when the seas were rough, but he thought better of it. He would have more than enough nights ahead when he felt the need to stay close to the controls. Tonight he would enjoy the comfort of the big bed in the stateroom, even though it would feel empty without Claire to share it with.

***

It was four in the morning when a noise dragged him from his dreams. Cursing as he struggled up into consciousness, Dan blinked the sleep out of his eyes, pulled on his jeans and a sweater, and made his way aft. The dream had been about Claire. She had been walking towards him on a stretch of white sand and he could hear her laughter, see her smile, and feel the softness of her touch on his skin. He didn't want to leave it, certainly not for a reality like the one that greeted him when he pushed open the cabin door to peer out into the impenetrable blackness.

The forecast wind was starting to build, the gusts making him shiver as they made their way around the breakwater and set the smaller boats dancing. The rain still wasn't much more than the few drops he'd seen earlier, but the air felt damp, pregnant with the promise of the coming storm, and heavy cloud blocked out the light of the stars. It was all a far cry from the snug bed and the warm dream he had just left.

A repeat of the noise pulled his attention away from the weather and back to the present. It was coming not from the float, but from somewhere down in the water. He leaned out as far as he could over the port rail and tried to see what it was, but the curve of the hull and the blackness of the night blocked his view.

He turned to go back inside and get the big flashlight he kept in the wheelhouse, but stopped as the noise sounded yet again, this time with an odd rhythm. Instead of a single loud bang, there were three or four quick raps and then a pause before the sequence was repeated.

Waves sometimes had that kind of consistent repetition, and waves sometimes brought in huge logs that had broken free from the log booms on the other side of the bay. If this was a log it could damage the hull and he would need to work fast to get it over to the float and secure it for the night.

He sighed and scrubbed his face with his hands, dreading the thought of what could be involved, then went forward to get the flashlight. On his way there he switched on the masthead lamp which bathed the deck in bright light but didn't reach where it was needed, the increased contrast only making the darkness seem even darker. He impatiently flicked the switch off again and stood shivering on the deck, waiting for his night-vision to return as he pictured Claire standing on a sandy beach under a hot sun. Why hadn't he gone with her? He could have booked time off, even two or three weeks, although the flights would have taken a lot of that. And the flights . . .

A sudden flurry of knocks interrupted his reverie, pulling him back to the present and triggering a memory. A couple of years ago Walker had once arrived unannounced in the middle of the night and had signalled his presence by banging on the hull with his paddle. It had been a long time ago and for him to be here now would be an incredible coincidence, and very unlikely. Plus now that Dan thought about it, the man had always come to the stern where he could hold onto the swim grid to keep himself from drifting away. There was no place he could hold onto the side of the hull and this noise was definitely coming from the side. In any case, Dan didn't believe in coincidence but still, he needed to check.

Even in the beam of the big flashlight it took Dan several seconds to realize the pale shape he could barely make out down on the water was actually the face of the man he had been thinking about and not some apparition he had conjured out of his dreams.

Chapter 7

It took a long time for Walker to lift himself out of his canoe and heave himself up onto the swim-grid, and even longer to reach the deck. For the first time since he and Dan had become friends, he was willing to accept assistance. And not just willing. It was a necessity. He had no choice.

Although his upper body still appeared strong and muscular thanks to his years of paddling out on the water, Walker was now hunched and bent and his legs, weak and twisted by his fall all those years ago, no longer supported him. When he was finally settled on the bench, a blanket draped around his shoulders and a cup of tea in his hands, he spoke for the first time.

"Pretty sorry sight, huh."

His face was lined with pain, and his eyes, usually filled with some private amusement, no longer had their sparkle.

Dan didn't answer right away. He didn't know what to say. He hated seeing his friend, always so strong and vibrant, huddled there like a tired old man.

"What the hell happened?" he finally asked.

"To me?" Walker gave a bitter snort of laughter. "Nothing much. Just getting old I guess. Soon gonna have to crawl into a cave like the bears do and wait till spring." He shrugged one shoulder and twisted his lips into a faint resemblance of the familiar smile, but it didn't reach his eyes.

"Don't give me that shit, Walker," Dan said. "We've known each other too long. What's going on?"

Walker shook his head, took another sip of tea, and looked out into the night. It was a long time before he spoke again, but Dan waited him out.

"Started a few months ago. Maybe a year, I don't know." There was another long pause. "Walking's always been hard since the accident—you know that—but I was okay when I was sitting. Even when I dragged myself up the beach to go ashore. It might have looked rough, and it took a lot of work, but there really wasn't that much pain. Now . . ." His voice faded away.

"You go see a doctor?"

"Doctor?" For the first time since he had arrived, Walker looked directly at Dan. "What the hell could a doctor do? Put me in some damn old folks home? Shove some pills down my throat?"

"Walker. . ."

"Look, they couldn't fix it when it happened, and that's been how long? Damn near eleven years? Why the hell would it be different now?"

He was shouting, his usually soft voice harsh with anger and resentment, but Dan could hear the pain running underneath.

"Yeah, guess you're right," he said, forcing a lightness into his voice that he didn't feel. It was obvious that Walker was not in any mood to listen to reason. "Might as well just give up."

Walker shot him a suspicious glance. "I didn't say I was giving up. I just paddled over forty kilometers in the goddamn dark to get here so don't tell me I'm giving up!"

"Sounds like you're giving up to me," Dan answered, keeping his voice light. "I don't think anyone who would rather crawl into a cave than try to help himself by going to see a doctor is working too hard at fixing things."

Walker gave a snort of derision and stared out into the night again, refusing to acknowledge the validity of Dan's statement.

"Look, that accident *was* almost twelve years ago, and a lot has happened since then." Dan could hear the frustration growing in his voice and fought to keep it in check. He knew he couldn't push this man, but he had to find a way to get through to him. "There's new technology. New treatments. New drugs. There's no way of knowing if the problem you have can be fixed unless you get yourself checked out."

He stood up and walked over to the rail. Beyond the breakwater he could hear the waves collapsing on the beach and slapping on the rocks at the base of the beacon. The storm was coming in fast.

"You were a con back then Walker. You would have been treated as a con. Sure you got some treatment, but do you really think you had the best medical attention possible? The best surgical team working on you?" He spoke into the wind, knowing it would carry his words back to the man sitting behind him. "And even if you did, I'm damn sure you never followed up with any check-ups after you got out. Hell, for all you know, there could be an easy fix!"

When there was still no answer, he turned back and sat down again. He had run out of words. Perhaps Walker was right and there really was nothing that could be said in the face of the agony he must be feeling. The man had already reinvented himself once. Would he have to do it again, this time tied to the land? To a chair? Perhaps to a bed. Could he? Would he?

For a long time the two of them sat there side by side, not speaking, simply staring out into the darkness, until finally Dan stood up.

"I'll make us some more tea," he said, then added as he stepped into the cabin, "This is going to break Claire's heart."

***

"Where is Claire?" Walker asked when Dan returned with two steaming mugs. "I figured she'd be here."

"Believe it or not, she's in Australia," Dan answered, glad Walker was talking even if it wasn't about his health. "She's studying some marine mammal called a dugong. Won't be back for three months."

"A dugong? That like a sea otter?"

"Nope. It looks kinda like a cross between a seal and an elephant. Weird looking thing. Lives in shallow bays and eats grass."

Walker thought about that for a while. "Three months huh? That's a long time. You're gonna miss her."

Dan gave a shout of laughter. "I already do, but I guess work will keep me busy . . ." He looked at the man sitting beside him. "And speaking of work, I've been hoping I would run into you. I've got something I think you'll be interested in. There's been a few thefts from some of the villages."

Walker stared at him in silence for a few moments, then suddenly his face lit up with a broad grin and for just a moment he looked like his old self. "And here I was thinking you didn't believe in coincidence."

"Coincidence? What the hell are you talking about?"

54

"You think I paddled all this way in the middle of the night just to chat with you?" The familiar smile erased some of the lines on Walker's face. "I mean you're okay—for a white guy—but I'm not sure you're worth forty kilometers in the dark."

His expression changed again and he turned serious. "Turns out I've got something I think you'll be interested in too."

Dan looked at Walker, huddled in his blanket, bent with pain, and realized that whatever it was that had brought him there, driven him through all those hours of cold and dark, it had to be something major.

"I'm listening," he said.

***

"So this happened two days ago?" he asked when Walker finished his story. The normally laconic man had taken the time to explain not only the basic events but also to describe everything surrounding them and the effect on the people of the community.

"One day since they found him. It happened the night before."

"And you were there?"

"No." Walker shook his head. "I was up the top of Dean Channel, near Kimsquit. They got a message to me and then one of the fishboats brought me down to the village. That was yesterday afternoon. Got a ride to Sointula then came over here."

Dan shook his head, not so much in confusion at the story he had just heard, but in awe of the journey Walker had undertaken in order to bring it to him.

"So you knew Jimmie personally?" he asked.

"Yeah. Not well, but I knew him. He was younger than me and still fighting his demons. I know Charlie better. He's a good man. A hard worker. Probably be made chief next year—although with this . . ." Walker looked off into the distance, perhaps seeing the ghosts of things that might have been.

"And they haven't reported it?" Dan asked. "Surely they know I'll have to call it in."

"That's why they asked me to come," Walker replied, coming back to reality. "They want you to be the one who investigates it."

He looked at Dan and the old familiar grin was back in place. "Must be the isolation getting to their brains. For some reason they seem to trust you."

Dan stared out into the night. It was good to hear Walker's sarcastic humour again. He had missed it, but this was serious. "I don't know who they'll send, Walker. It's not up to me."

But even as he said the words, he realized it *was* going to be up to him. This was part of the case he was already on. It had to be. It was the first murder, but it was the fifth robbery.

Suddenly what had simply been important had become urgent.

He turned to Walker. "I have to talk to my boss, but I have something to ask you. There's something I need your help with."

It didn't take him long to explain the other thefts in detail. By now he knew the list of stolen items by heart, and he described his trip to Alert Bay to try and get a better understanding of exactly what he was looking for.

"Vivien was great," he said. "And she gave me all kinds of books and photos, but I need to get specifics—and I need to get them fast. This is obviously escalating. We're not just dealing with a thief any more. This guy is willing to murder to get what he wants." He paused, trying to assess what Walker was thinking, but the proud, lined face, inscrutable at the best of times, was turned away.

"Look," Dan continued. "Jimmie's people have said they'll talk to me, but the folks at the other villages may not. Almost certainly won't."

He hesitated, suddenly not sure if it was fair to ask this man to go with him. It was certainly what he wanted, what he had been hoping for ever since Markleson had given him the case. It would not only make it easier for him to enter the villages and talk to the people, it would get him much more information. But Walker was obviously in pain, and it would take days of sitting as they travelled up and down the coast. The trip would take at least two weeks, and there would likely be some bad weather and rough seas to endure before it was over. Walker would have to maneuver himself in and out of the dinghy when they reached each village and as Dan had just witnessed, that took tremendous effort.

But would that be worse that sitting in a canoe with the coldness of the ocean seeping into his bones, or sleeping out on a beach?

He closed his eyes and made his decision.

"The way you are right now, I probably shouldn't ask, but they would talk to you," he said.

Walker didn't answer right away and Dan waited nervously to hear his response. If the man said 'no' then would he just get back in his canoe and disappear? Where would he go? Where *could* he go? He certainly wasn't in any shape to live the way he had been living: catching his own food, building his own shelter. If Dan let him simply paddle away into the night, would it be the last time he ever saw him alive?

The clouds had thickened while they had been talking, and now they obscured what few stars had still been visible, so even when Walker finally turned to look at him Dan couldn't read his expression. But he could hear the words Walker spoke.

"They're my people," he said. "I'll come with you."

* * *

By the time they were ready to leave with Walker's canoe tied down on the side deck and Markleson's promise to send one of the older, more experienced men out to collect the body and bring it to Port Hardy for examination, dawn was close at hand. The sky was just starting to lighten and a few breaks in the heavy cloud bank had appeared off to the east. As they headed out of the marina and turned north, a crimson sun slowly lifted above the horizon and lay a scarlet path across the water leading directly to the boat. It looked like blood.

Chapter 8

It was after nine that night when Dan finally dropped anchor in a small cove just inside the entrance to Dean Channel. The trip across Queen Charlotte Sound had been rougher than he had hoped and he and Walker still had a long way to go to reach Charlie's village, but it would have to be in the Zodiac. *Dreamspeaker* couldn't go any further in.

They both spent a restless night. Even though the cove was protected from the wind, the waves still found their way in and Dan made regular trips out on deck to check the anchor was holding. He had dragged an inflatable mattress out on the back deck soon after they arrived and made up a bed under the coach-roof, but Walker refused to use it. Instead, he spent the night on the hard bench, wedged between the coaming and the cabin wall, refusing to move, and Dan doubted he had slept at all. Each time he had checked on him, Walker had been staring out into the darkness, and not once had he acknowledged Dan's presence.

Light had barely seeped into the sky when Dan lowered the Zodiac into the water and helped Walker to lift his legs over the wide tubes and down into the bow. The roar of the big twin Mercury engines echoed off the rocky cliffs and sent a wide wake crashing off the steep shore as they made their way ever deeper into the inlet. The noise should have announced their intrusion long before they arrived, yet there was nobody on the floats when they reached the village. Dan ran the bow up on the beach, stepped ashore and led a rope up to a sturdy tree trunk.

"Where the hell is everybody?" he asked the man who sat unmoving and unconcerned, his arms draped over the glistening Hypalon tubes.

Walker's lips twisted into a lopsided smile, but he said nothing.

"Maybe they all took off somewhere," Dan said as he stared up at the trees lining the shore. "Figured they didn't want to talk to the police."

He thought he saw one of Walker's eyebrows lift a fraction, but there was still no response.

"Well perhaps they're holding a ceremony." Dan realized he was talking to himself. "I guess I'll go up and take a look around."

He started towards the path leading up from the float, but Walker's quiet voice stopped him.

"They'll come down when they're ready."

Dan turned and looked at him. "Walker you know I respect their customs, but one of their people has been murdered and they asked for me to come. I can't just sit around and wait."

Walker smiled again and let his eyes slide behind Dan as he inclined his head.

"Don't think you'll have to wait long."

Dan looked back up the path. A group of twenty or so people were walking towards the shore, some on the path and others filtering through the trees. By the time he turned back to look at Walker again, the man was almost surrounded.

The chatter faded as Dan approached and all eyes turned to focus on him. Not for the first time he felt a momentary surge of gratitude for a comment Willie Pete had made years earlier. Dan had been getting ready to leave the marina on one of his first assignments while Willie had been working on his boat.

"Looking pretty official," Willie had said as he watched Dan untie the lines. "Gonna try and impress someone important?"

At first Dan had been confused. He was wearing his RCMP uniform as he had often done before when he was heading up to the office for meetings, and Willie had never made any comment then.

"Just heading to one of the villages," he had answered. "Nothing major."

Willie had grinned. "Not going to win too many hearts and minds wearing that," he had answered, nodding at the tailored blue serge with its bright yellow stripe down the leg. "You guys aren't exactly popular with the people."

Dan had taken the advice to heart and since then had worn his normal jeans.

Now, as he walked back down the beach towards the inflatable, an older man stepped out of the group and walked towards him.

"*Gilakas'la*," he said as he held out his hand. "Welcome. I'm George. We are grateful to you for coming."

It was a formal greeting, and Dan responded in kind, then added, "I understand you need help with a problem? A member of your village has been killed?"

George nodded. "Yes. A young man. His name was Jimmie Alfred. He was my nephew."

For just a moment his voice trembled and he turned away and stood looking out over the water. Dan stood beside him, not speaking. Giving him time, and space, and respect.

When George finally spoke again, all the formality had gone.

"Thank you," he said. "This is . . . difficult. Not only for me but for everyone here. We don't understand how it can have happened. How we can have lost so much."

Off in the distance Dan heard the horn of a large boat sounding a warning as it entered the inlet.

"George, I don't want to rush you, but there are others coming. They need to take Jimmie's body back to Port Hardy so they can establish exactly how he was killed."

George nodded. "That too is a sad thing—that he will be given into the hands of strangers."

"I give you my word he'll be treated with respect," Dan said. "And he'll come back here for burial. But could I see him before he leaves? I need to try and understand what happened"

"Of course," George replied. "Please come with me."

They left the beach and climbed the path to a cluster of houses that sat in a circle facing inward, their backs to the sea or the forest. The door to one of them was wide open and George ushered Dan inside.

"He has been washed and dressed." George stood beside the table, his gaze focused on the young man lying there. "Perhaps we should have left him, but his mother needed to honour him, as do the rest of us."

Dan nodded and moved closer, his eyes roving up and down the body which was fully dressed and wrapped in a button blanket. It was what he had expected, and he understood the need to follow tradition, but it made his job more difficult.

"Are there any wounds?" he asked.

"Yes." George reached down and gently opened the blanket, then undid the shirt to expose four deep gashes. "These are the worst, but there are also cuts on his hands and arms and some scratches that perhaps he got from the salal where he was lying."

Dan turned up each palm and studied it. "He was brave," he said. "He fought his attacker."

In the silence of the room he picked up the first faint rumble of a big diesel engine and he turned to address the man standing beside him.

"The police boat will be here in a few minutes. They'll take Jimmie to the hospital in Port Hardy, but they will also want to take everything he was wearing—clothes, shoes, bracelets, rings—so they can examine them. It would help me if I could see them first. Do you know where they are?"

"I will show him." The voice was soft, with the slurred consonants of someone whose first language had been the traditional tongue of her people.

Dan turned in surprise and stared into the shadows. He had not known anyone was there.

"This is Jimmie's grandmother, Elsie." George placed his hand under the woman's elbow as she moved slowly into the light. "She has been staying with Jimmie to keep him company."

Dan bowed his head in greeting and reached out to take the bundle of clothing from her hands.

"Thank you, grandmother," he said. "I only need them for a few minutes."

She looked at him with eyes filled with sadness, and then her gaze sharpened and she tapped the back of his wrist.

"You're the one who found Billy last year," she said. "You wear his bracelet."

He nodded. "Always," he said. "It was a gift from his family."

Her face, seamed with wrinkles and framed with wisps of iron-gray hair that had escaped from her braid, broke into a gentle smile. "Yes," she said. "I am glad it is you who has come for Jimmie."

***

By the time Dan had examined the clothing, and Jimmie's body had been carefully carried down to the float and loaded onto the police boat for its trip to Port Hardy, well over an hour had passed and Dan still hadn't been to the site of the murder. As soon as the boat had pulled away, he went down to the beach to talk to Walker, who had been helped out of the inflatable and was now sitting on a log someone had rolled down onto the shingle.

"I'm going to be a while longer," he said. "I still have to visit the murder site. Are you okay here?"

Walker gestured to the plate of smoked salmon and bannock resting beside him, and the group of people still gathered around him. "Doing better than you. They're feeding me."

Dan laughed, but quickly turned serious. "Could you ask them about what was stolen? I'm sure you'll understand what it was better than me, and if I don't have a good description, I'm not going to be able to identify it when I find it."

Walker looked at him for a long moment, then nodded his head.

"Yeah," he said. "I can do that, but you need to talk to Charlie."

"Charlie?" Dan raised his eyebrows.

"Yeah. It was his regalia that was stolen."

Dan nodded and glanced around the crowd who had fallen silent and were watching and listening as he and Walker talked.

"There have been other thefts from other villages," he said, raising his voice so that everyone could hear. "But this is the first time anyone was murdered. Whoever's doing this, he's getting more dangerous and he needs to be stopped. I'm going to need your help to be able to catch him."

He looked at the faces that were all now focused firmly on him.

"Did anyone hear or see anything? Any strangers around? A strange boat? Anything?"

A low murmur filled the air as people consulted with each other. Heads shook and faces turned somber as eyes returned to focus on him.

"Nothing." A woman dressed in blue jeans and a heavy woolen sweater acted as the spokesperson. "There's been no strangers here for a long time. You're the first."

Dan couldn't help but smile. He was a stranger looking for a stranger, and in this tight little community, both he and any other outsider would be highly visible the moment they approached. So who was he looking for?

"How about someone from another village?"

Again heads were shaken.

"Any new crew members?" Dan nodded his head towards the boats tied out on the mooring buoys.

The response was the same.

"Okay, well I'm going to take a look at where it happened and have a word with Charlie before we leave, but if any of you can think of anything, no matter how small, it would really be helpful."

He started up the beach but was stopped by a lone voice that rose, loud and clear, above the rest.

"It was Man-eater."

He turned back as the conversation suddenly swelled, and listened as the comment was debated. Other names, some that Vivien had mentioned and others that he had read about, were discussed, but he didn't interrupt until he heard a word he was already familiar with: *Bak'wus*.

"Someone saw *Bak'wus*?" he asked. It sounded odd to be asking about something he had assumed was an imaginary creature, but it was a name he was hearing too often to dismiss.

There was a long pause and then a young man stepped forward and held out his hand. It held several strands of long, greenish-white hair.

Chapter 9

It was several hours later when Dan and Walker headed back down Dean Channel. Despite his visit to the murder site and his interview with Charlie, Dan had learned almost nothing useful. Charlie himself had been devastated by the theft and the shock had left him almost catatonic, the path to the murder site had been churned into a mud bog by the people who had been looking for him, and even the salal, with its tough stems and tangled branches, had been trampled and torn when they removed Jimmie's body.

The shed had also yielded no clues. The padlock had lain in the mud for several hours before being picked up and passed from hand to hand among the villagers, and the hasp had been touched by so many fingers the rust itself had been largely removed. The carved wooden hook where the stolen mask had rested was coated with oil from fingers still covered in the remnants of the previous night's feast. Even the white hairs would probably prove to be useless. They could belong to a Spirit bear, or perhaps to an ermine—although Dan thought they were too long for that.

Even Charlie's jacket was of no help. The smear of blood high on the sleeve couldn't have come from the murder: there was too little of it and it was in the wrong place, although that would need to be verified by forensics.

"Kinda wasted trip?"

They were sitting under the canopy on the stern deck drinking tea and watching the rain slant down. Walker, often silent himself, had taken note of Dan's unusual silence.

Dan looked at him and smiled. "Not wasted. It's true I didn't learn much, but it's always good to see where things happen and get to know the people involved." He shrugged his shoulders. "It's just . . . frustrating I guess. I was hoping to get a place to start."

They sat a while longer, watching as the shadows lengthened. The light faded early in these high, narrow inlets, and in the dusk small animals came out to search along the shore below the tide line.

"So what now?" Walker asked. After the silence, his voice was loud in the quiet air.

Dan shrugged. "Guess I'll head up north tomorrow. Talk to the people up there. Maybe there'll be something . . ."

The words hung on the evening breeze, and again, it was Walker that broke the silence.

"You got those pictures Vivien gave you?"

"What?" Walker's question caught Dan by surprise. "Yes, of course. Why?"

"Figure I might be able to give you a better idea of what was stolen. Got a pretty good description from the people on the beach."

Dan stared at him and then shook his head in disgust. Of course. While he had been getting more and more frustrated at the lack of information, Walker had been quietly collecting exactly what was needed.

***

"He pulls that cord there." Walker pointed to a photograph of a closed transformation mask. "And that opens the face and beak, and then the bottom of the beak drops down and reveals the face of his ancestor." He pointed again, this time to an open mask where a round, obviously human face appeared.

"And Charlie's the only one who's trained to use the one that was stolen?"

"Yeah. Only one person in each clan is given that right, and it comes with ceremonial privileges and obligations. For the *T'seka*, the red cedar-bark ceremony, that means dancing the mask. It's not easy. It takes a lot of time and practice to learn the dance, and the robe and the mask are both heavy." He shrugged. "We believe when it's danced, our ancestors temporarily return."

It was a long speech for Walker and a lot to take in for Dan. He stared at the photo for a long time, trying to imagine how the mask would look when worn by a dancer on the floor of the Big House. Trying to hear the sound of the drums and the shuffle of dancing feet. Trying to bring the ceremony to life.

"So is there a dance mask for this *Bak'wus* character?"

Walker laughed. "Not a transformation mask like this. *Bak'wus* isn't an ancestor. He's . . ." He paused and seemed to search for an explanation. "He's a sort of supernatural creature. A wild ghost-man of the woods. His mask is usually green and has long hair. He eats ghost food out of a shell, but if he offers some to you and you eat it, you'll become a ghost too." He peered at Dan. "Why?" he asked. "Did someone say they saw *Bak'wus*?"

Dan nodded, but his mind was still focused on something else.

"Long hair?" he asked.

"*Bak'wus*? Yeah. Same with *Dzunakwa*. She's the wild woman of the forest. She has crazy hair too, and big lips

69

like this." Walker pursed his lips and shouted, "Hu! Hu!" He grinned. "Kids hear that and they run home real fast."

Dan ignored him. "Is it always black?" he asked.

"What? You still talking about the hair?"

"Yeah. Does *Bak'wus* always have black hair like he does in this picture here?" Dan pointed to a book he was holding.

Walker shrugged. "Can be black, can be white, can be strips of cedar bark or moss, or even feathers. Depends on the person who makes the mask."

A fish jumped near the shore, and Dan watched as the concentric rings expanded and then slowly subsided leaving no trace of what had caused it.

He turned to look at Walker. Even sitting on the cushioned bench the man looked uncomfortable, his hips twisted and his left leg bent at an awkward angle.

"How about you stay aboard? I have to visit a couple of villages up north and then I'll head back down and talk to the two southern ones on the way home," he said, watching Walker's face for the resistance he had seen so many times before. It didn't come.

"How far north?"

"You know the Kitlope area?" Dan asked. "Had two thefts reported from up there. Two different villages."

When Walker remained silent he added, "Both of them mentioned seeing *Bak'wus*."

***

The next morning dawned cold and gray, the sky leaden and sulky with patches of thick cloud, but the worst of the wind and rain had passed. They were halfway up Fitzhugh

Channel when the satellite phone shrilled and Dan snatched the handset out of its holder.

"Claire?" He hadn't allowed himself to acknowledge his growing concern over the past couple of days when he hadn't heard from her, and now he couldn't control his eagerness. When she didn't answer right away he found himself shouting.

"Claire? Are you there? Can you hear me?"

"I'm here," she answered. "But there's a bit of a delay. Sorry I couldn't call sooner, but it's been a bit crazy getting everything sorted out. How are you?"

He closed his eyes as he felt tension he hadn't been aware of drain from his shoulders. "Damn it's good to hear your voice," he said. "I'm fine, but how are *you*?"

Her voice faded and swelled over the airwaves as she described the people she had met, the boat she had been given and the dugongs she was studying. He could hear the smile in her words and he found himself smiling too.

"It's so different from home," she said. "The earth here is red and flat, and all the houses have tin roofs. And it's really, really hot! Yesterday it was almost thirty-five degrees and it's supposed to get even hotter next month."

"Good thing you took your swimsuit."

"Yes, although I won't be doing too much swimming. Too many crocs around, although they told me as long as I swim off the beach and don't go too far out I should be okay."

"Crocs?" Dan didn't like the sound of that.

"They're supposed to hang out near the mangroves, not the beach," she answered. "But next month the jellyfish are supposed to arrive."

"Are you trying to scare me?" he asked. "Because if you are you're doing a good job of it."

She laughed. "Don't worry," she said. "I'm too busy to be lazing around on beaches, and the water here is crystal clear. If I need to have a dip I'll do it off the boat where I can see what's in the water."

"So are you on your boat now?" he asked.

"Yes. It's smaller than the one I had in Canada, but it's perfect for around here. It's got twin keels so I can go into really shallow water. It's actually sitting on the bottom right now!"

"Is there anyone there to help you if you run into trouble?"

She laughed again. Damn he loved that laugh! It was one of the things he missed most.

"I'm fine Dan. Really I am. And yes, there's someone here I can call on. His name's Waru and he's indigenous. He lives in Maningrida now, but he grew up on an island near Darwin and he knows the whole area as well as Walker knows the west coast."

Her voice faded for a few seconds and then returned. "Is that an engine I can hear? Are you underway?"

"I am," Dan answered, "and speaking of Walker, I picked up a hitchhiker. He'd like to say hello."

He passed the handset to Walker who had struggled up to the wheelhouse when he heard Claire's voice.

"Claire?"

"Walker? Is that you?"

"Yep. Figured with you away someone had better look out for this guy. Keep him out of trouble."

She laughed. "I think that might work both ways. We were talking about you before I left. It's been so long since we saw you we thought you might be lost."

He turned serious. "Only time I got lost was in the city. Never happen out here."

"So where's out here?" she asked.

"Heading north," he answered. "I'll let your guy explain."

He passed the phone back to Dan.

"Sounds like your boss really did have a nasty job for you," she said.

"Yeah. There's been a few unusual robberies. Traditional regalia from some of the villages."

She didn't answer right away and he thought he had lost her.

"Claire? You still there?"

"I'm here. It's just . . . odd. Waru was going to take me to a corroboree—a kind of ceremonial dance—but he got a call from his family on one of the Tiwi Islands, Bathurst I think, and he had to go back there. He was really upset. He said someone had stolen some of their sacred items."

Dan looked at Walker who was sitting at the chart table, listening to every word.

"Sacred items?" he said, his mind suddenly racing. What was the chance of these thefts happening in two different countries so far apart from each other?

"Yes. He didn't say what and I didn't ask him. I don't know much about the aboriginal culture here except that it's passed down much the same way as indigenous folk in Canada pass down their stories, mostly in song and dance and art.

When you said there had been traditional regalia stolen, it seemed such a weird coincidence, that's all."

Dan had to agree with her. It *was* weird.

They didn't talk for long after that. The satellite phone was cutting in and out, static often blurring her voice, and Fitzhugh channel narrowed and twisted forcing him to pay attention to his course. The call had been too brief, but it would have to do for now.

***

It was late the following afternoon when they anchored in Pruth Bay. Dan pulled a couple of boxes of the chocolate chip cookies Annie loved out of a storage cupboard, then went out on deck, lowered the Zodiac again and tied it to the swim grid.

"I'm going to have a chat with Annie while I'm here," he said, nodding his head towards the northeast where a channel led to Hakai Pass. "She doesn't miss much. Maybe she's seen or heard something about a stranger in the area. I won't be long, but I can make you a sandwich before I go, and leave you a box of these cookies."

"I'm not a complete cripple yet," Walker snarled. "And a sandwich and cookies aren't food. They're garbage. Food is salmon or mussels or kelp or something. I'll come with you."

Dan rolled his eyes. "You're going to be one of those damned difficult guests who's never happy with what's offered aren't you."

Walker's snarl turned into a grin and he pulled a length of fishing line wrapped around a stick out of his jacket pocket. "Maybe I'll catch something decent and teach you how to live right. You're looking kinda pale."

"Funny man." Dan stuffed the cookies into a waterproof bag. "Let's see you haul your ass off that bench while I go get the Zodiac ready."

It wasn't easy to stand by and watch as Walker made his slow, painful way down onto the swim grid, and it was harder yet to see him struggle into the rigid-hulled inflatable. Even though there was barely a breeze in the bay, the movement of the water made it difficult to hold the boat steady enough for him to get his legs over the wide tubes.

It took a long time, and by the time they reached Annie's boat, the light was starting to fade.

Dan ran the Zodiac up onto the shore beside the old plank that served as a walkway up onto the deck.

"You going to be able to haul yourself up there?" he asked.

"Don't have to," Walker answered. "You're the one who needs to talk to her." He started to manoeuvre himself towards the stern of the dinghy. "Gonna catch a fish for dinner."

"Pretty shallow to be fishing here," Dan said. "You're welcome to take the dinghy out further if you like."

Walker ignored him and started rolling out the line. "Probably have a couple by the time you've talked Annie into letting you on board—that's if she don't shoot you first."

Dan nodded. There was that. He turned and rapped against the hull.

"Annie," he shouted. "It's Dan Connor. Walker's here too."

There was no response, so he rapped again. "Annie? You there?"

"I don't see no Walker."

He hadn't heard her come out on deck but suddenly she loomed above him, balancing what looked suspiciously like a shotgun on the railing.

"And Dan Connor ain't got no fancy piece-of-shit dinghy like that either," she added. She despised fibreglass boats of any kind, referring to them in scathing terms as 'plastic bleach bottles,' and the Zodiac had a fibreglass roof.

Dan took a cautious step onto the ancient board that provided the only access to Annie's boat. "It's Dan, Annie. Walker's down here in the dinghy, and I've brought you some of those cookies you like." He pulled one of the boxes out of the bag and waved it in the air above his head.

There was a couple of moments of silence and then her disembodied voice called down, "What kind of cookies?"

He smiled. "Chocolate chip. Is there any other kind?"

The gun barrel was slowly pulled back over the rail and he heard the butt connect with the deck.

"Guess you can come up." Her voice faded as she turned and headed back into the cabin.

***

"Walker gonna make an appearance or is he sulking down there or something?" Annie had the kettle on the stove and was poking a piece of wood into the firebox.

"He can't make it up the ramp Annie," Dan said, and explained what was happening to the man they both loved and respected. "I'll take his tea down to him."

She didn't say anything, but he heard her follow him as he made his way back down to shore and over to the dinghy with the tea in his hand.

"You been to the doctor you stupid bastard?" she asked.

'Nice to see you too Annie." Walker kept his eyes on the line he was holding." How you doing?"

"Better than you from the look of it."

"Wouldn't be hard," he answered. "You want that?" He gestured to a fat coho salmon lying on the floor of the boat.

"Got my own," she answered. "But thanks."

They sat in silence, sipping their tea as night descended softly around them. A frog croaked from the bank of a nearby stream, then another. Birds chattered softly from the trees and out on the water, a fish jumped.

"So what the hell happened to you," Annie finally asked. "You look like shit."

Walker shrugged and turned his head away.

"Better do something about it," Annie said. "You ain't gonna be happy in one of them nursing homes."

Walker turned back and glared at her. "Guess everyone's an expert now."

"Better get used to it." Dan grinned to take the sting out of his words "And you know she's right."

Walker snorted, turned his gaze back out over the water, and refused to answer.

***

"So how come you're up here?" Annie and Dan had returned to the cabin to give Walker the space he obviously wanted. "Pretty lousy time to go cruising. Figured you and Claire would be tucked up nice and safe down in that marina."

"Not my choice Annie," Dan replied. "My boss sent me up to check on some thefts they've been having up north and Claire's over in Australia researching some weird creature there."

She stared at him for a while. "Australia? That's a hell of a long way away. When's she coming back?"

"Three or four months." Dan shrugged. "Too long as far as I'm concerned, but it's important to her, and I'll manage."

Annie stared at him some more before she nodded her head and poured another cup of tea. "Yeah, guess you will."

She pushed the plate of cookies towards him. "Must be some pretty major thefts to send you out this time of year. Can't them goddamn fancy police boats handle them?"

She had no love for the big RCMP catamarans that occasionally passed close by her anchorage and left her boat rocking in their wake.

Dan shook his head. "Too far up in the Kitlope for the big boats to travel—and they wouldn't be welcome if they did."

"Not welcome here either," she snarled. "Bloody useless waste of money charging around and disturbing everybody . . ." She stopped mid-sentence and stared at him. "The Kitlope? Can't be much up there to steal – unless maybe in Kemano?"

"Not Kemano. Someone's stealing regalia from some of the Haisla villages."

"Regalia?" Annie leaned forward and stared at him. "You talking masks and stuff? Who the hell would want to steal those?"

"Good question," Dan answered. "But whoever it is wants it badly enough to kill for it and he needs to be stopped. I was wondering if maybe you'd seen anything odd around here. A boat you haven't seen before nosing around?"

Annie had moored her boat in a small cove behind a point of land that almost hid it from anyone passing by, but from the deck she could see out through the thin screen of trees and had a good view of any activity either in Fitzhugh Channel or Hakai Pass.

She shrugged. "Few latecomers heading down from Alaska, but that's the same every year. Still some fishboats, but the season closed a while back so there aren't many of them now."

Dan sighed. He had been hoping he might finally get a lead.

"How about small stuff — dinghies or kayaks."

"Kayaks? You crazy or what? Who the hell would have a kayak out here this time of year?"

"Well they might have launched it from a mother ship anchored somewhere else."

Dan knew he was grasping at straws, but there had to be some way a thief had managed to sneak into these villages and a small boat was the only thing he could think of. Something silent that could slide up onto a nearby shore and allow someone to walk unseen and unheard into a remote community.

Annie cackled with laughter. "Only one I know crazy enough to paddle around out here right now is sitting down there on the beach and he don't look like he'll be doing much paddling anytime soon."

She poured them yet another cup of tea and Dan told her about Claire and her research.

"It took her almost two days to get there," he said as he described Claire's journey. "Can you imagine over twenty hours cooped up in a plane?" He shuddered. "I sure as hell can't."

"Better than one hour in a helicopter," she said. The mention of flying had obviously stirred an unpleasant memory. "Did that once and that was once too many."

"Yeah," Dan replied. "Can't say I'm fond of them myself. Damned noisy, uncomfortable things."

"Hey, that reminds me." Annie was frowning, a thoughtful look on her face. "Ain't seen no strange boats, but there's been this helicopter gone up and down a few times. Odd looking thing. Smallest one I ever seen. Had a weird symbol painted on it—bunch of lines and squiggles. Looked like a goddamn blue dragonfly."

"A helicopter?" Dan asked. That was something he hadn't considered, but even as he did so, he shook his head. "I don't think that's what I'm looking for. It would need a clear space to land, and these inlets are narrow and the cliffs drop straight down to the water . . . although maybe if there was a beach or foreshore area . . "

"It's got floats," Annie interrupted. "Don't need anyplace special to set down as long as the weather's good."

Dan still wasn't convinced.

"The noise would alert the entire community and nobody heard anything."

***

The sky had cleared and stars had appeared by the time Dan stood up to leave. As he pushed the dinghy off the beach their faint silver light glanced off the waves and lit the face of the man still sitting in the bow and staring out to sea. Annie, standing at the top of the ramp, called out his name.

"Hey Walker. You need some place to stay when the quacks get through with you, you're welcome to come here."

It was a surprisingly generous offer coming from someone as reclusive as Annie and a testament to the character of the man who sat hunched on the seat of the boat below.

Chapter 10

Walker made his laborious way up to the wheelhouse from the salon where Dan had made him comfortable on one of the settees.

"All that fancy electronic navigation stuff you got up there screw up?" he asked as he eased his way onto the bench behind the chart table.

"What are you talking about?" Dan had been staring out the window at a raft of Tufted Puffins diving for their dinner, the scales of their catch glinting in their fat red bills as they broke the surface.

"You're heading in the wrong direction. You said the next village was south, not north."

"It is, but I need to go to Rupert first," Dan replied. "I want to check something out."

They had spent the last two days visiting the two northern villages where thefts had been reported and had heard the same story in each of them: the thefts had occurred at night and no one had seen or heard anything. Dan's plan had been to head back south, but he had changed his mind. "You okay with that?"

"There been something stolen there too?"

"No," Dan answered. "But I've been thinking about that helicopter Annie mentioned. If it can land on water, maybe it could land far enough away from a village that it couldn't be heard, but close enough for someone to walk in. I'd like to get a look at it, and Rupert's got the airport."

"Why would it need an airport?" Walker asked. "If it's as small as Annie said it could land in a back yard."

Dan grinned. "It's got to refuel somewhere," he answered. "And when it does it needs to provide the pilot's name and a flight plan."

Walker snorted. "Yeah, right. Can't say I ever knew many thieves would file an honest flight plan. Might as well give you a map and tell you exactly where he's going."

"Doesn't matter. What we need to know is where it comes from and who owns it. It sounds pretty unique. If someone at the airport recognizes the description and has seen it, they may know who it belongs to, and we can get the pilot's name."

"Could come off one of them fancy yachts." Disdain filled Walker's voice. "Probably have some hired pilot."

"Maybe, but a pilot has to have a name and a licence, and he would know who pays his salary."

Walker shook his head. "Probably paid by some big company. Gets his paycheque deposited in the bank."

Dan raised his eyebrows and a corner of his mouth lifted in a wry smile. "You're sure full of helpful suggestions. Got any better ideas?"

"A helicopter could have a kayak on board." To Walker, who had spent so many years on the water, some kind of boat was the answer to everything.

Dan shook his head. "If it's really small, a kayak wouldn't fit."

"Could be an inflatable," Walker answered. "Not something I'd use, but I've seen a few of those this past summer."

"Possible," Dan agreed, "but it would be risky. Take a lot of time to inflate and deflate and the guy would be very visible while he was doing it—and he'd still have to walk in. Besides, no one said anything about seeing a kayak."

"Black rubber kayak pulled up in the trees at night?"

"Yeah, okay. Could have been done that way. But that makes talking to the people at the airport even more important. If anyone saw a small, blue helicopter with a kayak in it . . ."

"Think it'll be that easy?" Walker was proving to be a very good devil's advocate.

Dan grinned. "Hey. Got to get lucky sometime. Be good if it was now."

***

It was raining hard when they arrived in Rupert and the tide was low, giving Walker no choice but to stay on board. Even Dan didn't relish climbing the seventeen feet up the metal ladder leading up to the wharf.

"Could have timed that better," Walker said as he watched Dan pull on his jacket. "Those rungs are pretty slippery."

"Be fewer of them when I get back," Dan answered. "Tide's coming up."

He swung himself over the coaming and put his feet on the lower rungs. "Call me if there's any problem." He nodded towards the phone he had left lying on the cushion, but didn't wait for an answer. Walker hated phones, and there was no guarantee he would use it even in an emergency.

He had called ahead to the Prince Rupert detachment to ask them for a car and it was waiting for him in the parking lot, along with the report he had requested from the Coast Guard heliport at Seal Cove. No one there had seen a small helicopter of any colour, but there had been talk of something maybe built from a kit that might fit the description. A couple of the guys out at the airport had mentioned seeing it a few weeks ago, but nothing more had been said about it since.

The airport was located on Digby Island, only a short ferry ride away, but the next ferry didn't leave Prince Rupert until 1:15 pm and would only stay there a short time. It would give him less than twenty minutes to find whoever had seen the helicopter and get the information he needed and that wasn't going to be enough. Mentally crossing his fingers he contacted the detachment again for permission to take one of the small RCMP powerboats from the marina and was relieved when he received an okay.

The constable assigned to drive the boat was a fresh-faced young man only a few months out of the training academy. He was trying hard to come across as well-versed in anything and everything even though he was having trouble with the controls.

"You figure they used some crazy home-built bird to fly into these villages? Sounds pretty unlikely to me."

Dan smiled. "Yeah, I know what you mean, but right now it's all I've got."

"Maybe the perp walked in. Nobody would notice one more Indian skulking around at night."

It took Dan a few seconds to let the words sink in.

"What did you say?" he asked, not sure he had heard right.

The constable looked at him, sudden apprehension on his face, and haltingly repeated what he had just said.

Dan stared fixedly ahead, fighting to hold a rush of anger in check. The kid couldn't be more than twenty-two or -

three and looked as if he had only been off the farm a couple of days. He was large-boned and awkward, his straw-coloured hair cut short, and his hands red and rough. More than likely he had no knowledge of the coast, and no familiarity with the indigenous people who lived there.

"You haven't been here long have you?" Dan said, once he had himself under control. He kept his eyes firmly fixed on the water in an effort to avoid looking at the eager face beside him, and tried to keep his voice normal. "And I'll bet you don't come from anywhere near here."

"I—just got here a few weeks ago. I'm from the prairies." The forced bravado had gone, replaced by a wavering uncertainty.

Dan nodded, still not trusting himself to say very much.

"Did . . . did I say something wrong?"

The kid—that's really what he was—took Dan's headshake to mean he was in the clear, and he started to relax, but he was mistaken.

"Depends. If you weren't so new to the RCMP and the coast, I'd be tempted to kick your ass, but let me give you a piece of advice instead. Don't ever offer your opinion if you don't know what you're talking about. 'Indians' as you call them, do not skulk around. The Haida, and the Haisla, and the Tsimshian people were here long before us, and they know the land and the water far better than you or I ever will. And no one can simply 'walk in' to one of these villages. You need a boat or a plane and some damn good skills to be able to get there, and some serious knowledge to be able to live there."

He wanted to say more but the kid, as he thought of the constable, was already staring at him as if he'd grown two heads.

"Go visit Kitkatla. Hell, go to the band office right there in Rupert. Visit Ksan and watch the carving they do there. Go over to Skidegate and check out the museum and cultural centre. Get to know a few of the people. Learn about their history. You're supposed to 'Protect and Serve' them too you know."

The Digby Island dock was just ahead and he used it to distract himself. "I'll tie up and go talk to the staff up there. You wait here. I shouldn't be long."

"What's a Haisla?"

He ignored the question that followed him onto the wharf, but it seethed through his mind as he strode up the road. All the way to the terminal he kept hearing it, repeating over and over, until finally he stopped and lifted his face up to the sky, feeling the rain run over his skin.

What the hell was the matter with him? He was normally a pretty even-tempered kind of guy so it didn't make sense to be this angry. The kid was young, that's all. Young and ignorant, and he really hadn't meant anything offensive or insulting—but it had been both, and he should have known better. He was wearing the uniform, and it was officers like him that were the reason the RCMP weren't welcome in the villages. Why he, Dan Connor, always had to prove himself. Why he needed to drag Walker along with him to provide an introduction and give him credibility.

Ah, there it was! Dan shook his head and laughed. It wasn't the kid. It was him. It was all about him. About his annoyance at the extra time and effort he had to take at each village. He was the one who deserved a kick in the backside, not a youngster who was fresh out of college and who needed guidance, not criticism.

His anger evaporated as quickly as it had arrived. He would apologize when he got back to the dinghy, explain why he had been upset. Maybe even give that young man a little insight and understanding—although Walker would do a much better job of that if he felt so inclined, which, Dan acknowledged to himself, was highly unlikely.

Once on the tarmac, Dan headed straight for the fuel shed. He didn't want to waste time going through official channels and if anybody was going to be able to give him the information he needed, it would be one of the guys there.

"Help you?"

The voice came from behind him and he turned to see a tall, heavyset man wearing a vest that said "SECURITY" in large letters approaching.

"Dan Connor," he answered, holding out his hand. "I'm looking for one of the fueling guys."

"You got a plane here?" the man asked. "I didn't hear anything come in."

"No." Dan reached into his pocket and held out his badge. "I'm trying to track down the owner of a small helicopter. Maybe a home-built job. I figured if anyone would know it would be someone here."

"Well." The man made a quick decision. "You shouldn't be out here even if you are RCMP, but I guess it can't hurt. Got nothing moving right now. Head on over there to that shed. Joe's the one you need to talk to."

Even though there were three people crowded into the small shed, there was no missing Joe. He was huge, well over six feet tall, with his hair tied back in a ponytail, his blue overalls stretched tight across his belly and the word JOE stencilled across his chest.

"Help you?" They were the same words Dan had heard just moments ago from the security guy and he wondered if the two men might be brothers. They certainly looked as if they were related.

"I hope so. I'm trying to find the owner of a very small helicopter. Had one report saying it looked like some kind of blue insect. You ever seen something like that?"

"Yeah. I've seen something like that a couple of times, but it wasn't blue. It was black. Black with some kind of crazy gold painting on it."

"You know who owns it?"

Joe shook his head. "Nah, but the office should have a record of the registration number. Tell them it was the dragonfly."

"Dragonfly?" That was the same description Annie had given him.

"Yeah. Weird looking thing. Cockpit's all plexi with this black fibreglass shell over the engine. Flies pretty good though."

"You think it might be a kit?"

"I dunno. What do you guys think?" Joe looked at the other two men.

"Could be," one of them answered. "Pretty good job if it is."

"Gotta be local," the other one said. "Fuel tank's tiny. Only takes about thirty litres."

"Has it been here recently?" Dan asked.

"Nah. Not for a couple of weeks. I figure it came off some fancy yacht. Just some rich guy's toy. Probably filled it up on the way north, then stopped in again on the way south."

"Yeah. We get a few of those here during the season." Joe pulled out a chair and Dan heard it groan as the big man sat down. "But it wasn't a guy flying it. It was a girl."

"A girl?" Dan hadn't given any thought to the possibility of the thief being female, although he probably should have. None of the items reported stolen were particularly large or heavy and a woman usually moved more lightly than a man which would make it easier to slip unseen and unheard through the forest.

But on the other hand, it was unlikely a female had murdered Jimmie. Few women committed murder, and when they did, it was seldom with a knife, and almost never as vicious as this killing had been.

"You get a good look at her?"

"No, sorry. All I can tell you is she's small and black," Joe answered and when Dan continued to stare at him, he grinned and shrugged. "She had to open the cockpit a bit to show me where to fill the damn thing. Shoved her arm out and pointed. Blackest skin I ever saw!"

Chapter 11

"There can't be that many women with a licence to fly a helicopter, and even fewer black women, at least in Canada. Should be easy to find her."

Dan had returned to the marina to find Walker chatting with Charles Eden, a man he had met two years before when he had been investigating a murder at Kitsault, an abandoned mining town not far from Prince Rupert, and Joel, a friend of Walker's, had been a suspect.

"You think she's the one behind the thefts?" Walker asked.

"Seems unlikely," Dan replied. "It's not the same helicopter Annie saw—she said that one was blue—although come to think of it, it's odd to have two of these birds around here. They can't be that common. This was the first one the guys at the airport had ever seen."

He looked at the picture he had printed out from a website. The registration number recorded on the helicopter at the airport had come back to something called a Helisport CH7 and Dan had looked it up. It had been manufactured in Argentina and registered in the Dominican Republic, which made it likely that it had indeed come off a visiting yacht.

"Sure easy to see why both Annie and Joe said it looked like a dragonfly," Charles said. "It looks like a toy."

"Yes it does," Dan said. "And it can't fly far. It's only got a small tank – although it does say here it can have an auxiliary tank installed." He held up the print-out.

"So you going to hang around and check it out?" Walker asked. "Getting kinda bored sitting here doing nothing—and the food's lousy."

"No," Dan said, ignoring the jibe. "The guys here can follow up on it. I need to go talk to the people in those other two villages."

He didn't mention that he had used the phone at the airport to call a friend in Vancouver. Bryce Searles had been both a neighbour and a classmate when Dan was growing up and was now a neurologist. They had lost track of each other when Bryce went to University and Dan joined the police force, but had met up again when Dan visited a crime victim at the hospital where Bryce was doing his residency. They still didn't get together very often, but whenever Dan was in Vancouver they had lunch.

"Long time no see," Bryce said when he realized who was calling him. "You in town?"

"No," Dan said. "I'm up in Rupert on a case, but I need a referral to a good orthopedics guy."

There was a brief silence as Bryce took that in, then he asked, "Case turn nasty?"

The question made Dan realize Bryce thought he might have been hurt while on duty. "No, it's not for me. It's for a friend. He's a really good guy, but he's got a problem with his legs and hips. He can barely walk."

When Bryce didn't respond right away, Dan added: "He's unofficial, but he helps me out when I'm dealing with the people in the villages. I really need him." As he heard himself say the words, he realized they were true. He did need Walker, and not only to help introduce him to the villagers. In his own quiet way, Walker had become his teacher and his guide as well as his friend.

"I can give you a name," Bryce said. "But I can't guarantee he can fit this guy in. He's got a waiting list a mile long."

"Can you talk to him? See if he can shuffle things a bit?"

"That important huh? Okay, I'll see what I can do—but the next lunch is on you."

"You get me a fast appointment and the next two lunches will be on me."

The specialist Bryce recommended would of course be in Vancouver, and Vancouver was not only the place where Walker's life had started to go wrong, it was also a place he had vowed never to return to. But if he was ever going to get back his independence, Dan knew it was a vow he would have to break.

Assuming Bryce was successful, how Dan was going to get Walker to agree was something he had yet to figure out, but he would find a way. He had to. Even if he had to use his position on the force to coerce him he would do it. It might mean risking their friendship—almost certainly would—but if it meant Walker could get back on his feet, or even back into his canoe, then it was something he was prepared to do.

***

The trip south was nothing like the trip north had been. The winds had largely died down, but the seas had not, and *Dreamspeaker* sunk her bow deep into every wave, then lifted her stern high and often corkscrewed as a swell came in from the west. There was no way the autopilot could handle the motion and that kept Dan tied to the wheel. A couple of times he heard grunts coming from the direction of the salon, and twice he heard Walker yell a curse, something he had not heard him do before, but there was nothing he could do to help.

When they finally dropped anchor in Hartley Bay, he had been at the wheel for a straight ten hours and he was exhausted, his back aching and his arms like lead weights.

"Heard you cursing back here," he said as he eased himself down onto the settee. "Sorry I couldn't come and help."

"Didn't need help," Walker said. "Needed food."

"Give me a couple of minutes and I'll get us something. Won't be fancy but at least it will fill our bellies."

"Hell of a lot easier in a canoe," Walker muttered. "Just have to drop a line."

"I don't think a canoe would have been much use in this weather." Weariness tinged Dan's voice.

"Lots of fish near the shore." Walker was nothing if not persistent. "How about you put the canoe in the water and I'll go catch one."

Through the window Dan could see a black bear turning over rocks on the beach, and farther on, a family of otters playing on the bank.

"How about you just drop a line off the boat," he said. "Or wait till we've eaten and I'll lower the Zodiac."

He was leaning back against the cushions and didn't see the look of anguish flash across Walker's face.

***

It took them another day to reach the next village and Dan learned almost nothing new. Like the others, this theft had happened in the early hours of the morning from a home that was occupied at the time, the various family members all asleep. The house was small, a simple, old-fashioned clapboard building in poor repair, boards missing here and there and with a couple of broken windows that had been patched with pieces of scrap wood. The front door opened directly into a cramped living space where the family told him they had kept their regalia. They had been in and out the previous day, as had other members of the village, and no one had noticed anything amiss. No one ever thought about locking their doors, so it would have been easy for someone to enter once everyone had gone inside for the night. Easy, but brazen.

As before, Walker managed to get a much better description of the stolen items, but that was only going to help when Dan had tracked the thief, and so far he no idea of where to start.

"Anybody say they heard or saw anything odd?" he asked as they started back down the channel. He was pretty sure the entire population of the village had been down to talk with Walker and there was yet another pile of smoked salmon strips on the seat beside him and a woven basket filled with some kind of berries.

"You mean other than *Bak'wus*?" Walker asked, grinning. "Nope. Although one guy said he saw an odd looking woman in a big power boat down at Dawson's Landing a week or so ago, just a couple of days before the thefts."

"Odd in what way?" Dan asked.

"Said the woman was dressed in weird clothes—long sleeves, long pants, head and neck wrapped in some big scarf. Wide-brimmed hat. Gloves on her hands." He shrugged. "And she was wearing sunglasses even though it was raining."

Dan nodded. "Does sound odd, but Dawson's is a long way from here. No reason to think she had anything to do with the thefts."

"True," Walker said.

They stayed quiet for a while, hearing the water rush along the hull, watching the sun slide slowly down behind the aspen trees that lined the banks, its slanting rays caressing each leaf and bathing it with light. An eagle swooped down from a high branch ahead of them and snatched a fish from the water, the scales of his catch glinting silver as it lifted up again.

"He also said the boat she was in was blue and had this weird paint job. Covered most of the hull. He figured it was some kind of symbol or something." Walker's words carried back on the wind.

Dan kept his eyes focused on the water ahead. The slopes on either side of the channel were dark now, but the sky above still held the light and reflected off the waves. The air was cold and every now and then he could smell the clean, salt smell of fish.

"Annie said that blue helicopter she saw had a weird paint job," he said. "And Joe said the same about the one in Rupert."

Walker nodded, the movement visible against the sheen of the water. "Be good to get a look at them."

"Yeah."

It wasn't much, but Dan knew better than to pass it by. It was the first time since Markleson had assigned him this case that he had felt the adrenaline buzz of electricity shiver along his nerves. It was faint, but it was at least a hint that he might have found that first elusive loose thread.

The moon was up by the time he had winched the Zodiac up onto the coach-roof, and the water sluicing off the keel shone like molten silver. Walker had settled himself on a bench on the aft deck, and as Dan climbed down and headed towards the wheelhouse, he accepted the strip of salmon that Walker held out.

"Best meal around," Walker said. "You thinking of going back up to Rupert?"

"No. I'll call Joe and talk to him. See if he can come up with a better description of the paint job on the helicopter he saw." Dan broke off a piece of fish and savoured the rich, smoky, sweet-salty flavour he remembered from time spent in the villages.

"Damn, that's good," he said. "Can't be too hard to make. Maybe I should learn."

Walker snorted. "Gotta learn how to fish first."

Dan inclined his head and broke off another piece of salmon. "True," he said. "But it might be worth trying."

They sat in companionable silence beneath a patch of stars, listening to the water chuckle against the hull and the quiet hooting of a pair of owls calling from the shadows.

"Might go back and visit Annie again after we've finished with the next village." Dan's words mingled with the sounds of the night. "Won't take long and if she can remember the design she saw on that helicopter she mentioned, maybe I can figure out if it was the same one that was there at Rupert."

Walker didn't answer and when Dan looked at him, his eyes were closed, the lines of his face relaxed in sleep.

Chapter 12

Dan and Annie leaned on the railing of her boat looking out over the pass. Dan had anchored in shallow water as close as he dared, and set both the depth-sounder and the GPS to monitor *Dreamspeaker's* position. He had left Walker in the wheelhouse with the VHF beside him and instructions to use it if any of the alarms went off.

"Was there anything about the logo on that helicopter you can remember?" he asked her.

"Not really, except the colour. Guess it didn't really look like anything specific—just some kind of weird symbol or something." She shrugged. "I never really paid that much attention. Just wanted the goddamn thing to fuck off."

"Ah well," he answered. "It was a long shot anyway and it's probably not important."

"Right." She turned her head to look at him. "Guess that's why you came back here, huh? To check out something that's not important?"

He laughed. It was never a good idea to underestimate this woman. While he had no knowledge of who she was, or where she had come from, or even how she had come to live in this tiny, remote cove, one thing he had learned was that there was a lot more to Annie than met the eye, and there was not much she missed.

"Well hopefully the guy at the airport in Rupert will be able to help. He's seen one up there a couple of times and it sounds very similar."

He passed her the box of cookies he was carrying.

"Last one," he said. "I'll restock when I get back to the marina. Bring you up a carton next time."

She nodded her thanks and they started to walk to the top of the ramp leading down to the shore, but she stopped a few feet short of it and angled her head, a puzzled look on her face.

"What?" asked Dan. "Is there something wrong?"

"You know when I saw that thing, it made me think of a witchdoctor or something. Nothing I can put my finger on. Maybe a bit African, although I'm damned if I can think why." She looked at him. "Come back inside for a minute. I might be able to find something in one of my books."

Dan glanced across at *Dreamspeaker*, lying quietly at anchor where he had left her, and followed Annie inside. He had only been in Annie's salon once before, and that was over five years ago, but he remembered the surprise he had felt when he had seen her library. Hundreds of books had lined every wall, and there seemed to be even more of them now, stacks piled on two low tables with more on the floor beside an ancient leather chair.

Annie headed over to the wooden shelves that climbed from floor to ceiling on the starboard wall and ran her fingers along a row of hardcover spines until she found the one she wanted. She pulled it out and headed into the galley, beckoning him to follow.

"Maybe there'll be something in here," she said as she laid it on the table and opened it up.

Dan looked over her shoulder as she turned the pages. Each one was filled with symbols, some simple, some incredibly complex. A few he recognized, and some he could guess at, but most made no sense at all. Why she would have a book like that he had no idea, but it had obviously been opened many times as many of the pages were tattered.

"There!" she said, smacking her hand down on a bright yellow and gold design. "I thought I'd seen something like it before." She turned the book around and pushed it towards him. "Might not be exact, but it's close enough—and the colour's right. Probably why I thought of it: that bright yellow's kinda hard to miss."

"*Vèvè for Ayizan*," he read. "What the hell does that mean?"

"Voudou," she answered. "A vèvè's a religious symbol, usually a geometrical drawing that represents the spirits, and Ayizan's the most ancient of the loa. What?

Dan was staring at her in astonishment.

"How the hell do you know this stuff?" he asked. "You spend all your time reading?"

For the first time since he had met her she looked embarrassed. She shrugged her shoulders and said, "I like to learn about things. Just because I live out here don't mean I'm stupid."

"You're far from that Annie. In fact I think you're one of the smartest people I've ever met." He reached out and gave her a hug, feeling her stiffen with shock. "Thank you. You just might have started me on the road to solving a murder—although how the hell Voudou could tie in with this is hard to figure."

As soon as he was underway Dan called Markleson. "I need you to get someone up in Rupert to check something out," he said.

100

"Some reason you can't ask them yourself?" Markleson asked.

"Doubt if they'll follow through," Dan replied. "They don't know me, and it's kind of an unusual request."

"I see." There was a brief silence and Dan heard the snap of a lighter followed by a spasm of coughing. "Goddamn it, I gotta quit this shit. So what do you need?"

Dan explained what he had learned from Annie.

"So you want me to have someone look up this . . . what do you call it?"

"*Vèvè of Ayizan*," Dan said. "Yes, and then send it up to Rupert and ask one of them to take it out to the airport and ask the guys at the fueling shed if it looks like what was on that helicopter they saw."

"*Vèvè of Ayizan*," Markleson repeated. "You know how crazy that sounds?"

Dan smiled. "Yeah, I do. Seems weird to me too, but Annie was pretty certain."

"Well." Markleson sighed. "I guess at least it'll give the guys something to talk about."

"Might impress them with the breadth of your knowledge."

"Yeah, right. Listen, you headed back?"

"Got one more village to visit up the end of Seymour Inlet."

"Well come see me as soon as you get in. There's some other stuff came up."

***

The last village was a repeat of all the others. The items stolen, a chief's staff, two Raven rattles, and a bentwood box, had been kept in the chief's house, the theft had occurred

101

at night and no one had heard or seen anything or anyone unusual. Once again, the community came down to the beach and shared the descriptions with Walker as he sat in the Zodiac, and once again they brought him baskets full of dried salmon, packages of something wrapped in some kind of seaweed, and stems of some plant that looked a bit like asparagus.

"You want some of this?" Walker asked as they headed back down the inlet. He held out one of the small packages.

"What is it?" Dan asked, peering at it suspiciously. "The salmon's great, but I'm not sure about seaweed."

"Yeah, you said that about the salmon once, but I notice you're happy to eat most of what they gave us." He thrust the package into Dan's hand. "Try it."

Dan cautiously nibbled a corner, then took a larger bite. "This is good!" he exclaimed. "What is it?"

"Dried herring roe. They put in some salmonberry shoots and then wrap it in kelp. Beats the hell out of that canned shit you call food."

Dan didn't answer, but he found it hard to disagree.

***

In order to avoid putting Walker's canoe in the water, Dan carefully timed his arrival back at the marina for late afternoon. Markleson seldom stayed at his office later than 5:30 pm and having to go and see him before he left for the day was the best excuse Dan had come up with. He still hadn't figured out how he was going to get Walker to Vancouver, but he knew for sure if the man got back in his canoe, even crippled as he was, he would disappear.

"Sorry to rush off but I won't be long," he said as he jumped down onto the swim grid and stepped onto the float. "I need to catch Markleson before he leaves. Want me to bring you back anything to eat?"

Walker didn't deign to answer.

***

Two hours later Dan was still sitting in Markleson's office, a stack of photographs spread out on the desk in front of him, a haze of blue smoke drifting over his head.

"So what's all this got to do with me?" he asked.

While each photograph was very different, they were all identified as stolen traditional and sacred objects. There were carved throwing sticks, incised stones, woven baskets, and something called a *Pukamani* pole, all from an island somewhere near Darwin, and Markleson told him that an aboriginal man who had tried to protect them had been stabbed and beaten so badly he was in a coma and not expected to survive.

"The people down at Head Office think it has to be linked to what's happening here," Markleson answered. "And I tend to agree with that. Look at them. All traditional items taken from a remote, indigenous community and all items that can't be easily sold." He pointed to a report attached to a photo of what appeared to be a smooth stone incised with a pattern of lines and circles. "If you read the reports, they've even got a few of the locals there talking about seeing some kind of ghost spirit—and the timing's right too. Their theft happened just before the most recent of ours did. Pretty big coincidence if they're not linked."

Dan shuffled the photos for the third or fourth time, trying to make some sense of them.

"So you think that there's a single person masterminding all these thefts? A collector deciding who steals what from places half a world apart? Doesn't seem too likely."

Markleson lit another cigarette. "I don't think anything. That's not my job, as I was very clearly informed when I said I thought you would be more useful here. All I know is that the people at the National Contact Bureau down in Vancouver are very interested in both cases, and they want to talk to you about them."

"The guys from NCB are up here?" Dan had been involved with the National Contact Bureau, the Interpol liaison organization in Canada, several times during his years on the anti-terrorist squad, and it was not a time he wanted to be reminded of. "Have they found some of this stuff?"

"Not that I know of, but you can ask them yourself when you're down there tomorrow." Markleson slid an envelope across the desk. "You're due in Vancouver at 0930 hours. Your ride leaves at 0800."

"My ride?" Dan stared at the envelope in confusion, then reached out and opened it. An official form slid out." "They're sending a plane?"

It might not be his worst nightmare—that would be something happening to Claire—but it was close.

"You think I could drive down? Save them some bucks on the plane and that way I would be able to get around while I was down there."

Markleson shook his head. "Not possible. Even if you left now—and you look dead on your feet—you couldn't get there on time. The last ferry to Vancouver leaves from Nanaimo in half-an-hour and it would take you at least four hours to get there. Besides, last time I checked, you don't have a car."

Dan massaged his forehead. As he had told Claire, he hated flying. It was one of the few things that truly terrified him. Commercial jets were something he avoided like the plague, and even the thought of having to use one of the fleet of small planes the RCMP Air Services operated was enough to put him in a cold sweat. But on the other hand, if he absolutely had to fly, at least a small plane would be better than a helicopter. He could only pray they wouldn't send one of those. A helicopter would be unbearable.

***

The light had faded by the time he left the office, and haloes of mist hovered around the street lights. He debated dropping into Gus's pub for a quick beer but decided against it. He had already been away from the boat too long and it wouldn't be fair to Walker.

And speaking of Walker . . . was there any way he could turn this into an opportunity to get Walker down to the city?

Chapter 13

It took most of the night, but by the early hours of the morning Dan had Walker's reluctant agreement to accompany him down to Vancouver. It hadn't been easy, and he didn't feel comfortable with the knowledge that he hadn't been entirely truthful. He had spent hours convincing Walker that he was the only one who could give a good enough description of the stolen regalia to enable its return. That part was true, although he really wouldn't have to go down to the city to do that. What Dan hadn't said was that once the meeting was over he planned on driving Walker to the hospital and somehow getting him examined, if not by the specialist Bryce had recommended then at least by an emergency-room physician. The man was so obviously suffering there was a good chance he would be admitted, or at least given something to ease the pain.

It was three in the morning when he phoned Markleson to see if he could arrange a float plane instead of a fixed-wing aircraft.

"Do you have any idea of what time it is?" Markleson had obviously been pulled out of a deep sleep, and his words were slurred. "This had better be goddamn important."

"It is to me, and if you want me to continue working with the indigenous folks on this coast, then it is to you too." Dan was too tired to come up with a diplomatic response. "I need you to get hold of Vancouver and get them to send up a float plane for my trip tomorrow."

"Are you crazy? It's three o'clock in the morning. They'll all be home in bed sleeping—like I was and like you should be. Why the hell do you want a float plane anyway?"

"I'm taking Walker down there with me. I'll never be able to get him into a fixed-wing. Even a float plane will be tough. He's in rough shape."

"They're not sending a goddamn taxi! You can't take a civilian along for the ride just because you want to."

Dan looked back over his shoulder to make sure Walker wasn't listening.

"Then deputize him. Do whatever you need to do, but I need to take him with me. Tell them he's the only one who can identify this stuff. That's the truth, anyway."

"Damn it, Connor. This is not about 'this stuff', it's about an assault and thefts on the other side of the planet. He sure as hell can't identify those."

"So tell them to have someone from forensics, or better still from the museum out there at the University, to talk to him. Tell them it's cost efficient—two for the price of one. We'll get a good description of the items stolen here and the museum will be a good resource for when we turn anything up."

Markleson's sigh was loud and clear. "You're not going to listen to reason are you." It was a statement, not a question.

"No. Not if it means Walker stays here. He has to go down to the city, and he has to go with me."

"Shit. Okay, I'll see what I can do, but no promises, you understand? I don't even know if I can get hold of anyone in time to talk to them before the plane takes off."

Dan smiled as he felt a weight lifted off him. "Thanks boss. I appreciate it. I owe you one."

"You sure as hell do," Markleson growled. " In fact, you owe me more than one." The phone went dead.

***

"Why can't they come up here? Make more sense. This is where it happened."

Walker was slowly working his way down onto the swim grid. He looked as if he hadn't slept in a week, his face lined, his jeans and jacket stained and wrinkled. Dan knew that, like him, Walker hadn't eaten anything and was functioning on only a cup of coffee, and he also knew he himself didn't look much better. He should probably have changed into his uniform, but it was too late now and even as he thought about it, he realized he liked the message the state of his clothing sent.

"You ever known the big city boys to make it easy for us small town folks?" he asked. "They always figure their time is more important than ours."

Walker snorted derisively and grabbed the railing to steady himself. "They got an elevator to get me into that thing?" he asked. "Not going to be pretty if . . ." The rest of his words were drowned in the backwash of props as a Beaver float plane taxied up to the wharf.

***

It took time to get Walker onto the plane, and even longer to get him off, but with the help of the pilot and another RCMP officer who had come to escort them to the NCB liaison office, they arrived only a few minutes later than scheduled. They were taken to a small conference room on the ground floor where a breakfast of donuts, danish and a pot of

108

coffee had been provided, all of which Walker refused. It was only when a small, gray-haired woman with thick glasses was brought in and introduced as the curator at the University's Museum of Anthropology that he was willing to even acknowledge the other people present, let alone join the conversation.

The woman had brought several books and a box of photographs with her, and she placed them on the table, pulled out a chair beside Walker, and spread them out in front of him. Almost immediately they were deep in conversation, their voices warm and eager. After several minutes of watching the two of them, gray and black heads almost touching as they leaned over the material she had brought, Dan felt a tap on his shoulder and he was beckoned over to another table on the other side of the room.

***

"You have to be crazy! Why the hell would you want to send me over there?" Dan pushed his chair back and scanned the faces staring back at him. There were three of them, all in plain clothes, plus an Inspector who Dan thought looked vaguely familiar although he couldn't place him. None of them looked moved by his protest.

"You know I'm on a case, working on a murder and several thefts here. This is where I can be useful. This is where I know the people, know the villages, know how things work. I know absolutely nothing about Australia!"

The spokesman of the group, a short, thickset man with a crewcut and a long mustache, was unmoved by his protest. "Two weeks isn't going to make a difference, and Commander Markleson can have someone keep an eye on things while you're gone."

Dan heaved a sigh of frustration. "Two weeks can make one hell of a difference—and what the hell can I possibly achieve in two weeks over there? I have no contacts, no knowledge of the culture or how things work. It's crazy."

"You know how things are *supposed* to work on an investigation and we'll provide you with contacts. You can identify when there's something untoward going on. We don't expect miracles, but we need someone on the ground there to tell us what's happening."

"Something untoward? What the hell does that mean? You think there's something fishy about the investigation?"

"I didn't say that." The reply was sharp. "We simply want to be sure that everything possible is being done to find out who did this, and whether it's linked to what's happened here. With the current political climate, we need to get this wrapped up as soon as possible."

Dan stared at him before letting his gaze drift around the other faces. "The current political climate?" He was doing the same repeating thing he did with Walker when he felt completely out of his depth, and he didn't like it.

For the first time there were signs of discomfort in the group and Dan watched as they exchanged glances.

Crewcut spoke again. "I assume you are aware that the move towards Reconciliation is currently playing a leading role in Australia, just as it is here. It's important that everybody sees we are putting maximum effort into stopping these crimes and getting these items back."

Dan was too tired to be diplomatic. "So this whole trip is just for show? You want to be able to say you did everything possible? If it's about Reconciliation, shouldn't I be staying here? Taking care of Reconciliation on this side of the pond?

Why don't you use the guys from the anti-terrorist squad if someone from here needs to go there? They're all familiar with international stuff. Any one of them could handle this better than I could."

"It's not just for show, Detective Connor. We need someone who understands the unique issues that exist between a police force and an indigenous population. Someone who can recognize when things that should be being done, aren't. And it seems the powers that be don't agree with you as to your abilities." The Inspector had been quiet up till then, but now he reached out and flipped open the folder lying in front of him. "They say no one else has the unique qualifications and experience you do." He lifted out a sheet of paper. "You served in the anti-terrorist squad . . ."

"That was ten years ago!" Dan exclaimed. "Things have changed . . ."

"Eight years ago, and according to this you were very good at it."

He picked up another sheet of paper. "You are— informally of course—considered to be a 'Lone Wolf' and as such you are used to working on your own. You have a high solve rate and over the last five years you have received consistently high marks for both your ability to think independently and for your diplomacy when dealing with the public." He stared at Dan over the rim of his glasses. "An unusual combination I would say."

He looked back down and turned more papers over. "In addition, it appears you have earned the trust and respect of the indigenous people you work with who frequently welcome you into their communities—something none of the rest of us can claim."

There was a muffled bark of laughter from the other table where Walker, who was supposedly working with the curator, was apparently listening in to the conversation. The Inspector ignored it.

"And then of course, there is the best reason of all." He pushed everything back into the folder and looked directly at Dan, a smile playing at the corner of his mouth. "Your lady friend—I believe her name is Claire?—is already over there is she not? You could not possibly have a better cover than a trip to visit her. If there *are* problems within the investigation, no one will suspect you are over there to look for them."

Chapter 14

They gave him an official folder containing the report of the assault and the thefts, plus a return ticket from Vancouver to Darwin via Sydney leaving in three days. They also lent him a car for the afternoon as the float plane wasn't available to take them back until later in the day.

With the help of a constable, Dan got Walker into the car and for an hour they drove aimlessly around Vancouver until they found themselves parked at a beach in Kitsilano, staring through the windshield at the rain.

"You're awful quiet." Walker's voice broke the silence that had lasted since they left the station.

Dan shrugged. The beach was empty, the ocean beyond obscured by rain, but the air was filled with the raucous call of gulls.

"Plane ride bothering you?"

Dan leaned back against the seat and nodded. Yes, contemplating the plane ride was bothering him. It scared the hell out of him.

"Free trip. Probably have better weather over there." Walker gestured out the window at the slanting grey rain. "Get to see Claire."

Dan nodded again. "Yeah."

He knew he should be excited about that, but the truth was he couldn't get past the idea of having to sit in a metal tube, forty-thousand feet above the earth, crowded into an uncomfortable seat and breathing recycled air.

"Don't seem too happy about it."

Dan stared out at the rain some more, then looked at the man who sat beside him. This was a side of Walker he had never seen, but then neither of them had ever been in this position before. It had always been Dan supporting Walker—or had that just been his perception? His ego?

In any case, he owed both Claire and Walker an explanation. He hadn't been honest with either of them. Worse, he hadn't been honest with himself. And he had been downright dishonest with Walker about his motive for bringing him here. While he had admitted to Claire that he was afraid of flying, he hadn't told her why, and he certainly should have been open with Walker about his reasons for asking him to come to the city. He had brought the man down here under false pretences, and although it was certainly good to have the descriptions of the stolen items shared with the museum, Dan was in essence holding him hostage, deciding he knew what was best.

"There's a few things you don't know Walker," he said. "And I owe you an explanation—and an apology."

As he talked, the rain slowly eased and a few hardy souls made their way down onto the beach where a flock of shore birds probed the sand.

"So that's all of it," Dan said almost an hour later. "And I don't know which bothers me most, flying, leaving the folks in Tsatsquot hanging, or interfering in your life without your permission. Doesn't matter anyway. None of it's right, and for what it's worth, I apologize." He reached for the ignition. "Guess we might as well head back. Maybe we can find something we both consider edible on the way back to the airport."

114

They wove their way back through the wet streets in silence. Dan almost wished Walker would yell at him, swear at him, call him an asshole, anything to ease his guilt, but Walker only sat, staring quietly out of the window at the traffic.

They were approaching the airport again when he finally spoke, his voice sounding unnaturally loud after the long silence.

"So when's the appointment?"

"What?" The car swerved as Dan turned to stare at the man sitting beside him. "Why?"

"I'm already here, aren't I? Might as well go through with it. How about you?"

"How about me what?"

"You hate flying, right?"

"Yeah, I do."

"Scares the hell out of you?"

"Yeah, it does."

"But you're going to get on that plane anyway?"

Dan sighed and ran his hand through his hair. "I guess I don't have much choice."

"Then it sounds like we're both in the same boat."

***

The Capilano Reserve was a good hour's drive from the airport, but Walker said he had a cousin living there he could stay with. It was getting late by the time they arrived, and later still by the time they got Walker into the house. Dan was reluctant to leave but the floatplane wouldn't wait around once it returned.

"I'm sorry about setting up that appointment without your permission, Walker. I had no right to do that."

115

"True," Walker said, but there was no anger in his voice.

"If you have any problems, call Bryce. He's a good man. He'll sort everything out."

"Yeah."

"You need any money?"

"No."

"Okay, well take care. I'll be back in a couple of weeks, but I'll stay in touch with Bryce while I'm gone."

"You keep talking any longer I'll be thinking you're trying to miss that plane."

***

A few hours later, back aboard *Dreamspeaker* with only the slap of the waves against the hull to keep him company, Dan put a Mingus CD on the stereo, got a beer out of the fridge, and wandered out onto the deck. The jagged rhythms and harmonies of the music echoed his mood as he stared out over the water, watching its movement, hoping it would calm him as it had so often done before, but it didn't help.

The gibbous moon hanging above his head, its light diffused by a thin mist, lit a family of otters playing out on the float, and the soft calls of birds roosting in the trees above the marina played a counterpoint to the piano. Everything was as it should be—except for him.

He had promised Charlie and his people that he would do all he could to find the murderer and bring him to justice, and to bring the stolen regalia back to them, and while he hadn't actually said those same words at the other villages, it had been implied. If word got out that he had gone to Australia, would they all feel betrayed? Would he lose the trust he had built up? Worse still, would he lose that first hint of a trail?

If that helicopter was, in fact, linked to the thefts, and if it came off a yacht, then it would probably be long gone by the time he returned. A yacht big enough to carry that kind of dinghy would be capable of good speeds. It could easily be down in Central America somewhere and impossible for him to track down.

And what about Walker? Dan had deceived the man, coerced him into seeing the surgeon and then abandoned him in a city that Dan knew he both hated and feared. Hated because of the memories it carried, and feared because of the temptations it offered. If the specialist recommended surgery, would Walker be able to handle being in a hospital again? Perhaps learning to walk again?

And then there was the flight.

There it was simply his own fear he had to deal with. Even the thought of stepping into that plane and hearing the doors close sent a cold shiver of dread through his body. Just hours before he had shared the reason for his fear with Walker, the first time he had ever spoken it aloud, and it had been both easier and harder than he had thought it would be. Easier because the explanation was straightforward and Walker was a great listener. Harder because it was something he had locked deep inside himself for over thirty years, unwilling to revisit or even acknowledge the anguish he had experienced at the time.

His mother had died in a plane crash. There. Not difficult to say. Nothing to be ashamed of. So why had he buried that memory for all that time? Mary Connor had been heading to Ireland to see her own mother, a trip she had saved for and dreamed about for years, but she never arrived. Her plane disappeared into the ocean somewhere over the North Sea. It happened in late August when the sockeye were running along the west coast. After seeing her off at the airport, he and his father had headed out on their boat and they had received the news over the ship's radio. Dan was ten years old and he'd never seen his father cry before.

For weeks, the two of them simply drifted along the coast, stopping only when the supply of whiskey and beer ran low, surviving on whatever meager supplies were in the galley and the fish they caught. Winter storms finally drove them back to the safety of the marina, but still they stayed aboard, refusing to go back to the house where they'd lived as a family—the house they never lived in again because his father put it up for sale.

Dan closed his eyes and let the old memories wash over him. There was his mother, her black hair tumbling over her shoulders, laughing as he struggled to escape a hug he considered himself too old for. There was their boat, the *Mary Jean*, the boat they had all cherished, once bright with fresh paint and sparkling with polished metal, now slowly decaying until it became, like them, grubby and unloved. There was his father, aged fifteen years in a single month, bent under the weight of his sorrow.

It had aged Dan too. He had been a happy ten-year-old when it happened, carefree, excited by the idea of skipping a few weeks of school to be out on the boat with his father. Overnight he became the adult, caring for a man who no longer cared—or perhaps cared too deeply—to care for him.

He touched each memory tentatively, teasing it like a sore tooth, preparing himself for the raw pain he had once felt. It didn't come. Each one still hurt, yet they were softer now, further away, the faces and events blurred by time, the sorrow and the inevitable anger and resentment that followed blunted by the years.

And then, even as the images swelled and faded, another very different image imposed itself. Himself eight years ago, quitting the RCMP, disappearing onto a boat and losing himself in alcohol, and suddenly it all became clear. He had reacted to Susan's death exactly as his father had done when *his* wife had died. Had it been a learned behaviour or something genetic and why had it taken Dan so long to recognize it? And if he had been so blind to something so obvious, were there other things he had not seen or recognized? Other buried memories that might surface unexpectedly to trip him up?

His harsh laugh sent the otters diving into the safety of the dark water below. Just hours ago he had been told his solve rate was so good they were sending him to investigate the theft of items he knew nothing about from a culture he didn't understand in a country he was unfamiliar with. Hell, he couldn't even solve his own issues. How was he going to sort out problems in Australia?

And first he had to get there!

Seventeen hours. Seventeen hours locked in a plane. Another five to Darwin. Although acknowledging where his fear came from might be a step in the right direction, it didn't solve the problem. That was going to take time. A lot of time. Time he did not have.

It was the thought of Claire that finally brought him back to some semblance of sanity. She would be there to greet him, smiling, laughing, the sun dancing off that tousled mop of blonde hair. The sound of her voice, the scent of her skin, the feel of her hand in his. The curve of her hip as they lay together. The rise and fall of her breathing.

She answered his call on the second ring.

"Dan! It's so good to hear your voice! Are you back at the marina?"

They talked for hours and he told her everything: Walker, the plane crash, his father, the case . . . on and on. And she listened. And listened. And then she spoke. She said he might be thinking he was not the man he had thought he was, a man with strength and confidence, but she knew better. And he was the man she loved.

By the time they signed off he was calm enough that he thought he would finally be able to crawl into his bunk and sleep. He only had two days before his flight, but with her help he had figured out how he was going to use them.

Chapter 15

"This is how a condemned man must feel."
As Dan walked unsteadily down the jetway towards his plane,
he fought to keep himself from turning back. *"When I step
through that door I'll be incarcerated in a metal tomb and the
door will slam shut behind me!"*

He wiped a sweaty palm against the leg of his jeans
and hoped the flight attendant wouldn't notice the sheen of
sweat on his face.

From the time he had stepped onto the floatplane that
morning, exhausted by two sleepless nights and two endless
days spent talking to the people he would be leaving behind,
fear had been his constant companion. It was ridiculous and it
was annoying. He was a grown man and he knew the safety
record of planes was excellent, far better than cars and boats
and he wasn't afraid of either of them.

But even though he knew where the fear came from,
he couldn't find a way to ease it.

He forced a smile onto his face as he handed his ticket
to the attendant and she welcomed him aboard. The plane was
far from full and the clerk at the check-in desk had noted the
rank shown on his ticket and had upgraded him to first-class.
That meant a seat very near the front, although to his surprise
the 'seat' looked more like a private cabin. It came complete
with a desk and a TV screen and, as the attendant
demonstrated, an array of buttons that would convert the seat
into a bed long enough to accommodate even his long legs. It
even had a hood to ensure privacy. The smile of thanks he

gave her as he settled into the soft leather contours was the first genuine smile he had given for days.

***

A young constable had met him at the airport with a folder containing a detailed report of the theft he was supposed to investigate including background information on the town where it had occurred and a list of people to contact. He had stuffed them into a briefcase that was already filled with the Canadian reports and his plan was to read every word of every report as many times as was necessary in order to keep his mind off where he was. This 'cabin' would certainly help and perhaps would keep him sane. Maybe in seventeen hours he would even be able to see a pattern in the crimes. Recognize something he had missed before.

Yesterday, Markleson had promised to follow up on the helicopter and let him know if he learned anything. He also said he would send Dan the autopsy report when it came in, and make sure Jimmie was taken home by someone who would honour and respect the wishes and customs of the family. Dan had given his word and he intended to keep it even if he couldn't be there himself.

Bryce had agreed to keep him informed on what was happening with Walker—always assuming Walker actually kept his appointment and followed through with whatever treatment the orthopedic specialist recommended. That left only Charlie and his people at the village. Dan had tried to get a message to them by asking the skipper of one of the fishboats tied up at the marina to relay it to other fishboats from the Tsatsquot community, but there was no way he could be sure it had been received. There was nothing more he could do.

122

There was also nothing he could do to stop his fingers from digging into the armrests when the plane started to taxi, or to stop his heart from racing as the engines revved up for take-off. The only thing that helped was to keep an image of Claire waiting for him when this nightmare ended firmly fixed in his mind.

***

He stepped out onto the tarmac in Darwin almost thirty hours later, dazed and barely functional. He had spent eight sleepless hours in an airport hotel in Sydney after his arrival there, and five more on yet another plane to get here. He was exhausted and confused.

A quick glance at his watch, which he had yet to adjust for the time change, told him it was ten at night, yet a white-hot sun shimmered over his head and a flashing sign on a wall announced it was two-thirty in the afternoon. It also stated the temperature was thirty-four degrees. The contrast between this world and the one he had just left was so vast it left him disoriented. Gone was the cool, moist air he was familiar with, filled with the soft green scent of cedar, spruce and fir. Here the air was hot and dry, the earth red and parched, and there was a faint smell of eucalyptus. Briefly he wondered if the stress of so many hours in a plane had affected his brain, and he found himself running a mental checklist: name, birthday, boat name, marina. It all seemed right but he wasn't sure and he could hardly make out the faces of the people around him . . . but he couldn't mistake Claire's voice.

"Dan!"

Just hearing it was enough. His mind started to function once more, his heart rate settled, his eyes regained their sight, and when he felt her press against him and her arms wrap around his waist, he could finally smile again.

She led him out of the airport to a dusty jeep and they drove into the city along streets lined with trees he couldn't identify. The land was flat, the buildings a glaring white, and the glass in the windows reflected the sunlight.

"It all looks new," Dan said as he gazed at the multi-story apartment and office blocks.

"Well not new exactly," Claire answered. "The city was completely wiped out by a hurricane Christmas 1974 so it's all been built since then. The only thing left standing was an old stone church—I'll show it to you if you like. It's beautiful."

"Maybe later," he said. "What I need now is a shower and a beer, maybe two, and then we can relax and catch up on your work."

"And yours," she answered. "You didn't say much on the phone."

"Not much to tell, at least not yet."

He saw her glance at him and knew she had read the concern in his voice. He had never been able to hide things from Claire—only from himself, he acknowledged with a wry smile—and he found himself looking forward to explaining the situation to her. She, like Walker, was a great listener, and her insights often cut through the complexities he allowed to distract him.

***

Their hotel was on the Esplanade, and his room looked out across a white sand beach to the ocean beyond. It was a far nicer view than he had expected the Bureau to provide. Perhaps he had been too cynical about their motives and if that was so then he needed to give the case he was here to investigate more importance. But what exactly was he supposed to investigate? The crime? Or the local investigation?

"Interpol must have a pretty good budget," he said, staring out the window. "I hope I can give them their money's worth."

Claire slid her arm through his. "I suppose I'm prejudiced, but I don't think there's any doubt of that," she said. "They know what they're doing, and I'm sure they've done their research. They know how you work."

He leaned down and kissed the top of her head. "Thanks for the vote of confidence. I just hope it's not misplaced. They might know how I work in Canada, but I'm not so sure I'll be able to do the same here."

There was a bar fridge beside the bed, and he opened the door and took out two bottles of Toohey's beer. When he removed the caps and held the bottle up to the light he could see ice crystals clinging to the inside of the glass.

"Looks like they've thought of everything," he said. "How about we take these outside? That bed is calling my name, but I want to hold out as long as I can. I really need to reset my body clock if I'm going to be able to do anything at all."

They found a table under the shade of a palm tree in a wide courtyard where they could enjoy some privacy while they watched guests laze in the pool, and he gave her an edited version of the case he was here to investigate, carefully omitting the vicious beating documented in the Australian report. She didn't need to hear about that.

"This happened on Bathurst Island?" she asked as she beckoned to a waiter. "So that has to be why Waru left in such a hurry. You really need to talk to him."

"He's the guy helping you in Maningrida, right?"

"Yes, but I think I told you he was born on an island near here, and just last week he had to go home for some emergency."

Dan nodded. "Yes, I remember, but why would I need to talk to him?"

"Well the island he went to is Bathurst. His people have lived there for thousands of years. I haven't been there, but I know Wurrumiyanga, where you say this happened, is the only town. Waru didn't tell me what the emergency was, and I didn't ask, but surely it has to have been that theft."

As he watched the waiter approach to take their order, Dan tried to gather his thoughts and focus what she had just said, but his mind was too tired to cooperate. Nothing was making sense anymore. He had barely slept since he had first been told about this assignment, and he hadn't eaten anything except for a few snacks on the plane since he left Vancouver. He was tempted to order a steak, but the heat convinced him to follow Claire's lead and choose a sandwich and a salad instead. He didn't know if this was breakfast or dinner, but whatever it was, he was hungry.

"So this guy Waru is back in Maningrida now?"

"Yes, but he's often out of town for two or three days at a time. He's an environmental officer, always going off to check various sites. He calls it 'going walkabout.'"

"And he didn't say anything about a theft?"

"No, but he seemed very upset. All he said was to be careful because somebody—I couldn't understand the name—was angry and had sent out some kind of evil spirit."

Dan closed his eyes. Was it possible none of this was real? Could he be dreaming? He had flown almost 12,000 kilometers, crossed from one side of the Pacific to the other, gone from cold rain to hot sun, from green forest to red desert all in single day, but still he was haunted by spirits that didn't belong to the world he lived in and that made no sense.

He signalled to the waiter. "I think I need a drink."

Chapter 16

Dan was asleep two hours before the sun sank below the
horizon. He hadn't expected to sleep well, but whether it was
due to total exhaustion or the two glasses of whiskey he had
drunk that afternoon, he woke feeling refreshed and more
relaxed than he had in days. Outside his window the Timor Sea
lapped softly onto the sand and the air was filled with the
sound of birds. Not the piercing squawk of the seagulls he was
used to, or even the harsh call of ravens and crows. This was
the raucous screech of parrakeets darting through the pine-like
casuarina trees, their feathers flashing with brilliant colours.

Claire joined him at the window, her hair still wet
from the shower.

"I didn't think you'd be awake this early," she said.
"How are you feeling?"

"Better than I expected," he answered. "Maybe after
breakfast I'll even be ready to tackle those spirits your friend
warned you about."

She laughed. "Good luck with that! I hope you brought
some shorts. It's going to be hot again today."

It was late in the dry season, and the monsoon rains
had yet to appear. With them would come the humidity, but for
now the air was dry and the sky clear.

They wandered down to the courtyard again for
breakfast, and sat at the same table with the palm fronds
whispering overhead and a faint breeze coming off the ocean.
A waitress wearing only a halter-top and shorts came for their

order and this time Dan indulged his craving for a steak, adding two eggs, fries and toast to the order.

"Making up for lost time?" Claire asked as she watched him eat.

He grinned and beckoned the waitress for another cup of coffee.

"Nope. Stoking up for a busy day. I don't have to go over to Bathurst until tomorrow morning, but we've got a few hours until your plane leaves so I think we should make the best of it." His leer and raised eyebrows left no doubt about what he was referring to.

"I thought you wanted to go to the museum. Didn't you say you could get some information on those stolen items there?"

"It's on the way to the airport," he said as he pulled her to her feet. "We can stop there on the way."

The maid had not yet made up the beds, and he eased her down on the rumpled linen. In the little time they had been apart her skin had taken on a deeper shade and it glowed like gold against the stark white of the sheets. God, he had missed her! Missed this joining. This sharing. This merging of their bodies. It was not just sex, although the release that provided was more than welcome. It was so very much more.

***

It was hours later when they returned to the patio for lunch.

"You can't seriously want seconds," Claire said as she listened to Dan order another serving of grilled barramundi. "You won't be able to move!"

"I have to refuel after all my exertions this morning," Dan answered, his eyes betraying the laughter his face tried hard to hide.

"Yours? And what about mine?" Claire grinned and reached over to steal a tomato from his plate before changing the subject. "Anyway, I'll talk to Waru as soon as I can. See when he's going to be around long enough for you to meet him."

"I'd like to know a bit more about these spirits he told you about."

Dan, who had spent a lifetime dealing in facts, felt idiotic talking about spirits. "Maybe ask him if they have a name."

Claire stared at him in astonishment. "You can't seriously think a spirit had anything to do with these thefts! You must have spent too much time with Walker—and speaking of Walker, have you heard anything from Bryce?"

"No. I'll try and call him tomorrow morning before I leave, but do ask Waru about those spirits. I know it sounds crazy, but so far every one of these reports has mentioned some spirit or ghost being in the area, and right now that's the only thing I've got. That and a miniature helicopter with a weird paint job that probably has nothing to do with anything."

"A helicopter?" Claire nibbled the end of a slice of cantaloupe. "There's a guy who lives on an island in the inlet where I'm working who has a small helicopter."

"I imagine they're pretty common here," Dan said. "As far as I can tell the whole continent of Australia runs on planes or helicopters."

"True, but it's not so much the helicopter as the man who owns it that's interesting. Waru warned me to stay clear of Snake Island when I first arrived. He said it was private property and the owner doesn't like visitors."

"Private?" Perhaps Dan had been wrong to think this area was all now under aboriginal ownership. "You mean a white owner? But I thought . . . "

"Yes, I did too, but Waru said there's a few places not covered by the agreement the government made to turn the land back to the people. Most of them are industrial sites— gold and manganese mines over on the other side of Kakadu." She inclined her head to indicate the direction. "And there's a few others further south. But it turns out there's also a couple of places that were sold off to the private sector before the deal was signed, so they're grandfathered in. Snake Island's one of them."

The breeze had strengthened and it was ruffling Claire's hair. She had turned her chair to put her back to the other customers who were coming in for lunch and the light played across the smooth, bronzed skin of her shoulders. Dan reached out and trailed his fingers down her arm.

"Did Waru say this guy might be dangerous?" he asked, concern tightening his voice. "Is he someone we should be worried about?"

Claire smiled and patted his hand. "No, I think he's probably just a hermit. The whole island is posted with 'Private' and 'Keep Off' signs, and there's no wharf. As far as I can tell they've never seen him in Maningrida, but Waru said someone saw the helicopter in Darwin and they said a weird looking guy got out of it."

"Weird? Weird in what way?"

"They said he was tiny. Sort of hunched over, and he walked oddly." She laughed. "And they said he was wearing too many clothes!"

Dan stared at her. "Too many clothes?" he asked. "What does that mean?" It was the same comment Walker had told him was used to describe a woman at Dawson's Landing.

She shrugged. "I have no idea. It's just what he said. Maybe the poor man was hiding some disfigurement or something."

"I'm not sure I like the idea of you being out there alone with someone who's that reclusive. Those kind of guys can get violent if they think their privacy is being invaded, and it doesn't take much to set them off."

"I'm fine Dan. Really. I don't go anywhere near the island. Even the dugongs stay away. It has a steep, rocky shore and they like the shallow water along the banks where they can find grass to eat." She beckoned to the waitress. "Are you ready for dessert?"

He let her change the subject, but he still felt uneasy. Perhaps after he had dropped her off at the airport he would do a little checking into the owner of Snake Island. There was something very odd about having two people with a similar description in two different places.

***

They took a cab to the museum, which Dan had been advised could help him learn about aboriginal culture and art, but the only person who might have been able to help him was down in Alice Springs until the following week, and her assistant could only advise him to go to Bathurst Island.

"Guess you're headed to the right place," Claire said with a grin as they went back out into the sunshine. "Odd they don't know about the thefts. You would think someone would have told them."

"I think the police may be keeping it quiet," he said. "They told me in Vancouver the guys here think it might be local and they don't want to scare him—or them—off."

"Local?" Claire asked. "But Wurrumiyanga is an aboriginal village. Wouldn't that mean that one of their own had stolen those things?"

"Yeah, it would. Doesn't make any sense, but it's the same with the thefts back in Canada."

***

After he had watched Claire's plane take off, Dan made his way to the head office of the Northern Territory Police. Unlike the Darwin police department which covered the city, the Northern Territory police covered the entire state, a huge area of almost a million and a half square kilometers, and they also served as liaison for Interpol. He showed his credentials at the desk, and was immediately ushered into the Deputy Commander's office.

"You're certainly a long way from home. I can't say we have too many Canadians paying us a visit."

Deputy Commander Colin Harbinson leaned back in his chair and tented his fingers. Unlike almost every other male Dan had seen that day, Harbinson was wearing polished leather shoes instead of sandals, long tan-coloured trousers instead of shorts, and a white short-sleeve uniform shirt. The pants and shirt were both crisply pressed.

"I am of course aware of both the assault and the theft, but I must say I'm surprised that Interpol is taking such an interest." He nodded towards a file on his desk. "Assaults are unfortunately a regular occurrence in our aboriginal

133

communities, as I'm sure they are in yours, and it certainly isn't unusual to have an assault committed during a robbery." He opened the file, lifted out an airline ticket, and slid it towards Dan. "I doubt the value of the items stolen would even cover the cost of your flight to Bathurst. A rock, a couple of old sticks and a pole?" His sneer of dismissal was barely audible, but the meaning came across loud and clear.

"Well, there are collectors for everything," Dan replied, his voice carefully neutral. "The price they will pay for what they want doesn't necessarily conform to logic."

"And you think some collector would take an interest in this kind of thing?"

"It would seem so. There have been thefts of similar items from indigenous communities in both our countries, and the level of violence associated with them appears to be increasing. The only motivation we can come up with is personal satisfaction. It's hard to see any financial reward."

Something flitted across Harbinson's face and was quickly suppressed.

"Well, keep me informed of your progress, although I suspect you will find your perpetrators closer to home than half a world away. As will we." He closed the file, but as he did so Dan caught a glimpse of a sheet of paper with a bright yellow logo at the top. It looked familiar although it was only visible for a moment so he couldn't be sure.

"Was there anything else?" The tone was unmistakeably dismissive, but Dan refused to take the hint.

"Yes," he said, fighting to keep his tone even. "Two things. I would like to see the forensics report on the theft, and the medical report on the injuries sustained by the victim. I understand it was a particularly vicious beating and that he's still in hospital?"

Harbinson wrinkled his brow. "I'm afraid there isn't a full forensics report. There are only two police officers stationed on Bathurst Island, both aboriginal, and frankly neither one is capable of that sort of thing. By the time we heard about it and sent someone over there . . ." He left the rest of the sentence unsaid, but the implication was clear. Like the village where Jimmie had died, any evidence had been destroyed by the people themselves.

"And the medical report?"

"I'll have one of my officers phone the hospital. You can pick it up there." The interview was obviously over.

"One more thing," Dan added. "I was hoping you might be able to tell me who owns Snake Island."

"Snake Island?" Harbinson's head jerked up and his pale eyes focussed intently on Dan. "I wasn't aware of any thefts from out that way."

"None that I know of. It's just that I know someone working near there who mentioned the island is privately owned." For some reason Dan felt a reluctance to let Harbinson know about his relationship with Claire. "I didn't know it was possible to buy land here."

"I see. Well that really isn't anything we would have information on, and as it has nothing to do with your reason for being here . . . "

Again it was a dismissal, and this time Dan was happy to act on it. He needed time to digest what he had just seen and heard, and while he wasn't any closer to finding out who owned Snake Island, his interest had moved up several degrees.

After the chill of Harbinson's office, he found the heat outside the building welcome.

***

Five o'clock the next morning found Dan sitting out on the patio drinking his third coffee of the day as he waited for his call to be answered. The air was filled with the sound of cicadas, and even with the glow of the street lights along the Esplanade dimming his view of the stars, the night sky was spectacular. He was trying to identify the constellations when Bryce picked up his phone.

"Searles." The voice was brusque.

"Guess I didn't catch you on lunch like I hoped."

"Dan? Hell, lunch is just some crappy snack bar from the machine if I'm lucky, but thanks for trying. How was the flight?"

"Don't ask, and there's another one coming up in a couple of hours."

Bryce laughed. "Sorry to hear it, but you'd be better off talking to a psychologist about that. Anyway, I can't talk for long and I'm guessing you're calling about Walker, right?"

"Yes. I left him with a phone but he's not answering it." In the darkness Dan shook his head at his own naiveté. Of course Walker wasn't answering. He never did.

"Well so far the news is good. Mark—he's the orthopedic guy—says he can put in an artificial hip and knee and realign everything. It won't be perfect, and there's going to be quite a bit of rehab to get the muscles working right again, but it'll be considerably better than what he's got now."

The surge of relief Dan felt was short-lived.

"Of course that's assuming he actually turns up for the surgery. It's scheduled for tomorrow morning and Mark said your friend wasn't exactly enthusiastic when he laid it all out for him."

"Yeah, well if he does show, could you let me know? Or better still call me and put Walker on the phone. I'd like to talk to him."

***

Morning sprang to life with a suddenness Dan found hard to believe. One minute it was dark and the next a brilliant orange ball was lifting above the horizon, blinding him as he dialed Markleson's number.

"Where the hell are you?" Dan could almost smell the smoke from Markleson's pipe as the familiar voice rasped over the air. "You coming back any time soon? We need you here, not sunning yourself on some goddamn sandy beach."

"Too hot for that, and you already know where I am. I'm flying over to Bathurst Island in a couple of hours to check out the thefts over there." Dan offered a silent vote of thanks to whatever spirits had given him Markleson for a boss and not Harbinson. "I'll see you in a couple of weeks, but meanwhile I'm wondering if you've made any progress on that helicopter?"

"Yeah. Hang on a minute." He heard a match flair and an indrawn breath before he heard the answer.

"It belongs to a guy by the name of Jean-Jacques Chauvet and it's registered in the Dominican Republic."

"So it probably did come off a yacht," Dan said, disappointment colouring his voice. "Well there goes that lead."

"Not so fast. There's more. Remember you also asked me to check out that weird pattern you called the Vèvè of Ayizan?"

"Yeah. That's the design painted on that helicopter. Why?"

"Well I gave that job to Carstairs—remember him? He's that zealous young over-achiever more commonly known as the pain-in-the-ass. Drives everyone in the office nuts, but he outdid himself on this one." There was the sound of papers shuffling. "Turns out Ayizan is the high princess of Voudou. That vèvè-thing is her symbol."

"Well Haiti is next door to the Dominican Republic, and Voudou is the religion there so I guess that makes sense."

"True, but what's interesting is Chauvet owns a big chunk of land on Porcher island, up there near Rupert. He bought it a couple of years ago and apparently his daughter spends a lot of time there."

"And? Are you going somewhere with this?"

More paper rustled over the air. "Ah, here it is. Erzulie. That's what the daughter calls herself, although her real name is shown as Samantha. Carstairs says Erzulie is another one of the Voudou spirits. She's supposed to be a pale, white-haired woman associated with water and like all the spirits she's referred to as *mystère* or *invisible*."

"So . . .?"

"You ever ask yourself which one of us is the boss and which one the detective? Remember those white hairs you sent in to forensics? Well I just got the report. They come from a female with something called Xeroderma Pigmentosum. Carstairs looked it up. It means lack of pigmentation in the skin and/or the hair. An extreme case is albinism. Quite the coincidence, don't you think?"

It was indeed quite the coincidence, but Dan didn't have time to spend on it. His taxi to the airport had arrived.

138

"I have to go. Any chance you could scan all that and send it to me?"

Chapter 17

With his six-foot-two-inch frame crammed into a seat Dan figured was meant for a small child, and buffeted by what the pilot announced were turbulent air pockets, the half-hour flight from Darwin to Bathurst Island was a nightmare. To try to keep his mind occupied, he focused on the information Markleson had sent to his phone. There certainly could be a link, although just what it was he had no idea. The girl who had flown the helicopter they had seen in Rupert had been black, not albino, and any girl with either black or white skin and hair would have been very noticeable in any of the villages. It was also unlikely any girl could have thrown a body as big as Jimmie's into that salal. Finally, most if not all the villages were beyond the range of that helicopter so making any connection was almost impossible.

His mind drifted to the logo he had seen in Harbinson's office and he brought up the photo of the Vèvè of Ayizan. Could that possibly have been what he saw? It was hard to believe. As far as he knew Voudou wasn't popular in Australia, and even if it was, Harbinson, with his crisply pressed clothing and his dismissive sneers, would be the last man he would associate with it.

He put the phone back in his pocket and switched his attention to the medical report he had picked up at the hospital. The victim, one Ngarra Nungurra, an elderly aboriginal male, remained in a coma with severe head injuries likely caused by a heavy, blunt object. He was not expected to recover.

By corkscrewing his body in the seat and dropping his chin to his chest, Dan managed to peer out through the window at the Timor Sea sparkling below and, just coming into view, a tree-covered island fringed with white sand. It looked idyllic and much more like his vision of what northern Australia would look like than Darwin had done, but he didn't have time to enjoy his reverie. The plane lurched as they hit an air pocket and Dan's stomach lurched with it.

***

By the time the Cessna landed on the Bathurst Island airstrip, Dan's hands ached from gripping the armrest so tightly he was sure his fingers had left permanent indentations. He was also sweating profusely. He struggled out of his seat, almost fell down the steps onto the runway, and looked around. As far as he could see the land was flat, the ocean beyond shimmering under the yellow glare of the sun, the earth on either side of the smooth tarmac a rich red edged with what he thought were eucalyptus trees. A cluster of small white buildings with corrugated tin roofs glinted in the sun.

"Officer Connor?"

A man with the blackest skin Dan had ever seen, dressed in the uniform of the Aboriginal Community Police, stood by his side.

"That would be me," Dan answered, reaching out to shake hands. "But please call me Dan."

"Dan," the man acknowledged with a relieved smile. "I'm Wally. Welcome to Wurrumiyanga. The Elders are waiting to meet you at Patakajiyali."

He saw Dan's frown and laughed. "I think you will find our language hard to understand. Patakajiyali is our museum. It's where we try to preserve our history and culture.

141

Where we teach our children their traditions and their language."

His smile faded. "It is also where the thefts occurred and where Ngarra was beaten."

***

Driving through the streets of the town, Dan couldn't help thinking that except for the red earth visible on the roadside and the different vegetation, it reminded him of some of the communities he had visited back in Canada. All the faces he saw were indigenous, and most of the houses sat close to the street with no fences to keep out their neighbours and few cultivated gardens. There were also very few stores or businesses. These were a people who still lived largely by their traditional ways.

Five pairs of ebony eyes stared at him as Wally led him into a large meeting room. There was a brief round of chatter, none of which he could understand, and then a tall man with a full head of hair, shockingly white against the darkness of his skin, stood up and introduced himself.

"I am Sam Munkiri. *Akurupa*—welcome. We are grateful to you for coming." He gestured to the other four people sitting at the table. "These are representatives from our other skin groups—do you know about our culture Mr. Dan? Do you understand our skin groups?"

Dan shook his head. "I'm sorry but I do not, although I have a friend in Canada who has taught me about the moieties and clans there. Perhaps they're similar?"

"Moieties, yes. We have two moieties, but we also have eight skin groups or *yiminga*." He gestured to the others at the table. "Four of them are represented here, and then we also have country or clan groups." He waved his hand dismissively. "But that is not important now."

He took his seat and pointed to the folder Dan had brought with him. "You have been told what has been stolen?"

"Yes, but there's much more I need to know if I'm going to be able to help you. I have only been given a brief description, and there are no photos. I need to know what I am looking for."

He saw the looks of consternation on their faces, the evasion in their eyes.

"Is that a problem?" he asked. "I assumed that because the items were stolen from a museum they would have been catalogued."

Again, it was Sam who spoke. "Only the throwing stick was taken from the museum. Ngarra—he is the man who was beaten—had the *tjuringa*, and the *Pukamani* pole was taken from the cemetery. We can show you a Pukamani pole. They're part of our burial rituals, and there are many in our cemetery, but we also create similar poles to sell." He smiled. "They are very popular with the tourists. You saw one on your way in."

Dan glanced out the window at the oddly shaped pole that stood at the entrance. It was decorated with brightly coloured dots of white, yellow and red paint and flanked on either side by a wooden carving of a child. The designs were unlike anything he had seen before, yet at the same time there was something familiar about them.

"Have you ever seen a totem pole?" he asked. "I think these may serve a similar purpose. Do they . . ." He searched for a description. "Do they tell a story?"

There were smiles and nods around the table and one of the women answered. "Yes, they tell everything. That is our way. Our stories, our history, who we are, where we came from. It is all held in our art, and in our songs and our dances. The Pukamani pole we place at the burial site speaks of that person's life—their abilities. Their strengths. Their spiritual journey."

"And the ones that are for sale? What do they express?" Dan asked.

She shrugged. "They are just a pattern. They do not have meaning."

"And which kind was stolen, a burial pole or a pole that was made for sale?" Dan was pretty sure he already knew the answer, but he had to ask.

The atmosphere in the room changed completely, and for a moment he wondered if his question had been in any way offensive.

"It was a burial pole." It was Sam who finally answered. "A very old one. It had stood for many years."

"Was it for someone important? Did he perhaps have enemies who might have stolen it?"

"He was important, yes. A very powerful man. A *kurdaitcha*—what you would perhaps call a shaman. But any enemy would be long gone by now. That pole has been helping that man find his way back to the ancestors for many years."

Dan was writing everything down as fast as he could, so he didn't see the response his next question provoked, but he did feel the tension.

"What was his name?"

When no one answered, he looked up and saw all five faces staring woodenly back at him, their silence so complete

144

it filled the room with a weight Dan did not, could not understand, and had no way of lifting.

It was another woman who finally spoke. "We do not ever again say the name of a person who has died."

***

A flock of parrots flew past the window, their red and green feathers flashing bright in the sun, their shadows patterning the floor with movement. Dan let his eyes follow them, and wished his life could be as simple, as elemental as theirs. He had flown an agonizing distance only to find a repeat of what had happened back in Canada: the theft of traditional, sacred objects that could not be described and therefore could not be identified. He was getting nowhere.

"Are there other poles similar to the one that was stolen that I could see?" he asked, turning back to the group at the table. "And what about the other items—the throwing stick and the stone. Are there any photos of them?"

It took several minutes of consultation between the members of the group before he received a response, and again it came from Sam.

"The throwing stick was very old. We no longer use them but they are part of our history and it was on display. I believe there might be a photo of it. I will ask. The tjuringa . . ." His eyes scanned each member of the group as if seeking permission to continue. "The tjuringa is a stone with a totem inscribed on it. The totem is a representation of the *alcheringa*, the spirit, who lives in the place where a man was conceived, and it is sacred." He paused and looked again at the other members of the group. "Tjuringas come from the ancestors themselves, from the Creation time, and they have many powerful properties. Only the people to whom they are given

145

are ever allowed to see them. It would be sacrilegious to ever take a photo of them."

"But I thought this one was in the museum, on display." Dan said.

"No." Sam's shock of white hair danced as he shook his head. "When they are found, they are kept hidden in a special place. When a man is initiated, he is shown his tjuringa for the first time, and then he will learn the travels of the ancestral being who bought him into existence. Those travels are represented by the designs on the sacred tjuringa. We call them a dreaming or a songline." His eyes drifted to the window. "Ngarra, the man who was beaten, is the custodian of all the tjuringas belonging to this spirit. He was bringing it here to Wurrumiyanga for an initiation when he was attacked."

***

They showed him the place where Ngarra had been found, then took him to the cemetery to see the Pukamani poles standing like solemn guardians, some new with bright dots of colour, others old and weathered, a few broken and leaning or lying on the ground.

"You said the pole that was stolen was old?" Dan gestured to one that was shorter than the rest, its top section fallen long ago, the remainder graying with age. "Would it have looked like that or was it intact?"

"Like that," they all agreed and Dan nodded. It would have been very difficult to steal a full-sized Pukamani pole. Most stood well over two meters tall, and the ironwood they were made from was heavy. Even an old pole would need a strong man to carry it, and something large to take it away.

"So the thefts all happened during the night and no one saw or heard anything strange?" He had read the same line in all the reports, and had asked the same question at every site, but this time the response was different.

"The two young men who found Ngarra said they heard a cry or a yell," Sam answered. "But when they got to where they found him, they saw no one else there."

"Suzie Lowitja said she saw *Burga*." The whispered words were full of apprehension and Dan stared at the woman who had spoken. There had been nothing in the report about a witness.

"*Burga*?" Dan repeated. "Who's *Burga*? Is he local?"

The woman shook her head and wouldn't say anything more. Sam put his arm around her trembling shoulders. "*Burga* is a ghost spirit," he said, looking over her head at Dan. "He is only out at night. He has strange, pale skin and he will kill anyone he meets."

A ghost? First *Bak'wus* and now *Burga*? Nothing made sense. Dan felt as if he was walking on quicksand with no solid ground to give him a footing.

"But *Burga* didn't kill Suzie," he pointed out, hoping to reassure the obviously frightened woman. "So perhaps it was someone else she saw?"

"She was in her house so *Burga* didn't see her." Sam pointed across the road. "Her baby woke up and she went to calm her. She saw him through the window. She says it was *Burga*."

***

That afternoon Dan spent a couple of hours with Wally, wandering the town trying to figure out how a thief could have broken into the museum, attacked Ngarra, gone several blocks to the cemetery, and then left the island without being noticed. There were no security cameras, and the hard-packed red earth where the attack took place had long since been trampled by feet and driven over by vehicles. But ghost or no ghost, the stolen items had been real and even though it was old and broken, the ironwood pole would have been heavy and awkward to carry. There had to have been a vehicle involved, even if it was just a hand-cart.

Or a boat, he reminded himself when he looked at the dense mangroves lining the river bank. He had been warned to stay well away from the many rivers and creeks that crisscrossed the island because of salt-water crocodiles, but a boat might be able to navigate them safely. Even an inflatable kayak perhaps, like the one Walker had mentioned as a possibility, although that wasn't something Dan would personally want to risk and it certainly couldn't cross the ninety or so kilometers of ocean separating the island from the mainland.

"What do you think, Wally?" he asked. "This is your town and your people. Do you have any ideas on how it happened? Or on who's responsible?"

"I been asking myself that ever since it happened. Don't seem possible. All the people here? We be family. Only other people are government people—maybe a policeman come sometimes. Don't even have tourists no more. Not since the virus came."

Dan thought he had heard a note of disdain when Wally mentioned the police.

"You getting help from Darwin? Did they send anyone over to check things out?"

There was silence as Wally looked out over the ocean. When he turned back his broad face wore no expression. "Yes, they send someone. He very young, a constable. It be two days after we reported the theft that he come. He tell us the site had seen too much use to give him any leads to follow, and he say the items would be impossible to trace."

"Did he get a description of them?"

"We give him a list. He didn't have no time to talk to the Elders. Said he had to get back."

It was no longer disdain Dan was hearing. It was outright dislike.

"I'm sorry, Wally. I'll try and find out what they're doing when I get back there."

"Not your fault." Wally's grin flashed brightly. "I think you be different. You ask good questions. You show respect. The Elders like you."

"Thank you. I like them too. But may I ask you one more question?"

Wally stared at him. "Of course."

"This thing with *Burga*, the ghost spirit Suzie . . ." Dan checked his notebook. "Suzie Lowitja, says she saw?"

Wally nodded. "Yes."

"Do you believe her? Do you think she saw a spirit?"

Wally breathed in, his nostrils flaring, and glanced around. "Be careful when you speak that name. There be many spirits, and you must take care not to offend them."

He glanced around again, then looked directly at Dan. "All of my people know of the spirits, the alcheringa, but few have seen them. I do not know if Suzie saw the spirit she named, but I know she believes she did."

They walked back to the museum together and spent an hour looking at artifacts and photos and listening to the history behind them. It was all interesting, but it wasn't going to help find what had been stolen. What might help would be to talk to Walker. Walker, who was familiar with the ghosts and spirits interwoven into the lives of his people, and who would probably have some ideas about the ones who appeared here. But Walker hadn't called, and if he had shown up for his surgery, he wasn't going to be calling any time soon. Or answering his phone for that matter.

Even if he did, it would be useless, because solving this crime was not what Dan had been sent to do. He understood that now, and it made him feel like a fraud. His job here was political. He had been given neither the time nor the resources to do anything meaningful in a country where he was a complete stranger.

Towards evening he wandered down to the beach and sat on the white sand. The language and culture of the people here might be different from those he was used to, the trees unfamiliar, the sounds of the birds and their brilliant plumage all new, but the ocean was the same. He sat there watching it breathe: the long, slow inhale as the swells rose, the soft exhale as they slid up onto the shore and fell back into the depth. It was hypnotic and soothing, and it grounded him. He might have been sent here as window-dressing, but he would figure this out. Markleson was right. Whatever or whoever was doing this was also behind the thefts in Canada and somehow he would find them.

Chapter 18

The return flight to Darwin was not until the following day and Dan had been booked into the only hotel on the island, a place right on the beach that lacked phone service or television but had an exquisite view of the ocean beyond. The bathrooms and showers were communal, but the glass doors of his room opened onto a wide deck and he spent the night listening to the sound of the sea and imagining himself back aboard his boat.

Was there anything he had learned that day that could help solve these crimes? He now had a pretty good idea of what the stolen items looked like, and he had learned a little more about their importance to the people, but without specific descriptions or identifying marks they couldn't be identified even if they were located. And as for any witness . . .

He lay back on the warm wooden boards and gazed up at the stars. The Southern Cross wheeled over his head, and low on the horizon he could just see Ursa Major, the Big Dipper, the constellation he used to orient himself back home in Canada. It was as if the sky was reflecting his own reality, one foot back aboard *Dreamspeaker* in Port McNeill and the other here on Bathurst Island, linked by his job and by these damn crimes.

A sudden blaze of moving light caught his eye and he watched as a meteor shower streaked across the heavens only to disappear into the eastern sky. Would it have been visible if he had been home? He chuckled to himself and dismissed the question. Of course it wouldn't. It was early morning back on the west coast, daytime, and the planets and constellations and meteor showers, while undoubtedly there, could not be seen. The realization brought with it a sudden thought. Just as the skies above him remained the same whether it was dark or light, these thefts were the same no matter which side of the globe they occurred—and that meant they had to be linked. They had to be part of a plan. Like the Southern Cross and the Big Dipper, if he studied them carefully, they could point him in the right direction. Somewhere, hidden in the details, there had to be some hint of how these things were being done and who was doing them.

He remembered a time at Friendly Cove on Nootka Island, when Walker had shown him how to find a trail of footsteps simply by sitting down and moving his body from one side to the other so that the light lit the grass from different angles. It was something he would never have thought of doing until Walker taught him how, and it was a lesson he had never forgotten. Perhaps that was what was needed now. Another angle. Another way of looking at the problem.

***

Early next morning Wally arrived to drive him back to the airport, and before they climbed into the jeep he handed Dan two photos of the throwing stick plus several of various Pukamani poles.

"Wally, there's something I want to ask you," Dan said, staring at the images. "But I don't want to get you into trouble so if you have a problem with it, just let me know, okay?"

He watched Wally's face carefully as he spoke, looking for any sign of discomfort. What he was going to ask could be risky for him, but it would certainly be a bigger risk for Wally.

"I'm sure you've already figured out that I am not going to be here in Australia long enough to be of any real help, and there's no way I can find these objects before I head home, but the same thefts are happening in Canada and I think they're connected."

Wally turned his head and glanced at him.

"My official liaison is with the Northern Territory Police in Darwin," Dan continued, "but would you mind if I called you directly to see how things are going? Maybe between the two of us we can figure this out."

Wally's teeth flashed brightly as a smile dimpled his cheeks. "No problem Dan. I will give you my personal number."

***

Whether it was because he was intent on studying the photos or was finally becoming used to flying he didn't know, but the trip back to Darwin didn't seem to take as long or be quite as terrifying as before which boded well for his flight to Maningrida the following morning. It would be his last opportunity to spend time with Claire until her return to Canada, and it would give him the chance to talk with Waru. Fate, it seemed, had decided he was going to get used to flying whether he wanted to or not.

***

The heat was already building in Darwin when he headed out of the hotel in search of an aboriginal art gallery Sam had told him about. He walked six blocks, the sun burning his shoulders through his shirt, before he saw a sign with the now-familiar red and yellow dots announcing "Spirit Gallery."

The interior was blessedly cool and dim, small spotlights illuminating the paintings hanging on the wall. The quiet thrum of a didgeridoo accompanied by the sound of feet stamping on soft earth played in the background.

"You like that one?"

He had been admiring a picture composed of a series of concentric circles, each one a different colour, that reminded him of an underwater reef, and he turned to find a small aboriginal woman standing by his side.

"I do," he said. "But I'm not sure I understand it. Is it simply a pattern or does it have meaning?"

She smiled. "All of these have meaning. Each shape, each colour, how they're placed, tells a story. This here," she pointed to the outer wavy circle filled with bands of bright yellow and orange dots. "This is the Rainbow Serpent. She is from the Dreamtime, when all things were created. After she came out from under the ground, she travelled across the earth and the tracks she left filled with water. They created the rivers and the lakes." Her finger traced another line that flowed across the canvas.

She pointed to some smaller, irregular shapes. "These are the trees and plants that sprang up beside the water. And these," she indicated a small group of dots at the bottom. "This is a platypus that lives in that water.

"The stories and the designs go together. I can only paint the stories I own: the stories that have been passed down to me through song and dance by my family. My father's dreaming is *Ngalyod*, the serpent snake, and I can also paint fire, and lightning and thunder, and some of the animals, as I am the custodian of my mother's and grandfather's totems."

154

She led him to other paintings and told him the meaning of each one. Some were more graphic, and he could recognize kangaroos and wallabies and lizards and frogs, but others were entirely abstract. She—her name was Janet—was in the middle of explaining a particularly detailed set of dots in a vivid orange when they were interrupted by the sound of the door opening.

"Please excuse me for a moment," she said. "I like to speak to everyone who comes in."

Dan nodded and continued to stare at the pattern in front of him, trying to decipher what he was looking at. It was more like a code than a hieroglyphic he decided. Deceptively simple but conveying a complex message that he had no hope of understanding. All he could do was appreciate the design it created.

He was moving to the next painting when a single word caught his attention and he turned to see who had spoken. Janet was talking to someone dressed in a flowing crimson caftan whose back was towards him. Long dark hair, streaked here and there with strands of bright red, hung down over thin shoulders, and if he hadn't heard the voice, Dan would have thought it was a woman, but the voice was both male and arrogant.

"I am a scholar, madam. I am simply trying to learn more about your culture. Surely some tjuringas must find their way into the wider community. After all, some families have died out. What happens to the tjuringas they owned?"

"They are returned to the alcheringa. The ancestor. They are his." Janet's voice had become louder.

"And you have no photos? No records? Nothing that provides information on the various totems or the ancestors they refer to?"

"We do not. They are sacred."

"And what about the songlines? Surely you have information on those? Or on where the various spirits live?"

They were odd questions for a scholar to be asking in a small gallery, and the use of the present tense struck Dan as strange.

"I have heard people have written books that refer to our song lines." The chill in Janet's voice would have warned most people away, and every line and angle of her body was taut with dislike, but her words were rewarded with a sneer.

"Fiction! I am not interested in fairy tales. I am looking for facts."

One voluminous sleeve of the caftan slid back as a hand was lifted in dismissal. It might have been a trick of the light, but Dan thought something about the skin looked odd: rough perhaps, or scaly, but it was hidden too soon for him to be sure. He had been thinking of the man and his strange attire as being eccentric, but now he wondered if perhaps it was hiding some disfigurement.

"I need to know the actual routes the songlines describe in order to trace the journeys of the ancestral spirits. I am creating a map of the various locations these spirits reside."

Dan had met a number of academics over the years, many of them deeply immersed in their work and eager to share it, but there had also been a few whose arrogance made him wonder how they had ever been accepted by the institutions they worked for. It didn't take much imagination to guess which category this 'scholar' would fall into.

There was a slight pause, and then the man continued in what he probably assumed was a more conciliatory tone, but in reality sounded patronizing. "My work is intended to help you people protect your land. Ensure that your property rights are upheld."

There was no mistaking the anger in Janet's voice when she responded. "It is not our land. We do not own it. The land owns us, and it is sacred. Our songlines are also sacred. Even to walk in the wrong direction along a songline can be sacrilegious, and we must sing special songs when we wish to approach any site where a spirit resides so that we do not anger the one who lives there."

"What will happen if you don't?" There was a sudden eagerness in the man's voice that made Dan think that this was the real information the so-called scholar had come for.

Janet shook her head and glanced across the room at Dan. "I am sorry, but I cannot help you. Please excuse me," she said.

***

"Not a very pleasant sort," Dan said as he and Janet walked deeper into the gallery. "I hope he didn't upset you."

"He is a very rude man," she answered. "And very persistent. He always asks the same questions."

"He's been here before?"

"Several times. Sometimes he pretends he's interested in buying something, but he never does. He only asks questions about things that we do not share with white . . . with others."

"Do you know his name?"

She turned to look at him, anger still simmering in her eyes, turning them into liquid pools of darkness. "I have never asked him. I do not want to know. He makes me . . . " She shivered and rubbed her arms.

He nodded. There was indeed something troubling about the man.

"Do you think he lives here? In Darwin?" he asked.

She shrugged. "Probably. He's here too often to be a tourist—although I did see him at the airport once. He was with another strange-looking man."

"Another caftan-wearing academic?" Dan liked this unpretentious, straightforward woman and hoped his wry humour would help ease the tension still evident in her stance.

"No. Just the opposite." She threw him an apologetic smile. "Well, he might have been an academic, I suppose, but it was a very hot day and he was wearing a sweater and long trousers and gloves. He looked like he was dressed for Antarctica! He even had a scarf wrapped round his neck." She shook her head as if she still found it hard to believe. "Oh, and he was very small. Much shorter than me and kind of bent over."

For the second time since Markleson had given him the case, Dan felt a faint tingle of electricity shiver through his body. It was the feeling he always waited for. The thrill that kept him going. It was like an addiction. Something he needed and chased after no matter how long and difficult the journey.

Claire had told him the person who had seen the man who owned Snake Island at the Maningrida airport had said he was tiny, and 'wore too many clothes.' She had also suggested that perhaps he was hiding some disfigurement. Surely there couldn't be two men who fit that description. It suggested that the 'scholar' who was interested in tjuringas and songlines was somehow connected to the recluse who owned Snake Island.

And the man who owned Snake Island flew a small helicopter very like the ones seen in Canada. Dan had no idea exactly what the connection was, but he was sure it was there. He could feel it.

Chapter 19

That afternoon Dan again ate lunch in the courtyard of his Darwin hotel, shaded by the swaying fronds of the tall palms. The pool was full of laughing tourists and noisy teenage kids, their pink skin glistening with suntan oil as they batted a ball back and forth. The ball splashed unnoticed into the water and the laughter and noise stopped when a young, smartly-dressed aboriginal man walked past them and approached the table where Dan was sitting.

"Detective Connor? I'm Ernie Gamma with the Aboriginal Police. I was asked to bring you some information." He held out a large envelope. "It's all in here."

His words were formal and he stood very erect, but his eyes kept sliding towards the pool and his shoulders twitched as if he felt the eyes of the people there boring into his back.

"Thanks." Dan took the envelope from his hands and gestured towards a chair. "Have a seat. I'll get us something to drink."

Ernie shook his head. "Uh, no. No thanks. I need to get back to the station."

"I'll only keep you a few of minutes. I'm hoping you can help me answer a couple of questions and you may as well be comfortable while we talk." Dan signalled to a hovering waiter. "Could you bring us some juice please, and some ice water?"

He watched as Ernie reluctantly lowered himself into a chair. "Don't let those people in the pool bother you, Ernie. You belong here. They don't."

Ernie's smile gleamed in his dark face. "I don't think either they or the hotel would agree with you, but thank you. So what were your questions?"

"I assume you work here in Darwin?"

"Yes, sometimes, but only at the old mission out in Parap, or at the places where my people gather. I don't go to places like this."

"You mean places where white people are?" Dan smiled when he saw Ernie nod his agreement. "It can be the same in my country, Ernie, but it's changing. It will change here too." He poured them both a glass of juice. "When you do come into town, have you ever seen a white man with long, dark hair wearing a caftan—a long robe?"

"Oh yes, we've all seen him wandering around in his red caftan. He's always asking questions about the ancestors and the spirits and where they live. Sometimes he goes to the old mission the day after welfare day and asks people there if they want to sell him a tjuringa."

"The day after? You mean when he knows there will be people who have been drinking? Who are maybe short of money after a night on the town?"

Ernie nodded. "It's no secret that many of the people who live there have a problem with alcohol. Most grew up in a white man's residential school. Alcohol is how they deal with their memories."

"Do you know this man's name?"

"He calls himself by many different names and none make any sense. I've heard Dantor, Met, and Kalfu – or at

161

least that's what they sound like. Maybe he's foreign, although he speaks good English. I think perhaps he's a little crazy."

Dan pulled a napkin out of the holder and scribbled the names on it. He would check them later, but something about them sounded vaguely familiar.

"Have you heard of anyone who's sold him a tjuringa?"

Ernie let his eyes stray to the pool where the kids had started their game again. "No. That would never happen. The people he talks to are lost. If any of them ever had a tjuringa, it would have been taken from them long ago. Now? Now they've probably forgotten what a tjuringa is, just like they've forgotten who they are and where they came from." Ernie's eyes had a faraway look, as if he was remembering his own roots and wishing he could return there, and once again Dan was reminded of Walker.

"Your home around here, Ernie? You get to go back sometimes?"

A flock of Rainbow lorikeets erupted from the fronds of the palm trees, their deep blue heads, orange bellies, and the scarlet bars under their wings brilliant in the sunlight, their raucous calls drowning out the noise coming from the pool.

"Not really. My country is over east, below the Daintree in Queensland. Takes a long time to get there."

Dan signalled the waiter to bring another round of juice and water.

"Any idea where this caftan fellow lives?"

Ernie shrugged. "I don't think he's local. He seems to just come and go. I know he's been seen at the airport a few times, and I saw him down on the wharf a couple of weeks ago. One of the regional people was talking to him."

"One of the regional people? You mean the regional police?"

"Yes, but not the regular fellas. One of their administration people. White shirt and long pants. I don't know his name. I don't have much to do with the regionals."

Dan closed his eyes. The description could fit any senior officer, but senior officers did not go out and question people, and if it was Harbinson . . .

***

Dan ordered lunch to be sent up to his room and he read the contents of the envelope Ernie had given him while he ate. It seemed he didn't need Harbinson's cooperation to get the information he needed: the guys back at the Interpol office in Sydney had come up with everything he had asked for. A copy of the deed for Snake Island showed the owner as a man called Emile Dahonney. According to an attached document pulled from Australian immigration records, Dahonney was an American, originally from Louisiana. He had taken out Australian citizenship three years earlier and then purchased the island from a biologist who had spent most of his life working in the area. Dahonney was fifty-eight years old and unmarried. His profession was listed as geologist. He had no criminal record and had met all the financial requirements for citizenship.

It wasn't until Dan saw Dahonney's passport photo and read his physical description that he found anything of interest. Dahonney's height was listed as 1.5 meters, his face showed a mouth distorted by crowded teeth, and his skin was covered by odd brownish patches. It stated the man suffered from both dwarfism and something called Porphyria or an extreme sensitivity to light which could cause blistering on exposed skin. This was obviously the man both Claire and Janet had mentioned, but why on earth would someone who was sensitive to light move to northern Australia?

The second group of papers was even more interesting. Information from the Darwin airport listed frequent visits from Emile Dahonney including re-fueling records showing he landed there often and normally took on between 40 and 50 liters of fuel, plus 30 liters in an auxiliary tank. There was even a photo showing a bright red helicopter, undoubtedly the same kind of chopper both Annie and the guys at the Prince Rupert airport had reported seeing. It, too, had an odd pattern painted on it, but there the similarities ended. The design was nothing like the Vèvè of Ayizan.

Later that evening Dan walked down to the beach and watched the sun disappear into the ocean. The night sky turned black above his head and even with the loom of lights from the city behind him the stars shone with an intensity he had seldom seen before. He stretched out on the warm sand and spent a couple of hours trying to find a new way of looking at what he had learned. Both Dahonney and Chauvet came from places where Voudou was practiced and both had a helicopter with some kind of symbol painted on it. They weren't the same symbols, but they were similar. Could they be simply a kind of logo Chauvet put on the helicopters he sold or was there another meaning?

***

The flight to Maningrida was blessedly short and uneventful. No air pockets caused him to dig his fingers into the armrests and both take-off and landing were smooth enough to make him believe he might someday be able to get over his fear of flying—although it would certainly never be his favourite form of transportation.

He climbed down the stairs onto a smooth, tarmac runway which, like the runway at Wurrumiyanga, was edged by wide strips of bright red earth. A small group of people sat on plastic chairs pushed against the wall of a tin-roofed building, all but one of them almost indiscernible in the deep shade.

"Good thing you're blonde," he said against Claire's hair as he pulled her close. "I almost missed you in the crowd."

"Idiot," she said, smiling as she gestured to the man with aboriginal features and dark hair but lighter skin who was standing behind her. "Dan, this is Waru. Anything you want to know about this land and what lives here, he can tell you—and about what's in the water too."

The two men shook hands and Waru led them to a dusty jeep and drove them through the smooth, red dirt streets that made up the town.

"I never thought it would be so flat here," Dan said, "nor that there would be so few trees. I always figured the coast would be really tropical."

Waru grinned. "We've got a few mountains and lakes—we call them billabongs. Even got some waterfalls in the Kakadu—and there's lots of trees down there at the bottom of the inlet where the river comes in below Snake Island."

"And is this the only town?" Dan asked.

"Nah, there's a few others," Wally said. "Yirrkala, Gunbalanya, Jabiru. But they're all smaller than this and it's probably not a good idea to go exploring. Most of them are inland, and they don't welcome outsiders."

Dan nodded. "Still true for some in Canada," he said. "And probably for the same reason."

***

The road ran out onto a beach where a boat sat on the sandy bottom a few feet offshore.

"Welcome to Larapan II," Claire said, removing her shoes and wading into the water. "She's named after an old mission boat that used to supply the mission over on Bathurst Island." She turned to smile at Dan. "You should feel right at home seeing you've just come from there."

"She's a great boat for this job," Waru said as they watched Claire clamber aboard. "The original owner was a real character. When he retired he sold the Larapan I, but he missed the sea so he bought this one." He nodded towards the boat now starting to lift with the waves as Claire started the engine. "Lived aboard for a few years, but he died without a will and no one could find any relatives so she ended up with the government and they gave her to us."

"*Us* being Maningrida, or the dugong program?" Dan asked.

"Actually neither. I work with an environmental group run by several of the Arnhem Land aboriginal nations. They made me the government liaison officer, probably because I'm a 'coconut'—dark on the outside but white on the inside." He laughed. "I was sent to school in Darwin then went to university in Sydney so my people figure I can see things from a whitefella's point of view."

"And can you?" Dan asked.

"Usually, although I don't often agree with them." Waru's wide smile took the sting out of his words and Dan

166

could see why Claire liked the man. He, like Walker, was completely comfortable in who he was.

"Claire told me you come from Bathurst Island," Dan said. "Do you know anything about the thefts that happened there?"

"I know they happened." Waru's tone turned sombre. "Nothing more. I didn't believe it when I first heard about it. It still seems impossible."

"Do you have any idea how anyone would know when and how the tjuringa was being brought into town? From everything I've been told, that information would be kept from everyone except the custodian and the person that owns it—although 'own' is perhaps not the right term?"

"Close enough, and you're right, that information would not normally be known, at least not officially. All the tjuringas that 'belong' to a particular spirit are kept in a secret place by the man we call the custodian, but the tjuringa that was stolen had been removed because there was to be an initiation."

Dan nodded. "They told me it was to be shown to the initiate for the first time."

Waru rubbed a hand over his hair and let his eyes follow the flight of a gull. Dan heard him take a deep breath and slowly let it out. "Many would have known there was to be an initiation, and that always means a tjuringa will be brought in from wherever it is kept. Some would even know who the custodian of that tjuringa was, but no one would have known where he stored it, the route he would take, or the time he would arrive."

"Someone knew," Dan said. "You've heard what happened to the custodian?"

Waru nodded. "I heard. He's a member of my skin, my family. I checked with the hospital a couple of hours ago. He's still in a coma."

Chapter 20

It felt good to be back on a boat, breathing in the salt air, watching terns and gulls wheel overhead, feeling the rise and fall of the ocean under his feet. Dan, Claire and Waru spent the rest of the morning and most of the afternoon cruising the coastline and exploring the inlet where Claire spent her days. Several times they pulled into shore to check on a group of dugongs and she pointed out individuals she had already identified, while Waru pointed out various birds and animals, identified the trees, and related some of the stories he had grown up with. Twice, in order to satisfy Dan's curiosity, they went a short distance up mangrove-lined river estuaries to see the salt-water crocs that stared silently at them from between the roots and then sank below the surface as they approached.

"Some say a Yawk Yawk lives near here," Waru said, watching for Dan's reaction as he pointed to a small trickle of water running out from between the roots of a mangrove with twisted, moss-draped branches. "She lives in waterholes and streams, and has long green hair made of algae and the tail of a fish, but she can change into a crocodile or a snake or even a dragonfly when she wants to."

"Have you ever seen one?"

For the first time Waru looked a little uncomfortable. "I thought I saw one a couple of times when I was younger," he said, "but not recently."

"Does she have any special powers? What does she do?" Dan asked and watched Waru relax when he realized he was not going to be laughed at.

"Mostly she controls the weather; brings rain for people to drink and to water the plants, but when she's angry she can bring a storm, and she can take different forms, mostly as a dragonfly." He paused. "She's also associated with fertility. My sister says she became pregnant after she saw a Yawk Yawk at a waterhole near Mandorah." He stared out over the water. "It was her husband who was to be initiated."

A vein began to throb in Dan's head. How much weirder could this case become? Was it all coincidence? The only thing that linked the various crime scenes, other than all the thefts being of traditional regalia, were the consistent reports of sightings of spirit beings. Was that only the result of the beliefs of people who had grown up listening to their traditional stories, or was there something else going on? And now there was a spirit who could take the form of a dragonfly, a description given to the helicopter he was looking at as possibly being involved, and a link between that spirit and the man who was to be initiated. The man whose tjuringa was stolen.

A breeze stirred the leaves of the mangroves and carried with it the fetid odour of a swamp. Dan stared out over the bow and pictured himself on his return to Vancouver, trying to explain it all to the people who had sent him here. He was not looking forward to it. They were not men who would be interested in what they would consider flights of fancy. All they dealt with were cold hard facts.

***

It was late afternoon, with the sun well past its zenith, when they turned back towards town. During the course of the day, they had completely circled Snake Island, staying well off the rocky shore with its numerous warning signs sprouting like a palisade erected to keep out a marauding army. The whole island appeared to be covered with low-growing trees and scrub.

"Have either of you ever seen anyone there?" Dan asked. "I can't see any sign of construction. No house, no helicopter or boat, no dock. Nothing."

"Saw a helicopter a couple of times, but only from the beach after it had taken off," Waru said. "Looked like it was heading for Darwin."

"Must be some low ground in the center," Dan said. "Be interesting to see a satellite shot."

They were altering course to take Waru back to the beach when Dan caught the glint of light flashing off glass or metal.

"Well, there's certainly someone there,' he said, nodding towards the island. "And whoever it is knows we're here. We're being watched."

***

That night he and Claire lay out on deck on a blanket, watching the stars wheel above them in a black velvet sky. After the heat of the day, the cool onshore breeze that had arrived with the disappearance of the sun had been too pleasant to abandon for a narrow bunk, and now they lay quietly, arms touching, letting the air cool their overheated bodies.

"I wish you didn't have to leave tomorrow." Claire voiced what they were both thinking.

"Unfortunately, I have no choice. That's the date on my ticket and there's no way I'm going to get any support from Harbinson with a request to change it."

"You don't like him much, do you?"

"It's not a question of like—although I'm pretty sure he doesn't like me."

Claire's comment had brought an unwanted image of Harbinson's narrow face into Dan's mind and threatened to spoil a previously pleasant evening.

"There's something about the man . . ."

Claire pushed herself up onto an elbow and peered down at him. "You think he's part of these thefts you're investigating?"

"No. There's no indication of that. It's just . . . something's not quite right." He laughed and reached for her. "It's probably something simple. Maybe he just doesn't like Canadians invading his turf. Let's forget him and get back to more interesting things."

He pulled her down beside him and slid his hand over her smooth stomach.

***

The next morning they woke to the sharp cries of terns wheeling overhead. Claire brewed a pot of coffee and they ate a leisurely breakfast sitting out on the deck before heading slowly back to Maningrida. There were still a few hours until Dan's plane left, and he wanted to visit the local Arts Centre where he hoped to learn more about aboriginal art and culture.

Claire drove the boat up into shallow water until the twin keels rested firmly on the sandy bottom and Dan took her hand when they waded ashore, savouring their last few minutes alone.

"Be careful." He kept his voice quiet so his words would not reach Waru who was waiting on the beach. "There's something going on here. I don't know what it is, but I'm

172

pretty sure it involves the guy who owns Snake Island, so keep well away."

Her fingers tightened on his. "I will," she said. "You don't have to worry." And then she smiled as Waru came down to join them.

***

Two hours later they walked into the tiny airport terminal and sat outside in the shade under the same tin roof, in the same plastic chairs Dan had seen on his arrival. He had added two paintings to his luggage, and a good deal more knowledge to his understanding of both aboriginal spirituality and art, but while it intrigued him, it also frustrated him.

He now knew that an Alcheringa was a mythical ancestor who had taken the form of a geographical feature like a lake or a mountain, and whose spirit was believed to still reside in that site. He also knew that a tjuringa represented whichever Alcheringa spirit resided in the place someone was thought to have been conceived. But the people at the Arts Centre had told him that while each spirit was represented by designs made up of symbols, those symbols had different meanings in different designs. A concentric circle like the ones in the paintings he and Claire had purchased meant a waterhole in one, and a camping place in the other, although both paintings represented the journey, also known as a songline or dreaming, an Alcheringa spirit had taken to get to its resting place. It obviously made complete sense to the people he was talking to, but how could he, or any other white police officer, ever understand? And if they couldn't understand, and if aboriginal police officers were only assigned to routine work, how could they ever hope to solve the theft and get the stolen items back to their owners?

Dan was certainly grateful for the information. He had enjoyed meeting the artists and loved the paintings he had bought, but nothing he had learned helped him know exactly what he was looking for, and it certainly wouldn't help identify it. What it did do was make him wonder about the man he had seen in the gallery in Darwin, asking about songlines and tjuringas.

***

The sound of a plane coming in for a landing brought him back to the present and he reached for Claire's hand.

"Stay safe," he said, standing up and pulling her to his side. "I'll phone you from Darwin before I leave."

She nodded. "I'll be back in Canada in a couple of months. Make sure you have the heater on in the boat. I'm going to need it!"

He stepped out into the sunlight, then stopped and turned back as a thought suddenly struck him. He might never know the name of the man whose Pukamani pole was stolen, or be able to see a tjuringa, or even know its shape or size, but some of the information he had been given might help him follow the trail—or at least point Wally or perhaps Ernie in the right direction. If there was one thing he was sure of, it was that Harbinson and his regional police would be doing absolutely nothing to help.

"Waru," he called. "Do you know where the man who was to be initiated was conceived?"

Chapter 21

Dan stepped off the plane in Vancouver completely exhausted yet at the same time elated. He was home. In just a few hours he would be back on his boat, breathing the cool, damp air of the north-west coast, inhaling the scent of pine and cedar drifting on the breeze, hearing the familiar rhythms of the sea as it broke on the shore. He had spent the first hours of the interminable flight thinking of what he had learned in Australia, the last hours thinking about the thefts in Canada, and he now felt it was beginning to come together—but only beginning. He still had nothing definite.

In between he had slept a little and dreamed of Claire. Now, as he moved through the long corridors of the Vancouver terminal, he found himself thinking of Walker. Where the hell was he? Bryce had told him he had checked himself out of the hospital after the surgery and no one had heard from him since.

***

The same constable who had met him before, met him again and drove him to the same office, where the same Interpol men sat at the same table. Dan handed them his notes and gave them his verbal report, watching for raised eyebrows and quickly hidden smiles as he repeated the stories he had been given.

"So you're saying we're dealing with ghosts and spirits?"

Dan looked at the officer who had spoken.

"No," he answered. "I'm saying we're dealing with some very smart people who are using the cultural beliefs of

the local indigenous people to steal their traditional artefacts."
It was a realization that had come to him during his hours on
the plane and from the puzzled looks around the table, it was
not something that had occurred to them here.

"Think about it. You and I may not believe in spirits
and ghosts, but they do. So if someone dresses up like a
spirit—maybe uses a wig, or a costume with long stringy hair
on it . . . Hell, even if he uses a bedsheet and makes a few
moans, then it would be easy to convince everyone in the
village."

"But surely that would take more than one person." It
was the Inspector who spoke. "So are we looking at a group of
collectors working together? An organization created to get
what they want?"

"No. At least I don't think so."

Dan couldn't say why he felt so certain it was a single
person masterminding these thefts. Like so many cases he had
been on, the solution started with little more than a hunch, a
feeling. If he thought about it, he would probably say it grew
from tiny seeds planted in his subconscious that sprouted and
grew into an idea. A word here. A description there. A name
perhaps, or a series of occurrences that didn't quite fit.

"So you think it's just one guy flying back and forth
between these two countries?" The man who spoke had grey
hair, wore a dark suit and thick, black-framed glasses that
distorted his eyes. He pointed to a pile of file folders stacked
on the table beside him. "Must have a fast plane and a pretty
good network of spies."

"Maybe it's a network of spirits."

This time it was the youngest of them and he followed
his words with a nervous giggle.

Dan ignored the comment as did the rest of the group. "There are certainly a lot of people involved, both here and in Australia," he said. "But I think it's one person directing it all."

"Any ideas on who or where?"

"Not really, but I think he or she has recruited not only some very good, and in some cases very violent thieves, but also some officials, certainly customs agents and maybe even police."

A silence fell around the room.

"You have any proof of that?" Again it was the Inspector.

"Not yet," Dan answered. "But think about it. These items are being stolen from remote locations, all places difficult to get in and out of, and they need to be moved. That means they have to be packaged and shipped. Someone—and probably a few someones—have to be turning a blind eye."

Several of the group had followed the Inspector's lead and begun scanning Dan's report.

"You seem to mention Snake Island quite often."

"Yes. There's something going on there that I think might be linked to the theft on Bathurst Island, but when I tried to ask about the guy who owns it, I got stonewalled."

The Inspector frowned. "By who?"

Dan smiled. "Colin Harbinson. He's the Deputy Commander at the Darwin office of the Northern Territory Police."

***

The RCMP float plane flew him back to Port McNeill that evening and he struggled onto his boat, his body aching and his head pounding. Many hours later he awoke, made himself a cup of coffee and a piece of toast, and took it up to the wheelhouse. His coffee cooled and his toast got soggy as he stared out over the float at the dark sea. At the fine rain slanting down like strands of fine silver. At the intricate pattern of the trees on the mountain slopes. Letting it all flow back into him after his time away. A long time later he started the engine, released the lines and headed out. There was a tiny cove he and Claire had visited several times before. It was a place that would be both quiet and deserted at this time of year, where his frayed nerves would have a chance to find the peace he craved.

It was four o'clock in the morning when he reached the cove and stepped out onto the deck again. He took a breath of the cool, sea-scented air and felt his spirits lift as the stress of the last few days fall away. His eyes searched the darkness for the familiar outlines of spruce and cedar stabbing up into the night sky, for the glimmer of surf along the shore, and when he finally saw it he knew for sure that for him, this was home. Australia had its own beauty: the red soil, the eucalyptus trees, the mangroves, the beaches, the birds, but this was where he belonged.

As soon as it was light enough to see, he lowered the dinghy and rowed himself ashore. The tide was going out, and the exposed seaweed glistened in the soft light of dawn. Clams announced their presence with a soft pop as they cleared sand from their siphons and out beyond the narrow entrance, a rocky islet floated on a silver sea.

He sat on a log under the drooping branches of a cedar tree, letting his thoughts drift. He had given the Interpol people everything he could think of, both facts and hunches, but he knew that his comment regarding Harbinson would make their job more difficult. In the natural order of things, Harbinson would be their liaison, but if, as Dan had intended, the man now had a question mark by his name, they would have to find some other way to continue the investigation. He had pointed them towards the aboriginal police, given them both Wally's and Ernie's names, but both of them worked under the authority of the Northern Territory Regional Police which Harbinson ran. It wouldn't be easy to get past him. Dan had also mentioned Waru, although he doubted the man was in a position to help, and as he worked so closely with Claire, Dan would rather he not be involved. Both the remoteness and the distances involved made it even more complicated than it would usually be, and all he could do now was hope he had given them enough that they could continue what he had started. There was nothing more he could do there to help until the case was solved. He needed to get back to the people here. His people.

The thought made him smile. When had they become 'his people'? Certainly not ten years ago, or even five. Then they had simply been people that existed on the edges of his awareness, people he knew little about, people he might have to investigate or even arrest one day. Now they were his family, his friends, their safety important to him, and that was thanks to Walker.

Walker. Where the hell was he? Even someone as mentally tough and stubborn as he was could not possibly have returned to the life he had been living so soon after surgery. A healthy man without Walker's problems would take weeks of physio to get back in shape. For Walker, it was more likely to be months. Maybe years.

After his arrival in Vancouver Dan had borrowed a police car and driven to the Capilano Reserve, but the cousin who had taken Walker in for the surgery said he had neither seen or heard from him since. There was no one else Dan could call.

A salmon jumped a few feet from shore. It was spawning time, when the returning fish swam hundreds of miles upstream, battling the currents, fighting the rapids, until they arrived at the spawning grounds. Watching the ripples left behind made Dan think about the effect thefts such as the ones he was investigating had on the various communities. They weren't simply the loss of something irreplaceable, passed down over generations and holding treasured memories, although they were certainly that. But they were also much more. These thefts stole the history of a whole community. An entire people.

As he had learned at Tsatsquot, Charlie's mask didn't belong to Charlie alone, even though he was the only one who could dance it. Every family in the village, every individual from the eldest to the youngest, was inextricably connected to it. It represented their story, confirmed who they were, and its loss set them adrift, disconnected from their past.

But while he understood both the scope and the pain, he couldn't allow himself to dwell on it. The question he had to answer was why someone would take them. Was it a collector with a particular passion for traditional indigenous regalia? But then why the throwing stick and the rattles? They were certainly traditional, but the Australian people hadn't used a throwing stick in a long time and did not consider it sacred, and here on the coast of British Columbia, the rattles, while holding an important place in ceremony, were not the most important part of regalia. A bentwood box might be appreciated simply for the skill it took to make it, but an incised stone? And where would a Pukamani pole fit in?

None of it made sense. The items stolen were not famous works of art that a collector could sit and admire, maybe share with close friends with similar taste and low moral character. Nor were they unique gems, or exquisite jewelry, to be desired simply for their rarity. These items would show their age, perhaps with faded paint or with cracks and chips: the Pukamani pole was in a state of disrepair, well on its way to returning to the earth. No, he was missing something, and he needed to figure out what that something was.

The mist that filled the air dampened his skin and he could almost feel his pores, dried out by both the arid air of Australia and the recycled air on the plane, open to accept it. He stretched out his arms in welcome as the raucous cries of a flock of gulls drew his attention to a bloom of phosphorescence on the water, its presence announcing a school of fish.

Phosphorescence wasn't common here on the west coast, and when it occurred few looked beyond its almost magical appearance, but it spoke of something far greater— water currents, plankton, algae and crustaceans—and it had the power to call both fish and birds from vast distances. As he stared at it, he felt the beginnings of an idea nibble at the back of his consciousness, but, like the phosphorescence, it dissolved almost as quickly as it had appeared.

A coastguard helicopter flew low overhead, the beat of its rotors filling the air with noise and bending the tree-tops as it lifted over the peak of the island. This late in the year Dan figured it had to be checking on fishboats working out of season, but it made him think of those other helicopters he had heard about, although not yet seen. All of them had been designed and built by a company in Argentina and sold by a company in the Dominican Republic which was owned by a man whose daughter lived on Porcher Island. A daughter who had given herself a name from the Voudou pantheon, which in turn had provided the design painted on at least one of the Canadian helicopters and possibly the one from Snake Island too. Those facts in themselves proved nothing, but when he added in the glimpse he had caught of what he thought was the same design in Harbinson's office, it certainly made it all worth checking into—and it was the only practical thing he had.

While he had been sitting there letting his mind wander, the sun had risen above the trees and now its light shone on the droplets of water still clinging to the branches after last night's rain, turning them into sparkling diamonds. He was wasting time. He needed to get back to work. A murdered man's family were waiting for answers.

Chapter 22

By noon Dan was back at the marina and he spent the afternoon working on his boat. *Dreamspeaker* was solidly built, designed to handle the west coast, but it was now late October and he would be heading north, alone. It was unlikely he would make Rupert without running into at least one major storm.

He had learned caution on his father's boat, and had grown more cautious over the years, and he didn't want to have to deal with an engine failure or the radar dying while he was in the middle of bad weather.

Yet there was something about storms that both excited and, in some odd way, grounded him. The strength of the waves that rose up from the depth, forced high when they met the steep wall of the continental shelf challenged and awed him. Together with the power of the wind as it howled across the vastness of the ocean or swept down off the mountains, it demanded respect while at the same time putting things into perspective. In the face of a storm Dan became aware of his place in nature, and the realization of his insignificance cleared his mind of all the clutter it had accumulated. It was a feeling of awareness and calm he tried to recreate when he practiced his katas, but it was never the same.

He had spoken with Markleson earlier that day to get an update on the results of the autopsy on Jimmie Alfred.

"Nothing too surprising in the cause. Those cuts were deep. One of them penetrated his liver and the loss of blood killed him. What's interesting is the weapon that was used."

"They came up with an identification?" If they had, Dan's job would be made considerably easier.

"Nothing specific, but they say it was done with a Kris knife."

"A what?"

Markleson laughed. "That's what I said. Turns out it's some fancy traditional weapon from Indonesia or the Philippines. It's got a wavy blade, but here's what's going to make your day." He paused. "It's supposed to have magical powers."

Dan closed his eyes. Was there nothing about this case that was normal? He already had apparently invisible thieves stealing unsellable items from inaccessible villages, and now he had a murder committed with a magical weapon. It was all insane. He dealt in hard facts with maybe a hunch or two thrown in. Walker was the one who could navigate the spirit world.

"Great," he said. "That sure helps a lot. How about that Vèvè of Ayizan thing. You heard anything back on that?"

Even that was related to the spirit world, but at least the helicopter it had been painted on was real. Annie was much too down-to-earth to have imagined that, and the one seen at the airport in Rupert had been documented. And there had been one in Darwin too, he reminded himself, and that was important to remember. It meant that whoever was behind this was not just a collector of west-coast traditional objects. There was too much money involved. Too much organization. There had to be a different motive.

"Not really," Markleson replied. "At least nothing definite. Got the expected smart-ass comments, but there was one response from the captain of the big ferry. He said he'd seen a small helicopter with what he thought might have been similar markings heading east near Bella Bella, but it was too far away to be sure."

"But no more thefts? Or murders?"

"None that have been reported." Markleson was well aware that many of the remote communities kept their own counsel and dealt with things their own way. "Of course that might change now you're back."

Dan replaced the microphone and stared out over the breakwater. Markleson was right: there might have been other crimes committed while he was gone. The RCMP had only learned about Jimmie's murder because the village had been able to contact Walker who in turn had contacted Dan. Without Walker, and with Dan away in Australia, it was unlikely they would have reported a theft, and maybe not even a murder if one had occurred.

"I'll drop in on a couple of the villages on my way up to Rupert. See if anyone has heard anything."

"You sure you have to take your boat to Rupert? It's pretty late to be out there on the water and I can always book you on a flight."

Dan shuddered. He had done enough flying in the last few weeks to last him a lifetime.

"Thanks, but I need the boat. It lets me go places the plane won't take me." He didn't add that arriving in an RCMP float plane would pretty well guarantee the villagers would tell him nothing.

***

185

He had spent the summers of his youth on these waters, fishing with his father, and he knew and respected its moods. Knew the way the water rose in steep, sharp waves when the wind was blowing against the current over the sandbars. Knew the way a breeze curled gently into the bays, only to pick up speed as it swirled around a point. Knew the way the seas rolled across the Pacific to lift themselves up over the continental shelf and smash against the rocks of the shore.

Walker had taught him more. Taught him to read his position by a change in the swell. By the rhythm of waves. By the flight of birds. Taught him to read the current by the ripples on the surface. By the scent of fish. By the presence of whales and dolphins.

He didn't rely on any of it, but he used it all to confirm what his electronic equipment told him. Whether it was plotting his course on a paper chart, or searching the night sky with his sextant, there was both satisfaction and comfort in reading the signs nature provided. It made him feel as if he was where he belonged.

But he wouldn't be reading the stars on this dark night, and he already knew the tides and currents for the morning. Combined with the forecast wind, none of it promised an easy start to his trip.

He left at 5:00 a.m., long before night had relinquished its hold on the sky, but not before the wind had stirred the surface of the sea into a mass of white-caps. For now, they were moving in his direction, but as soon as he hit the open water of Queen Charlotte Sound that would change and he knew he was in for a long, hard day. With luck he would reach the protection of Pruth Bay by nightfall, set the anchor, and get a good night's sleep, but that meant close to a hundred miles of rough seas. Meanwhile, he could only set the steadying sail on the mast, fill a thermos with coffee, and wedge himself into the captain's chair.

***

Night had fallen again by the time he reached the safety of the bay, and when he rolled out of his bunk the next morning he was stiff, sore and hungry. He put on a pot of coffee and stretched muscles knotted from the long hours spent at the wheel. Rain drummed on the cabin roof and pock-marked the surface of the water. Briefly he considered skipping another visit with Annie, but it was something he needed to do. So far she had been his best source of information, and he needed to know if she had seen that helicopter again; the one the ferry captain reported seeing.

As he drank his coffee and ate a peanut-butter-and-honey sandwich he recalled Walker berating him over his choice of food, and it made him think about the day-to-day reality of the life Walker had chosen to live. There would have been no loaves of bread in the freezer ready to thaw at a moment's notice. No convenient jars of peanut butter or jam. No cans of soup or stew. Calm or storm, Walker would have had to go out in his canoe and find his own food. That would be impossible for him now, so where was he?

After he had cleaned up the galley, Dan rowed the dinghy over to the shore, hiked through the trail to West Beach, and spent an hour running along the sand. It was good to feel his heart and lungs pumping hard again, and rather than returning to *Dreamspeaker* for the Zodiac, he decided to head straight over to talk to Annie. The rowing would do him good and he could spare the time.

It took longer than he had expected. The wind came off the open ocean and funneled through the pass and by the time he reached the cove where Annie's boat was moored his shoulders and arms were aching again and he was soaked to the skin. He rapped on the hull and waited, miserable and shivering, hoping Annie would be in a good mood and would welcome him aboard.

"You thinking of moving here or what?"

Once again he had not seen or heard the woman come out on deck, but she had obviously seen him approach.

"Gettin' to be like a goddamn hotel around here, people comin' and goin'. Gonna have to start chargin' room and board pretty soon."

He had no idea what she was talking about, but if she had seen other people in the area, he wanted to hear about them. "I wasn't planning on staying over Annie," he said. "I just wanted to drop by and say hello."

"Yeah," she said. "Might as well come on up. At least you've got a real boat this time, not that goddamn stupid rubber and plastic thing you had last time you were here."

Dan grinned. You could always trust Annie to say exactly what she thought.

"Hell of a lot more work to get here in this one," he said as he pulled the dinghy up on the shore and tied it to a tree, but she was already heading back towards the cabin, her boots thumping along the steel deck, and he knew she hadn't heard him.

It wasn't until he had taken off his raingear and stepped into the cabin that he saw the man sitting on the bench behind the table, a cup of tea in his hand and a smile quirking a corner of his mouth.

Chapter 23

Dan stood there, unable to move, the rain beating on his head and soaking the back of his sweater, his mind refusing to accept what his eyes were showing him. Walker, the man he thought had disappeared, the man he believed would need to spend months in physiotherapy, was here with Annie, looking completely happy and relaxed. It didn't seem possible, and yet it made perfect sense. Walker had a habit of doing the unexpected and Dan had been with him when Annie had offered him the invitation. He hadn't taken it seriously, thinking Walker would never take her up on it. Obviously he had been wrong.

"You going to stand there all day lettin' the rain in?"

Annie's voice brought Dan to his senses.

"No. Sorry. I just . . ."

"Yeah. I felt the same way when he arrived, but here he is." She poured another cup of tea and handed it to him. "Didn't expect to see you back here for a while either. There been more thefts? Another murder?"

"Nothing we know of." Dan slid onto the bench beside Walker. "I'm hoping you can help me solve the ones that have already happened."

"You talking to me or to him?" She nodded towards Walker, who still hadn't said a word.

Dan smiled. "Both of you would be good," he said, and it was true. While Walker had taught him to see and appreciate the world around him, Annie had shown him the value of respect. Of not making assumptions based on looks or lifestyle. He was a better man thanks to the two of them, and better at his job as well. He valued both their friendship and their perspective.

***

They spent the rest of the morning catching up. Walker had arrived on a fishboat and had been carried aboard. He spent his first few days hobbling around the deck, using the railing to support himself, but was now strong enough to do three or four laps with no assistance. He still limped badly, and always would, but the improvement from the last time Dan had seen him was remarkable.

"That doctor you set me up with did a real good job, even if you did trick me into seeing him. Wanted me to stay and have a bunch of physiotherapy, but I figured I could do that myself." He grinned. "It ain't like I haven't done it before."

"So how did you manage to get on board a fishboat?"

"Called Charlie. Remember him? He's the guy who lost his regalia. He's waiting for you to bring it back."

"I'm working on it, Walker. That's what I need help with—but you didn't answer my question."

Walker grinned. "Used that fancy phone you left with me and asked him to come down to Vancouver and get me. My cousin sprang me from the hospital and got me down to the wharf at Steveston."

"The cousin I went to see when I got back, who told me he hadn't seen you since I dropped you off?"

Walker's laughter was good to hear. "I told him not to tell anyone where I was."

"Glad you found a use for the phone," Dan said. "I was kind of hoping you would call me."

"Figured you would find me, you being a detective and all." Walker's smile took the sting out of his words. "So what happened in Australia—and how's Claire?"

"Claire's fine. She's enjoying her work and she'll be glad to hear you're okay. We've both been worried about you."

"And the thefts? You think they're connected?"

Dan nodded slowly, but didn't answer. He did believe they were connected, but exactly how was something he had yet to figure out. His eyes drifted to the window where rain streaked down the glass, but the air inside was dry, warmed by the woodstove Annie kept going night and day. It was all so very different from Australia, yet the link was undeniably there.

"I don't have much to go on, but that helicopter Annie saw may have something to do with it. One very like it was seen up in Rupert, and there was another one I heard about in Australia. They're not common, and the one in Rupert may have come off a yacht. It was registered to a guy in the Dominican Republic, but his daughter lives on Porcher Island. She uses a name from Voudou, and that graphic on the helicopter is from Voudou as well."

"So you got helicopters, Voudou, traditional regalia, and two countries half a world apart?" Annie lifted the kettle from the stove and refilled their cups. "Pretty odd mix."

"Yeah. And, and it's always sacred objects stolen."

"They say they'd seen a helicopter over there in Australia?"

191

"Not where the theft occurred, but there's one not far away that sounds like it's the same kind as the one seen here."

Annie leaned back and looked at him through the steam rising from her cup.

"If that's all you got, this one's going to be pretty hard to figure out. Maybe you need to take a break for the winter. Go on back to that marina of yours where you'll be safe, and hope something else turns up."

"He's already got something else." Walker had remained silent while Annie and Dan were talking, but now he leaned forward and glared at Annie. "He's got those reports of spirit sightings to follow up on. And Jimmie's family shouldn't have to wait until the weather gets nice to learn who killed their son."

Annie's eyes held sympathy as she looked at him across the table. "No, they shouldn't, but Dan shouldn't have to risk his life out there in Hecate Strait either. Maybe he can get the information he needs while he's tied up at Port McNeill."

Walker shook his head. "The answers are going to be out here, not down there."

"Thanks Annie, but Walker's right." Dan had come to get information, but it felt good to be sitting here chatting with two of the three people he cared for most, realizing that they cared for him too. They were his family. The only one missing was Claire and if the gods of the airwaves were looking on him favourably, he would talk to her later.

He smiled at Walker. "I don't think those spirit sightings are going to be of much help. There's no way a spirit stole any of these things—and it's pretty easy to dress up as a spirit. Dye your hair green and put on some weird outfit that would scare any local who happened to see you."

"So that's what you think happened?" Suddenly the old Walker grin was back in place. "Got some crazy guy running around in a white sheet shouting Hoo Hoo?"

Dan stood up and moved to the window. "Something like that." He was quiet for a moment and then he turned back and let his eyes roam over the now-familiar space; the scarred wooden table, the worn cushions on the bench seats, the cast-iron woodstove. "I spent a lot of hours crammed into that sardine-can they call a plane thinking about all this stuff. I still don't know who, or why, or even how, but I know it wasn't spirits and I'm pretty sure it's associated with Voudou, and that means I need to talk to a woman called Samantha Chauvet up on Porcher Island."

"You think she's the one doing all this? One woman? Collecting traditional regalia from all around the world and killing people if they get in the way?" Annie's face was a picture of incredulity.

"Probably not, but she may be able to help me figure out who is." He looked at Annie. "You got any books on Voudou in that library of yours?"

"Might have something on it somewhere, but it wouldn't be much. Why?"

He reached into his pocket for the notebook he always carried, flipped to the page he wanted and passed it to her.

"There was this guy in Darwin. Called himself a bunch of different names. I think they might belong to Voudou."

"Darwin? Darwin, Australia?" She gave him a puzzled look, picked up the notebook and disappeared into the salon. It took a while but finally she returned with a thick book on the religions of the world.

"Like I said, there ain't much on Voudou here, but I checked out the index." She lay the book on the table, opened it to the index, and lay Dan's notebook beside it. Then she pointed, first to one name, *Dantor*, and then to a second, *Kalfu*. "Got two hits. Nothing on that other one."

"Well, I might have written it down wrong. They were just names I heard."

They sat there quietly, each caught up in their own thoughts as they stared at the open book.

"You going to tell us why you figure Voudou is mixed up in this? I know they have a bunch of spirits, but it seems like a pretty big jump. Maybe there just wasn't enough oxygen on that plane and you got confused." It was Walker who asked the question, and Dan was pleased to hear the familiar sarcasm was back in place.

He smiled. "Well every theft involves sacred items, right? And every sacred item has a special meaning, its own kind of spiritual power, at least to the people that own it."

"Yeah, sort of, but not to anyone else."

"No, not to anyone else, but maybe there's someone out there who doesn't understand that. Someone who thinks they can use that power themselves. Who doesn't understand it's not really power as much as tradition and culture and belief."

"So you're saying maybe it's not a collector? Maybe it's someone who really believes in spirits? Who thinks wearing a mask and shaking a rattle can give them some kind of magical power?"

"Something like that," Dan agreed. "I know it sounds crazy, but then all of what's happened is crazy, and at least it provides some kind of motive. Some kind of trail I can follow."

***

Annie stood up and pushed another piece of wood into the stove.

"You want to stay for lunch?" she asked. "Got some soup here and it's getting pretty late in the day to start up north."

She lifted the lid of a pot and the rich aroma of fish chowder filled the air. It was a hard offer to refuse and Dan didn't bother trying. Within minutes she placed three steaming bowls on the table, then added a plate of warm bannock that had to have been freshly made that morning.

"I can see why Walker never appreciated the food I gave him," Dan said as he grinned at the man he was talking about. "You keep giving him meals like this he may never leave."

"Kinda helps when he's the one catching it," Annie replied.

Chapter 24

In Prince Rupert five days later, the weather had finally improved enough to allow Dan to put the Zodiac into the water and head for Porcher Island. It was still raining—it hadn't stopped since he had left Annie and Walker in Hakai—but the wind and sea had died down enough that he figured he could get there and back safely. It was a good sixty kilometers one way, part of it exposed to the treacherous waters of Hecate Strait, and the woman he wanted to talk to lived at the end of a long, shallow inlet that almost cut the island in half. He would need to be quick as the weather was forecast to worsen again later that day, but this was a trip he needed to make. Samantha Chauvet just might be the key he was looking for.

It took him well over three hours before he pulled the Zodiac up onto a gravel beach. Even under a gray sky the lagoon had the lush look of a tropical paradise. A white sand bottom turned the shallow water turquoise, and overhanging branches reminded him of the palms he had seen in Darwin. It was completely deserted. There was no wharf, not even a float of any kind, and no formal path led to the house he could glimpse through the trees. To get there he would have to follow a loose trail that wound past patches of salal and wild berry bushes. It wasn't well used and could have been made by deer rather than human foot traffic.

The house was much bigger than he had expected. It sat in a wide clearing, its windows and doors protected from the elements by a deep, wrap-around verandah. Beside it on a cement pad sat a tiny black helicopter with an ornate, yellow design painted on it: the *Vèvè of Ayizan*.

The woman who answered the door was certainly not the woman who had been flying the helicopter when it was seen at the airport. She was perhaps the largest woman Dan had ever seen. She was not tall, but her flesh hung from her in folds, overflowing down her body in cascading tiers to puddle over feet encased in worn, felt slippers. He thought she might be Asian, but he couldn't be sure because her eyes were almost hidden by her inflated cheeks.

"What you want?" The accent quickly confirmed her ethnicity. "This house private. You leave now."

Before he had a chance to answer, the door was slammed in his face. He knocked again, and when she failed to return, he went over to a window and tried to peer in. A heavy blind blocked his view. He went back to the door and knocked hard enough to rattle it in its frame but again there was no response. He was heading around to the back when he heard it open.

"You go away! You not come here. I call police."

Dan pulled his credentials out of his pocket and held them out. "I *am* the police. I'm here to speak with Samantha Chauvet."

"She not here. You go away."

The door was starting to close again, and Dan put his foot against the jamb to hold it open.

"How about Erzulie?"

He saw the flicker of uncertainty and decided to capitalize on it.

"If she doesn't talk to me now, I'll be back with more police. A lot of them. And we'll search the house."

She stared at him. Her eyes, already mere slits in her swollen face, narrowed even more, and then she gave a sharp nod.

"You wait here," she said as she turned and shuffled down a long hall, her gait crablike as her body rolled heavily from side to side with each step.

She disappeared into a distant doorway and Dan stepped inside. The house was even larger than it had first appeared, with numerous rooms opening off the dark hallway, and Dan wondered how many people lived there. Certainly more than Samantha Chauvet and the woman who had greeted him and considering how remote the place was, that was odd. In the distance he could hear the sound of hand-drums and that too seemed out of place. Could this be some kind of Voudou religious centre where people came to study or reflect? But if so, how did they get here? That helicopter was barely big enough for a pilot let alone a passenger.

A painting hanging on a wall inside the first room caught his eye and he moved inside to study it. It reminded him of the vèvè symbol on the helicopter, but the design was different and so was the colour: this was white on a bright red background filled with birds and what looked like gourds or rattles.

The drumming swelled and then receded as a door opened and shut, and footsteps sounded in the hall. As he turned to meet whoever was approaching, he saw the other walls were also hung with paintings and banners, all with different symbols on them, and the chairs were ornately carved to represent figures with their arms forming the armrests.

"You wished to see me?"

Although the voice was soft and carried the lilting tones of the Caribbean, it did not sound friendly. The woman was tall and slim, her skin a warm gold, her eyes bright green and her hair, hanging in soft waves over her shoulders, a pale, reddish blonde. She was wearing a rose-pink dress and she would have been beautiful if not for the petulant sneer on her heavily painted mouth and the hard look in her eyes.

"Samantha Chauvet?" Dan hoped he had kept his surprise hidden. He had been imagining her as the pilot of the helicopter but he was obviously wrong. Joe had told him the pilot had been black.

"Yes," she answered. "And before you ask, yes, I am also sometimes called Erzulie. It is a title bestowed by my religion." She gestured towards the end of the hall. "We were holding a service when you threatened my housekeeper and I would like to return to it."

"My apologies," Dan said. "I will try not to keep you long." He had come to ask about the helicopter, but her obvious hostility was raising his interest. He pointed to the side of the house. "I assume that's your helicopter out there?"

"It is. They are made in Argentina but my father, who lives in the Dominican Republic, is a distributor. Surely you didn't come out here just to ask that."

He ignored the comment. "And are you the pilot?"

She laughed. "No Officer . . . I'm sorry. I don't know your name. I suppose I should have asked to see some I.D."

Dan pulled out his wallet again and showed it to her.

"Thank you. Well, Detective Connor, I would certainly like to be able to fly my own helicopter, but it seems the authorities do not think people with my disability are capable of doing so." She lifted the long skirt of her dress to reveal an artificial leg. "Something you didn't already know perhaps?"

"I'm sorry." The words were inadequate but they were all Dan could come up with.

"Thank you. Now if that's all, I really would like to get back to the service."

"Just a couple more questions." Her sarcastic tone annoyed him. "You have your own pilot then? Someone who lives here?"

"Obviously. How else could the helicopter be here?"

"Does he ever take the helicopter out alone?"

She sighed. "SHE follows my orders. Occasionally I may ask her to go over to Prince Rupert without me to pick up groceries, but then she usually has one of my workers with her."

"And you're sure she doesn't go anywhere else when she's on one of those trips?"

"Where could she go Detective Connor? It's a very small helicopter. It isn't capable of going very far. My father gave it to me so I could get supplies more easily. If I need to go further, I take a plane." She moved her eyes to the open door behind him. "If that's all, I really do need to go now."

"It's all for now Miss Chauvet, but I'm investigating a murder. If I have more questions I'll be back."

He watched her face closely for any reaction, but saw nothing and that too was odd. She should have been either surprised or worried, but she didn't appear to be either. Instead she simply turned and started to walk away, heading back down the hallway, the scent of her perfume drifting behind her, but she stopped abruptly, her back suddenly erect, when he asked another question.

"Does your father sell helicopters in other countries? Australia, perhaps?"

She didn't turn but instead threw the answer over her shoulder before continuing on her way. "I have no idea where my father sells helicopters, Detective Connor. You would have to ask him. Goodbye."

He debated whether he should call her back. She was not as composed as she intended him to believe. That momentary hesitation had given her away. But he had absolutely nothing to go on and until he had figured things out a little more there was really nothing he could do.

Dan was stepping off the veranda when he heard the sound of the drums swell, then quiet again as she re-entered the room she had left.

He didn't return directly to his boat. The helicopter was still sitting on its pad only a few meters away and he wanted a closer look at it. It really did look like a dragonfly, small and delicate with the oversized plexiglass cockpit and the black engine casing with its bright gold design tapering down to the tiny tail rotors behind it. It had two seats, although he thought it would be pretty uncomfortable for two people of even average size, and the landing gear consisted of four tube-like legs attached to what looked like a pair of thin metal rods. There was no way this machine was going to land on water. He was walking around it taking photos when he saw the housekeeper. She was staring at him from behind a closed window and her look made him feel uncomfortable.

The rain was getting heavier and the wind had increased by the time Dan got back to the Zodiac. He pushed it back off the beach and slid it into the water, grateful that he had installed a windshield and a fibreglass roof to protect him from the worst of the elements. As he climbed aboard a sudden movement in a thick clump of grass up on the shore caught his attention. He watched it for a moment, waiting for it to happen again, but there was nothing more. It must have been some small animal taking shelter, but he couldn't shake the unease he had been feeling ever since he arrived. Even though he felt an urge to hurry, he found himself checking the boat to make sure nothing had been tampered with.

With the wind blowing down from Chatham Sound, he fought the sea all the way back to Georgy Point, the Zodiac bouncing off the top of one wave only to slam into the next, until finally he felt the change in motion as he reached the silt-laden outflow of the Skeena river. Even with his wet-weather gear zipped as tight as he could get it, he was soaked to the skin. His hands, encased in heavy, water-proof gloves, felt frozen in place, the fingers locked around the wheel. He was almost through the smoother water and back into the heavy chop when the engine quit.

Chapter 25

For more than an hour Dan was at the mercy of the sea, clinging to a wheel now made useless, praying that the next wave would not cause the Zodiac to overturn. Over and over he called Mayday until his voice was hoarse. Finally, just when he was about to give up hope, he received an answer from a fishboat on its way from Oona River to Rupert. It took another half hour to reach him, almost as long again to get a line attached, and then an agonizing three hours wallowing in its wake at the end of a towline. He had thought flying was his greatest fear, but now he knew better. He had never been so terrified or felt so helpless. By the time he fell into his bunk after a stiff shot of whiskey and twenty minutes in the shower under the hottest water his skin could tolerate, it was almost morning.

He woke at noon, took another shower, and drank a pot of coffee before heading over to the Coast Guard base. He wanted one of their mechanics to check the engine out before he called the marine repair shop.

"Plugged line," the mechanic said as he closed the cowling and wiped the oil off his hands. "Looks like you had some dirt in the tank. Maybe get a new fuel filter."

"That one's new. I changed it before I left Port McNeill a week or so ago."

The mechanic shrugged. "Dirt coulda gotten into the tank a while ago and been sitting there on the bottom. All that bouncing around stirred it up and when you hit smoother water it lodged in the fuel line. Seen it happen before."

The way he made it sound was straightforward: something with a simple explanation and easy to fix. But it could easily have cost Dan his life and although it might well have happened the way the mechanic said—unpredictable but accidental—Dan couldn't help but remember that movement he had seen in the tall grass just before he left Porcher Island. Had the Zodiac been deliberately sabotaged? It wouldn't have been difficult. He had been gone long enough to allow someone to open the tank, but who? And why?

The two women he'd talked to had been more than unwelcoming, but he had made no accusations and had issued no threats except to tell the housekeeper he could return with more support if she refused to ask Samantha Chauvet to talk with him. And all he had asked Chauvet was to do with the ownership of the helicopter and who the pilot was. Had that been enough to provoke someone into wanting him dead?

As soon as the work on the Zodiac was finished and he had tested the engine, he winched it up onto the cabin roof and secured it on its cradle. It was too late to phone Markleson and too early to phone Claire and an evening spent doing nothing, surrounded by the familiar sounds of his favourite jazz musicians, lulled by the gentle rocking of the boat, was too tempting to resist.

He woke just before dawn to the sound of rain on the roof and Miles Davis still filling the warm air of the cabin with the haunting notes of *Blue in Green*. Considering the events of the previous day, he felt surprisingly relaxed—at least mentally, although the twinge of pain in his shoulders when he tried to move let him know his muscles needed more than one night's sleep to recover.

Rolling out of his bunk, he pulled on a sweatshirt and pants and padded barefoot out onto the covered back deck. The tide was high and up in the town streetlamps glimmered through the mist, their light reflecting on a thousand puddles. He performed a basic kata to loosen himself up, then moved to more advanced routines. By the time he had finished he was sweating, his body was back to normal, and morning was slowly seeping into the sky.

***

He called Claire over a breakfast of toast and coffee.

"All good there, babe?"

"Dan! It's so good to hear your voice. It's been a couple of days. Are you okay?"

"I'm fine. Got hung up with some nasty weather." No way was he going to tell her about his recent adventure with the engine failing. "How about you?"

He could hear her smile when she answered and he found himself smiling in return. She always had that effect on him. It was if she carried sunshine within herself and it radiated from her voice.

"It's all great here. The weather is perfect and the dugongs don't seem at all bothered by my presence—in fact I think they're getting to know me!"

"No problems with that fellow on Snake Island?" Dan asked.

"I still haven't seen him, although I have seen his helicopter a couple of times. It flew right over my head yesterday when I was taking samples of sea-grass."

That was news Dan wasn't happy to hear.

"Let me know if he starts bothering you. I think there's something fishy going on there."

She laughed. "As they say here in Oz, no worries, mate! And at least he's got a pretty paint job on it."

Dan pinched the bridge of his nose to stop the headache he felt coming on and rolled his shoulders. The stiffness he had felt when he first got out of bed had returned.

"What kind of paint job?" he asked, trying to keep the tension out of his voice.

"Would you believe fire-engine red? Not exactly what I would have expected from someone who keeps himself locked away on an island like he does, but it looks really good. Oh, and it's got this crazy pattern on it, all bright yellow lines and squiggles."

The ache in his shoulders was getting worse. He wanted to ask her if she could take a photo of it next time she saw it, but he didn't dare. If Emile Dahonney was a part of the group organizing these thefts—and he was pretty sure he was—there was no way of predicting how he would react if he realized he or his helicopter were being photographed. And if he had played a role in the theft and assault on Bathurst Island, his reaction could well be violent.

"Certainly sounds different," he said, hoping he sounded less concerned than he was. How the hell could he convince her to be cautious but at the same time not scare her? "Maybe he has a yellow submarine as well? Better tell the dugongs to be careful too."

***

As soon as his call with Claire ended, he phoned Markleson.

"Any way we can find out more about this Chauvet guy that sells the helicopters?" he asked. "Maybe get a photo of him?"

"He's the guy from the Dominican Republic, right? Got some fancy yacht?"

"Right now we're guessing about the yacht, but yes, he's the helicopter sales guy."

"You talk to his daughter yet?"

Dan reached for the coffee pot and poured himself yet another cup, his fourth of the morning.

"I talked with a woman who said she was the daughter. Don't know if she was telling the truth or not. That's one of the reasons I need to know more about Chauvet."

"Well if he's brought a yacht up here he has to have a passport, so we can probably get what you want from the passport office. I'll put Carstairs on it."

"Thanks."

"You sound a little off. Something bothering you? Something I should know about?"

Markleson might be a bit of a slob, overweight and out of shape, and he might have bad eating habits and a worse smoking habit, but he didn't miss much.

"Yeah." Dan's eyes followed the flight of an eagle as it glided towards the top of a wooden piling, watching the delicate movements of its wings as it adjusted its forward motion to time its landing perfectly. "Had the engine on my Zodiac quit on me when I was coming back from Porcher yesterday. It might have been an accident, but I don't think so. I think someone over there put sand in the tank."

Markleson was quiet for a while. "So you think this Chauvet woman is involved?"

Even though he knew Markleson couldn't see him, Dan nodded his agreement. He had asked himself the same question and realized that was exactly what he believed, although he had nothing solid to base his belief on. The woman was no longer just someone on the edge of his focus. She was right in the centre of his lens.

"Yeah, I do, but that's all I can say. I can't even tell you why I think so. I have absolutely nothing to prove it. I don't have motive or opportunity for the thefts. Hell, I don't even have the means. No one saw or heard anything or anyone, and that helicopter of hers doesn't have the range to get to any of the sites."

"So not exactly a solid case."

He laughed. "No, not exactly, but I'll keep working on it."

***

Twenty minutes later, his coffee left cooling on the counter, Dan was on his way to the Prince Rupert university campus which was known to be research-intensive and had one of the best computers labs in the province. He should have thought of it sooner. While the helicopters had been the first thing to catch his interest, it was the designs on them that held it. The designs linked everything: Samantha Chauvet, her father, Emile Dahonney and even Colin Harbinson, because it had been one of those designs on the letterhead Dan had seen in his office. He was sure of it, but all he knew about them was that they were somehow linked to Voudou. He needed to know more and he figured the university computer lab was the best place to go.

A few hours later Dan returned to his boat with a stack of documents to study: long lists of Voudou spirits or loa, each with his or her own special colour and symbol or vèvè. It was going to take him a couple of days to go through it all, but he had already learned a lot.

Erzulie Freda was a *Loa* or spirit with tremendous power who was feared as much as she was loved. She was the Voudou goddess of not only love and beauty but also of jealousy, vengeance and discord, all of which Dan thought might well fit the image Samantha Chauvet presented. Her dress had been pink, her hair and skin were both fair, and she used a strong perfume, all attributes assigned to Erzulie.

But why was the design painted on her helicopter the symbol of a different loa, Ayizan? And the colour was wrong too, yellow, not pink—so how the hell did that fit in?

What if the symbols and colours on the helicopters were simply the fanciful whims of a rich man and his daughter who came from a land steeped in Voudou? What if all the helicopters sold by Jean-Jaques Chauvet had the same kind of paint job? What if . . .

But that wouldn't explain the symbol on the letterhead in Colin Harbinson's office—and the more he thought about that, the surer he was that it had been the Vèvè of Ayizan. No, he was on the right trail, but he was missing something. He just hoped he could figure out what that something was before there was another theft, or worse still, another murder.

Chapter 26

Tom Markleson had been in the police force a long time. He had spent his early years working in cities across the prairies where he not only learned his job but also that he was a small-town boy at heart and he missed the ocean he had grown up beside more than he had thought possible. Another thing he had learned over time was that the higher up he moved within the force, the harder it was to maintain either a marriage or a friendship. He was on his fourth marriage now, and could count the people he considered friends on the fingers of one hand. Dan Connor was one of them, and while he both admired and perhaps even envied Dan's independent lifestyle, he worried that it often put the man in danger. As he stared at the report in his hand, he knew this was one of those times.

There had been yet another murder and it too was connected to the theft of traditional indigenous art. This time it had been a man from a remote village called Ahas'wit and the report had come from the Waglisla detachment. They had been told about it by the brother of the murdered man, who had braved the seas in an open runabout to report it. As with the other crimes, this one had occurred in the middle of the night and it had taken the man two days to get to Waglisla, which meant it had happened three days ago. A coast guard ship was already on its way to pick up the body, but someone from the RCMP had to go in and investigate.

Dan Connor was heading back south now, and should pass right by Waglisla the following day. But Waglisla was on the inner coast, protected from the worst of the weather, while

Ahas'wit was on the outside, tucked into a tiny cove protected by only a sliver of land. To get in there he would have to take the Zodiac and Markleson was uncomfortable asking him to do that, especially at this time of year, and especially after Dan had told him about the engine failure on his way back to Rupert. But what other choice was there?

***

Dan was one day out of Waglisla enjoying a brief respite from what had been lousy weather. The skies had finally cleared, the winds had died down and the night brought with it a brilliant display of stars. He would have liked to be out on deck to watch them, but the cold would make that uncomfortable and darkness brought with it the risk of unseen danger from collisions with floating logs and other debris. Navigating demanded his full attention and it wasn't until he was safely anchored that he could revisit what he had learned from his research and his visit to Porcher Island.

Markleson had told him the white hairs found in Tsatsquot had belonged to an albino female, but Samantha Chauvet was not an albino. On the other hand, Erzulie, the Voudou spirit whose name she used, was said to be a pale woman with pale hair. It was a description that the largely black population in the Dominican Republic would probably consider described Samantha accurately, and perhaps it was they who had given her the name.

His own research had taught him that Ayizan, whose vèvè adorned Chauvet's helicopter, was the senior priestess of Bondye, the Voudou supreme being, and a loa who was seldom seen. Nothing in her description sounded sinister or violent but her colours were yellow and gold, so it was

211

possible the symbol painted on the helicopter was simply in her honour. A tribute from a devout believer.

If that was the case, and if Erzulie was simply a nickname given to a girl with skin and hair much lighter than was common among her peers, then there could well be no connection to the crimes. Perhaps he had been on a wild goose chase and needed to let this whole voudou thing go—but then, why had Chauvet been so hostile? She was certainly not a recluse—there was not only the housekeeper and the helicopter pilot but also whoever was playing those drums. And her reaction when he told her he was investigating a murder had been odd. Usually that announcement resulted in either increased cooperation or some indication of guilt, but there had been neither. A sociopath perhaps? She had certainly shown some of the signs. And then there was the possible sabotage to the Zodiac . . .

Dan leaned back against the cushions and ran his hands through his hair. He hadn't had it cut for a while and it was getting long. *Soon be able to braid it like Walker*, he thought and then laughed out loud at the image that created. He planned on stopping to visit Annie again on the way down to see how things were going. Perhaps between the three of them they could come up with a new idea or two.

He was listening to the soaring notes of Santana's *Europa* and sipping a whiskey when Markleson's call interrupted his thoughts.

***

"G'wanis is a tough place to get to at this time of year." Dan was looking at a chart of the area to the west of Waglisla.

"Yeah, and I don't like the idea of you risking your neck to get there, but it sounds the same as the other one, so that makes it yours." Markleson answered. "The coastguard has collected the body, but they're headed down south now to help a fishboat in trouble, otherwise they could have taken you out there.

"Might take me a few days." Dan was reading the weather forecast. "Looks like a couple of squalls coming in."

"Like I said, don't take chances. Hole up in Waglisla if you have to. Talk to Sergeant Matthews. He's the one who sent the report. Maybe the brother will still be there—his name's Richard. It's going to be pretty hard for him to get back to his village in this weather."

***

The Government Wharf in Waglisla was almost empty when Dan arrived the following day. He tied up to an inside float, put on his raingear and walked the couple of blocks to the detachment office. He hadn't been there for several years, and while the town looked as if it had grown and prospered, the weather certainly hadn't changed. The rain was now a continuous drizzle from a uniformly grey sky.

"You made pretty good time."

Sergeant Matthews was a heavyset man with a pale complexion probably made even paler by the local weather and the need to stay at his desk and work through the stack of paperwork that covered most of its surface. He leaned back in his chair, pushed aside a thick file he had been studying and pointed to a coffee pot.

"Help yourself. It's fresh. I just made it a few minutes ago."

Dan poured himself a cup and sat down on the other side of the desk. "Any more information?"

"Nope, and we're not going to get any until this next weather system clears off. Coast Guard took the body up to Rupert for an autopsy, but I doubt they'll find anything other than the obvious. They said there were a couple of deep stab wounds and the guy was slashed as well. Pretty vicious."

"And nobody heard or saw anything?"

"Not according to Richard—he's the brother—and that's odd because the seven or eight families that still live out there are pretty close and there were two masks stolen from inside a house."

"Richard say what kind of masks?"

Matthews flipped open a file. "Says here that both of them were *Crooked Beaks of Heaven*, if that makes any sense."

"Both the same? I think that's unusual. And this happened when?"

"Four days ago. Richard said it happened sometime during the night but they didn't find the body until the next morning."

Dan grimaced. It sounded like a repeat of Tsatsquot, and it annoyed him to think he had wasted a lot of time following what might well turn out to be a non-existent voudou connection: four days ago he had been on Porcher Island talking to Samantha Chauvet and checking out her helicopter. There was no way either she or her tiny chopper could have been involved in this.

He pushed his chair back and stood up.

"Okay, thanks. I'll be at the Government Wharf if you need me."

He wasn't looking forward to spending the next couple of days cooped up on *Dreamspeaker* listening to the storm howl, but he had no choice. It was darker outside now than when he had arrived, the sky almost purple and the wind and rain were already picking up. All he could do while he waited was try to figure out a new lead—although if he was lucky the autopsy report might tell him something.

"You could talk to Richard yourself if you like." Matthews had already started back on the stack of papers. "He's staying with his cousin down by the water, but you can probably find them both in the café there by the wharf. I think he's hoping to get a ride down south once the weather clears. Said he needs to let family down in Vancouver know what happened."

***

Richard wasn't hard to find. There were six tables in the small café but only one was occupied and it was surrounded by a cluster of people all focussed on one man who was sitting with his head in his hands. The buzz of conversation died as Dan approached.

"Richard Mack?"

One of the men put his hand protectively on Richard's shoulder and glared at Dan.

"Don't know who you are, but this is not a good time."

"Dan Connor. RCMP. I know the timing's bad, but I need to ask Richard a few questions."

"You don't look like RCMP and he's already told them everything."

The hostility around the table was palpable. This was family business and Dan was an outsider. He wasn't wearing his uniform and he briefly considered going back to the detachment and getting Matthews to come back with him to verify his identity, but he was pretty sure that wouldn't help and even if it did, would Richard have anything to add? It might be better to leave it for now and try again later. He had learned over years spent visiting these small communities that respect and patience got him far more cooperation that pushing too hard—which often got him nothing at all.

A voice interrupted his thoughts.

"That your boat down on the float?"

"Yes it is."

"Pretty nice paddle you've got up there in the wheelhouse. That yours?"

The tone was challenging, but the hostility was turning to interest.

"Yes. It was a gift from a friend up on Haida Gwaii. His name's Joel."

There was a low buzz as the group conferred among one another, and then a solitary voice rose above the rest. "This is the guy Walker told us about. He's the one who brought Billy home last year. He's wearing Billy's bracelet."

Every eye dropped to Dan's wrist. The kelp-vine had obviously been hard at work, sharing information up and down the coast, and it seemed Walker didn't even have to be present to provide an introduction.

***

They made a space for him at the table and a glass of some kind of juice magically appeared in front of him.

"Don't think there's anything more I can tell you." Richard's voice was muffled and filled with pain.

"You told Sergeant Matthews two masks were stolen, and they were both Crooked Beaks of Heaven?"

An older woman sitting next to Richard answered for him. "That's what he told us. There's always two of those masks used in the Hamatsa, a big one and a small one. They're two of the four servants of Man Eater at the North End of the World."

Dan had heard that name before. One of the women at Charlie's village had said something about Man Eater. He would have to check the information Vivien had given him.

"Did anyone see or hear anything? A stranger? A motor? A scream? A whistle? Anything."

Richard's head moved slowly back and forth. "No. Some kid said they heard *Bak'wus* earlier but it was blowing hard."

Bak'wus again. Just like Tsatsquot. If Dan was right in thinking Jimmie's killer had used the cultural beliefs of the community to cover his tracks, this had to be the same man.

"Did they say they saw *Bak'wus* as well as hearing him?"

The intensity in Dan's voice made Richard lift his head and look at him for the first time.

"No, not that I know of. Don't think anyone was outside then anyway. It had to have happened late and everyone was asleep."

"So the masks were in your brother's house and he was killed trying to protect them? Was there anyone else there at the time?"

For a minute Richard looked confused and then he shook his head again. "Leonard wasn't killed in the house. We found him down on the beach." He started to sob again, his shoulders heaving. "He wasn't there when Birdie—that's Leonard's wife—got up and she figured he'd gone out to get some more wood. When he didn't show up for breakfast she went looking for him. Pretty soon we were all looking for him." He heaved in a shuddering breath. "I saw him first. He was just lying there like he was asleep. At first I figured he'd fallen, maybe gone out to collect some clams or kelp or something. I couldn't see any blood even when I turned him over. I guess the rain had washed it away."

He dropped his head again and Dan waited quietly until he saw his breathing steady.

"Richard, I know this is hard, but I need you to try and remember everything that happened. Was there anything different? Anything unusual? Doesn't matter how small it was. A sound. A strange boat. Someone where they shouldn't have been. Something out of place."

Richard had been shaking his head as he listened to each of Dan's questions, but when he heard the last one, he stopped.

"Well I don't think it's anything important but Len had this bit of cedar rope in his hand when I found him. Looked like something a kid might have made—it wasn't woven very well. We all figured he must have picked it up off the beach, but he didn't usually pick up junk like that."

"Do you think your folks will still have it?" Dan tried to keep his voice neutral. The last thing he needed was word to spread that something important had been found, but his heart was beating so fast he found it hard to stay still.

Richard shrugged. "Don't know. I guess they could have kept it. Seemed like just a piece of garbage, but when the hand holding it belongs to your husband or son. Or brother . . ."

Sobs racked his body again and Dan stood up and laid his hand on a shaking shoulder as his glance ran over the gathered faces.

"Look after him," he said. "I'll be down on the boat for a while if any of you need to talk to me. I'm going to head out to Leonard's village but I might need some help launching the Zodiac."

Chapter 27

The rain made launching the Zodiac difficult but Dan had more help than he needed. He also received more offers to join him than he could possibly accept, but this was a trip he had to make alone. The risk was too great to involve others and he would have neither time nor energy to spend on passengers. He was going to need speed, total concentration and more than a little luck in order to reach Ahas'wit in this weather but if, as he hoped, he could gain the first real evidence as to how these crimes were being committed, and by whom, then the risk was worth it.

The wind had veered ahead of the oncoming storm and with luck he could take advantage of the confused seas to make it to the village before the worst hit and then use the wind and waves to help him on the way back. It was risky and if it didn't work he would have to find a place to run the Zodiac up onto the shore and ride out the weather as best he could. He hoped it wouldn't come to that, but he needed to plan for the worst and he stowed a sleeping bag in a waterproof container, an extra tarp, several bottles of water and a handful of snack bars in one of the lockers. Thanks to Walker, he knew how to find clams and mussels to eat, and with luck there would still be some cloudberries and the bearberries Walker called kinnikinick as well as salal. And then there was camus root and seaweed. He would survive— although he wished he knew how to catch a fish!

The thought made him smile, and he realized that even though he had spent the last few weeks wishing Walker was with him to share his knowledge, the man had already taught him most of what he needed to know. Now it was up to him.

***

A strong gust of wind pulled his mind back to the present. What was important now was to get out to Leonard's village as soon as possible. That meant speed was of the essence, and not only because of the weather. Dan wanted that piece of cedar rope. It might have been just a piece of flotsam washed up on the beach but he thought that unlikely. Cedar rope, even if it wasn't well made, took time to create, and he doubted it would be lightly discarded. Either way, why would Leonard pick it up? Something had to have made him leave his house in the middle of the night and head down to the beach, and Dan thought that whatever it was could well have been related to the theft. If Leonard had seen the thief and struggled with him, perhaps that piece of rope was somehow involved. If so, there might still be traces that could be used as evidence.

He was about to let go the lines when he felt the Zodiac rock and Richard stepped aboard.

"I'm going with you."

"I can't take you, Richard. It's going to be too dangerous."

"I made it here, didn't I?"

Richard's tears had stopped and his twisted grin reminded Dan of Walker.

"Hell. Look, I may have to spend a night ashore, maybe more, and I don't have enough food for two. And I only have one tarp. I can't take you."

"You think I don't know how to fish? How to live in the forest? Shit, it was us Indians that taught you white guys how to survive—and looking back on it that may have been a mistake."

Richard softened his words with another quick smile before turning serious again. "Besides," he continued. "Leonard was my brother. I'm the one who found him."

It was a hard argument for Dan to refuse and having Richard come with him had several advantages: he would provide an entrée to the village, and he was obviously familiar with the local waters and could act as a guide.

"You're right," Dan said. "Thank you."

If Matthews found out he had taken a civilian along and reported him he could be in trouble, but he had already crossed that bridge with Walker and although this was police business, it was still a private boat. Sort of.

***

At first they stayed out in the middle of the channel, but as the waves built, the Zodiac spent as much time in the air as in the water and the propellers started to cavitate. That forced them to move closer to shore where the surge hid the jagged rocks beneath in a maelstrom of seething white water. It was Richard, standing shoulder to shoulder with Dan, both of them locked onto the console, whose directions helped them avoid tearing the hull off.

"Steer in a bit," Richard said as they bounced and rocked wildly on the chaotic sea. "You can stay closer here."

Even with the wind shrieking around him, tearing the words from his mouth, he stayed calm, his feet planted solidly on the deck, his eyes fixed ahead, and Dan once again marvelled at the skill and knowledge that came with this ancient culture.

By the time they reached Ah<u>a</u>s'wit the muscles in Dan's hands were frozen into claws from fighting with the wheel and his face was set in a rictus grin. He was so cold he wasn't sure he would be able to speak even if he found someone willing to talk to him. With his white face and hunched, shivering body they would probably think that *he* was *B<u>a</u>k'w<u>u</u>s* and slam the door in his face. That thought triggered another and he stopped for a moment and stared off into the distance, but the cold pulled him back to the present before he could flesh it out.

Richard led him to a house set deep in the trees and even before he opened the door he could hear the sound of many voices rising and falling above the moaning of the wind. They all fell silent when Dan stepped inside.

"This is Dan Connor," Richard announced as he moved through the crowd towards an older couple sitting at the far end of a table. "He's that cop that Walker told us about."

So even here, knowing Walker gave him credibility.

The babble started up again and within minutes Dan had shaken hands with every male there, been greeted by the women, and was sitting down with a mug of hot tea in front of him.

"Tough trip." The speaker was a man who had been introduced simply as Richard's uncle. "Surprised you took it on in this weather."

"I wasn't planning to," Dan admitted. "But I didn't want to wait three or four days until the storm blew itself out. It's already been too long. You and your family deserve better."

"Well, I appreciate you coming—we all do—but I'm not sure there's anything you can do. There were four people in that house and at least three of them didn't hear a damn thing. Leonard . . .? Guess we'll never know."

"So the masks weren't stolen from this house?"

"Nah. Leonard's house is down there closer to the water. His wife's there now with her parents. They all live there."

Dan looked at Richard. "Any chance you could take me over? I don't want to intrude but I'd like to see where the masks were taken from, and I need to see where your brother was found."

Richard glanced at his uncle and they both stood up.

"Shouldn't be a problem," the uncle said. "I'll go down and tell them you're coming—her parents don't speak much English—and Richard can take you down to the beach and show you where he found Leonard."

They excused themselves to the rest of the group, put their raingear back on, and went outside. They didn't speak as they approached the beach. The tide was high and between the sound of the waves crashing on the shore and the wind screaming through the trees like a whole family of the angry banshees he and Claire had talked about before she left, it would have been impossible to hear anything.

Dan knew that even if there had been any evidence left behind on the beach, it would have been washed away long ago, but other than the cedar rope it was not physical evidence he was hoping for. He wanted to see where Leonard had met up with his killer.

Richard's uncle turned off the path and entered a clapboard house sitting in a small hollow protected from the spray by a line of wind-stunted trees while Richard and Dan continued on towards the ocean.

"He was there." Richard pointed to a rocky outcropping a little way back from the point, where centuries of wave action had created a sandy space between a group of large boulders. "Looked like he had fallen asleep."

"Was he face-down or on his back?" Dan asked. He had never liked asking these questions of witnesses. He hated seeing the looks of pain such memories brought with them, but if he was to understand what had happened, it was something that had to be done.

"Face-down towards the water." Richard had turned away, unwilling to keep re-living the scene, and his answer was muffled by the wind. "We should go back."

"I need to go down and take a closer look, but you go on and I'll join you. I won't be long," Dan said. He started down towards the beach then stopped and called back. "Those rocks are a long way from where this path comes out. Is there another path that goes that way?"

Richard turned around and stared at the rocks. "No," he said. "This is the only way down unless you scramble down that bank over there, and it's pretty steep."

***

Someone had put green wood on the fire at Leonard's house and when Dan entered a haze of smoke hung over the five people sitting huddled there, but no one seemed to notice. The uncle said something in a language Dan didn't understand, and the older woman stood up and went over to an old woodstove where a kettle sat steaming. Moments later, she placed a cup of tea in front of him, said a few words and sat down again.

"Rose wants to thank you for coming. She says you are welcome here."

"Please tell her I am honoured to meet her although I wish it was in happier circumstances." He smiled at Rose then turned back to the uncle whose name he still didn't know.

"I know this will be difficult, but I need to ask some questions. Could you interpret for me?"

"Sure. We all want to find who did this."

Dan looked around the small room, at the sagging furniture and the smoke-stained walls. At the blanket-hung opening screening a space he guessed was being used as a second bedroom. At the dark entrance to another room where he could just make out an unmade bed.

There was poverty here, but there was also pride and love. He could see it in the carefully hung jackets, the boots lined up below them. In the gleaming black top of the woodstove and the silver shine of the kettle. In the photographs that hung on the walls, all of them portraying people standing close together, smiling.

"Was anything other than the masks stolen? Anything out of place?"

There were headshakes all around.

From his seat at the table Dan could see the place where the masks had hung. Two pale outlines on a smoke-darkened side wall towards the back of the room screamed their absence. In this house, the interior dark even in daylight and crowded with furniture, whoever had taken them had to have known exactly where they were.

"Have there been any strangers around here recently? Maybe a new crew-member on one of the boats? A friend of a friend? A guest? Anyone?"

It was Richard's uncle who answered. "There's always a few new crew-members when things open up, but that was back in spring and they all came from one of the other villages. No one from outside."

Richard himself had remained quiet since Dan had entered the house but now he spoke out.

"Leonard had that white guy pulling shrimp pots when the season first opened back in March or April."

"You remember his name?" Dan asked.

Richard shrugged. "Only met him once or twice. Didn't last too long."

"Do you know why Leonard let him go?"

"Short season—but I don't think Len liked him too much. Said he was lazy. He sure looked weird. Had this long hair with red streaks in it."

Dan sucked in a breath of the smoky air and fought to keep the surge of excitement in check. It was too soon to be making assumptions. There could be more than one person who fit that description.

"Would there be a record of his name anywhere? I think crew have to be registered with Fisheries don't they?"

Richard glanced briefly at his uncle before he answered. "Pretty hard to keep track of everyone with all the openings and closings," he said.

Dan heard the evasion behind his words. Fishing had been a way of life for the indigenous people of the coast for thousands of years. It was how they survived, the staple food in their diet, an intrinsic part of their culture, and they had never welcomed the white man's intrusion into their affairs. In these remote communities the restrictions and regulations arbitrarily placed on them by an organization they neither

227

respected nor wanted would often be ignored. They would fish when they determined the time was right and they would take who they wanted on their boat.

"How about other crew members? Is there anyone who might have known this guy's name?"

The uncle was looking at him oddly.

"You're very interested in this man. You think he might have had something to do with this?"

Dan shrugged. "I'm interested in anything out of the ordinary. Leonard having a white crewman on his boat was out of the ordinary, so yes, I'm interested. Do you know if he ever came here, to Leonard's house?"

"Might have. Manny might know. He's worked on Leonard's boat for years. He might even remember the name. Richard, you want to go ask him?"

A cold gust of wind blew in as Richard opened the door and stepped outside. It made Dan shiver. Birdie, Leonard's widow, put more wood on the fire, and smoke once more swirled in the room, only to be sucked out again when Richard returned a few minutes later.

"Manny says it was a weird name and he can't remember exactly, but it sounded like Kung Fu. They used to tease the guy by calling him that and it would make him mad."

For a moment Dan was back in Darwin, the shade from the palm tree dappling the courtyard and Ernie sitting across from him as they talked about the man with the long hair and the caftan. *He calls himself by many different names and none make any sense. I've heard Dantor, Met, and Kalfu—or at least that's what they sounded like.*

Chapter 28

It was still raining when Dan left the village, the wind now blowing hard into the channel from the open ocean. He hadn't stayed long after hearing the name, too eager and impatient to get back to his boat and check his notes to take up the offer of a bed for the night.

"I think this is the best chance I'm going to get for a few days," he said. "It looks like the weather's only going to get worse. I need to go before the sea get a chance to build." He held out his hand. "Thank you for your help, and please tell the women how sorry I am."

He had asked for and been given everything Leonard had been wearing and had put it all into a waterproof bag he had brought with him.

"It will all be brought back to you," Dan promised. "You have my word it will be treated with care, as will Leonard."

Birdie offered him a watery smile and clutched her mother's hand as she watched him pick up the woven cedar basket she had given him containing a heavily engraved silver ring, a medallion on a chain, and a cedar bracelet. There was no cedar rope even though he had specifically asked for it.

He told himself that it had been a long shot anyway and probably would have told him nothing—a piece of flotsam dying fingers had scrabbled from the rocks—but he knew he was deceiving himself. The possibility that the rope would somehow offer the first piece of tangible evidence was what had driven him to challenge the storm. But while he didn't have that, he had something that might be even better: a name.

He was halfway back to the Zodiac, the rain a solid curtain of gray that made it hard to see more than a few meters ahead, when he sensed a presence and turned to find Richard at his side.

"Thought you might need my help again," he said. "Gonna be a rough ride." He held out a plastic bag containing a scrap of frayed cedar rope. "And you might want to put this with the rest of Leonard's stuff. Birdie wanted to keep it because it had been in his hand, but if it would help find his killer . . ."

***

It was a nightmarish trip back to Waglisla and when they finally arrived they were both exhausted. Richard collapsed onto a settee while Dan spent ten minutes under the hottest water he could stand before falling into his bed. He fell asleep with the never-ending sound of rain beating on the cabin-roof above his head. How long had it been since he had sat with Claire under the blue skies of Australia and felt the heat on his shoulders? He still wouldn't trade the west coast for the desert, but a sunny day now and then wouldn't go amiss.

He woke just before dawn with the bag containing Leonard's belongings lying unopened on the table to remind him of all that needed to be done.

He stared at it as he sat in the wheelhouse trying to reach Claire on the satellite phone and while he was waiting for her to answer he input the crewman's name into the computer. It took only minutes to confirm that *Kalfu* was indeed the name of a voodoo loa. He was associated with

Satan and was responsible for misfortune, destruction and injustice. Red was his colour and Dan smiled as he recalled the man in the Darwin art gallery with his flowing red caftan and the bright red streaks in his hair. His instincts had been right all along. These murders and thefts *were* all somehow linked to Voudou.

Dan tried calling Claire a second time but she still wasn't answering and he didn't want to look at Leonard's clothing until Richard had left. The man had already suffered enough. He didn't need a reminder of what he had lost. Perhaps Dan should wake him, but that didn't seem fair— although the idea brought with it a new thought. Why had Leonard been the only person to wake up? And why had he not woken the others in the house?

Suddenly it was clear. He had to have been deliberately targeted. This murder wasn't about a thief trying to get away after he had been discovered. This murder had been planned. Leonard had been deliberately lured down to the beach. The killer had almost certainly arrived in some kind of boat, maybe a kayak as Walker had suggested all those weeks ago, and Leonard had either followed or chased him. That was why he had been so far from the path. And the killer knew exactly where to find his victim: he had crewed on Leonard's boat. Finally Dan had a solid lead. He only hoped Kalfu/Kung-Fu had not already returned to Australia. If he had it was going to be very difficult to prove anything at all.

***

The peal of the phone woke Richard and made Dan smile. Claire! But it wasn't her. It was Markleson.

"Just heard from the coroner's office. Looks like that same weird kind of knife was used to kill both Leonard and Jimmie."

"Yeah, and I think I might know the name of the man wielding it," Dan replied. "Or at least the alias he uses. We need to get someone checking arrivals at Vancouver International. If I'm right, this guy flew in from Sydney a week or so ago. It would be good if we could stop him from leaving again."

He wanted to start the process as quickly as possible but knew it would take involving the Bureau to convince Immigration to start checking arrival records. Their office at the airport was understaffed and they would be reluctant to spend the time required to sort through thousands of photographs of incoming passengers. To make it worse, Dan could only provide a general description of a man he had glimpsed just once, which meant that all passengers on flights arriving from Sydney would have to be checked. And if the man they were looking for had worn a suit and tie instead of a caftan, or if he had washed the dye out of his hair or cut it, he would be hard to identify. It would all take time. Time Dan didn't think they had.

He also needed to get word to Wally and Ernie in case Kalfu had already returned to Australia. While Harbinson and his regional police force would undoubtedly hear about the search through official channels, there was no way the aboriginal police were going to be informed and if Dan was right, they needed to know.

***

Ernie answered his call almost immediately.

232

"Haven't heard anything of him for a couple of weeks," he said, "but I'll ask around. Like I told you, he's usually been seen down at the wharf or out at the airport and those aren't places they send me."

"Thanks Ernie, and maybe keep it to yourself. If I'm right, it'll be the airport this time, probably arriving from Sydney after an international flight. I'll call you back in a day or so.

Wally answered just as quickly and was more direct.

"You think he's the guy who killed Ngarra?"

"Killed? Ngarra was in hospital in a coma last I heard."

"Not any more. He died just after you left."

So yet another theft had turned to murder, and while motive was still missing, there was no doubt that caftan-man had been in the area at the time. Dan had seen him for himself.

"Just keep an eye out and let me know if you see him. I don't think he'll come back to Warrumiyanga. If he *is* the guy then he's already taken what he wanted—but just in case . . ."

He thought about calling Waru as well. Waru had seen Kalfu at the Maningrida airport and if he flew there again, either on a commercial flight or on Dahonney's helicopter, Waru would almost certainly hear about it. He might not be a cop but he could keep a close eye on Claire. She was out there alone with a man who could well be a murderer—and she still wasn't answering her damned phone!

Dan cursed as he replaced the microphone yet again. He had not thought to get Waru's phone number and that meant the only way to contact him would be to have Claire pass on a message, but then she would want to know why and he didn't want to scare her—although perhaps he should. He hated the idea of her being anywhere near Snake Island, Emile Dahonney or any of his associates.

He dialled her phone yet again, but she still didn't answer even though he let it ring a good dozen times.

***

After Richard had left, Dan opened the bag of clothing, carefully removed each item and spread it out on the table. It had been dried in front of a fire and the smell of cedar smoke gradually filled the salon. There would be little if anything left for forensics, but as Dan hadn't been able to see the body, there might still be things he could learn from it.

There was a heavy coat, a flannel shirt, a t-shirt, jeans, a pair of long-johns and a leather belt with a raven engraved on the buckle. It was a lot of clothing for someone pulled out of bed by a strange noise and all of it had been slashed, long gashes slicing across the fabric. Even the belt had been cut. The only thing untouched was a pair of blood-stained boots.

This had been a vicious attack with a long, sharp knife. A Kris knife the attacker had brought with him. Leonard hadn't had a chance.

Dan refolded everything and placed it back in the bag. The storm was forecast to ease later on with the winds shifting to the northwest. It would make his trip back down to Port McNeill considerably easier, but it would be at least two days and probably three before he got there. He still hadn't heard from Claire and he was about to try calling her again when the shrill peal of the satellite phone called him back to the wheelhouse. He smiled as he saw who was calling.

"Claire! Good to hear from you. I've been trying to reach you. How are things going?"

"Dan?" Her voice was almost hysterical. "I'm coming home. Someone sank my boat!"

Chapter 29

Twenty-six hours after receiving Claire's call, Dan tied *Dreamspeaker* to the float at the Port McNeill marina. He hadn't slept, and other than a cup of cold coffee and a package of dry crackers, he hadn't eaten. She was coming home. Waru had driven her to Darwin and put her on a plane to Sydney, and she was booked on a flight to Vancouver arriving the following day. He was going to be there to meet her.

He had spent his time at the helm fighting the sea and trying to figure out exactly what he had said or done that could have triggered the sabotage of her boat. Harbinson had to have been involved. Dan hadn't mentioned Snake Island to anyone else, and he had told him he had a friend working near there. It wouldn't have been hard for the commander of the Northern Territory Regional Police to find out who that friend was.

But Claire didn't pose a threat to Harbinson— or to Dahonney for that matter—so why sink her boat? It had to have been a message, a warning intended for him just as the sabotage to the Zodiac had been. And in both cases that warning had come with at least the possibility of death. They might have taken care to ensure Claire was not aboard when they planted the explosives—although he was far from sure of that—but whoever had put sand in his gas tank had certainly known the risk. Maybe had even hoped for the worst.

***

His call to the National Contact Bureau in Vancouver lasted well over an hour and resulted in them re-routing the

RCMP plane to Port McNeill to pick him up. He used the two hours before its arrival to grab some much needed sleep, used the roar of its prop as his alarm, and climbed eagerly aboard without a single tremor of apprehension.

"We can't bypass Harbinson. He's our official liaison for the area. Everything goes through his office."

Dan had already given the group all the details of his trip to Darwin and Wurrumiyanga
and now he told them about his visit to Porcher Island and the subsequent engine failure on the Zodiac. He knew he had convinced them that his suspicions were worth following up, but now they seemed to have reached a stalemate.

"How about the aboriginal police?" he asked. "They're the ones on the ground where we need them."

"Not possible. They don't have the authority, and besides, it's Harbinson who commands them. We would have to go through him."

"Shit." Dan ran his hand through his hair in frustration. He hadn't had it cut for months and he hadn't combed it since Claire had called. He hadn't even shaved for three days and the scar that ran over his cheekbone was stretched tight against his skin. He probably looked like a criminal himself but he didn't care. "Surely there's something you can do."

"We can arrange satellite surveillance on both places." It was the commander speaking. "That will keep track of the helicopters and any unusual activity, and meanwhile we'll get the federal guys over there to start an internal investigation into Harbinson."

"How about here? Anything you can do to identify who's helping them at this end?"

"How? Until we know where the stuff ends up there's nothing to check. The last theft was over a week ago. If those masks were shipped anywhere, they would have already gone, and we can't start checking the bank accounts of every cop and customs agent unless we can provide a good reason."

They were right, and it was the best he was going to get. He needed proof, not conjecture, and right now that probably meant waiting for another theft to occur. He could only hope that didn't also mean another murder.

**

He found a hotel near the airport and slept for another couple of hours before meeting Bryce for dinner.

"You look like shit," Bryce said as they headed into the dining room. "You working undercover?"

"No," Dan laughed. "Just haven't had time to clean up."

"Must be something important. What does your lady think of it? I can't imagine she would be too happy with the look."

"She's been in Australia for the last couple of months. I'm picking her up here at the airport tomorrow. She's pretty easy going."

Dan planned on going to a barbershop before Claire's plane arrived. The shave would be welcome but he had yet to decide about a haircut. Barbershops were few and far between on the coast and a ponytail or braid might make more sense. It might even make it easier to connect with the people in the villages just like wearing jeans did—although he wasn't sure he wanted to give Walker such a good opportunity to practice his unique blend of humour and sarcasm.

On the other hand, he needed to find a way to convince Claire to stay with him onboard his boat, at least for the short term, and if she came with him to any of the villages that shock of blonde hair would hardly blend in.

He couldn't let her stay ashore. These people, whoever they were, had already proved they would stop at nothing and until this case was wrapped up he needed to keep her close, both for her sake and his.

She was one of the last to exit the big jet, and seeing her looking so shaken and wan broke Dan's heart. The exuberant, confident, outgoing woman he loved seemed somehow diminished, and he vowed once again that he would find whoever was doing this and put them behind bars.

They stayed in Vancouver overnight then flew back to Port McNeill the following morning. Claire was quiet, offering little about what had happened, and Dan didn't press her. She would talk about it when she was ready and meanwhile she obviously needed sleep.

It was on the second day, after he had spent the morning with Markleson and brought back a lunch of grilled halibut and steamed vegetables, that she told him what had happened. She and Waru had been on the beach, coming back from buying supplies in town, when there had been an explosion and the boat had simply disappeared under the water.

"It almost sounded like someone beating a huge drum," she said. " A kind of *whump*. Sort of dull and deadened. Not like a big eruption with a loud bang and sparks and flames. Nothing flew up into the air. The boat just kind of broke apart and . . . sank."

"And you didn't see anyone else on the beach?"

"No. It was completely empty. Almost surreal. Even the birds were quiet. It took me a while to understand what had happened."

He felt her shiver and pulled her close, his anger surging.

"I need to talk to Waru and warn him," he said. "Ask him to keep an eye out for that helicopter. I don't suppose you saw it did you?"

She looked at him in confusion. "The helicopter? You mean the one from Snake Island? No. Like I told you it was totally quiet. No people. No movement. No sound except that weird boom, although . . . " She paused, a thoughtful look on her face.

"Although what?"

She looked at him. "Now that you mention it I did see it earlier, before I went into town, but I only got a glimpse of it. It was flying really low, and then it disappeared. I think it must have landed on the island." A worried frown wrinkled her forehead. "Why are you asking? Do you think it's somehow connected to what happened?"

He didn't want to upset her any more than she already was, but he couldn't lie to her, and if he was going to keep her safe, she needed to know the truth.

"Yes," he said. "I do. And I think it's connected to what's happening here as well." And he told her about the engine on the Zodiac quitting.

She looked at him in horror. "You could have died!"

He nodded. "Yes, I could. And maybe they hoped that would happen. Or maybe they figured I'd be picked up. I don't know, but either way it was a risk. And it was the same with you. Did they know that charge would go off when you were ashore?" He saw her close her eyes and shudder and he reached out and grabbed her hand. "I'm not trying to scare you, but we need to be careful. These are dangerous people, and they obviously think I'm a threat."

Her eyes were wide and much darker than usual as she stared at him. "You think they'll try again."

"Could be." He pulled her into his side. "It's you I'm worried about." He ran his fingers through her hair. She'd cut it very short before she left for Australia, but hadn't cut it since and it was starting to curl again, turning into the tangled mop he loved. "I need you to stay aboard with me. It's the only way I can keep you safe."

She didn't say anything for several long moments and then he saw her eyes turn to look out over the breakwater to where a flock of gulls sat preening themselves.

"You mean not go back to work. Not take up another contract until this is over. Just sit on the boat." It was a statement rather than a question but he answered her anyway.

"Yes," he said. "But you wouldn't be just sitting. You could help me. And we could maybe catch them quicker that way."

The idea had come to him during the night while he was lying beside her, watching her breathe, thinking about how close he had come to losing her, thinking about how he would find whoever was doing this and make sure they never did it again. How they would never murder another son, or brother, or husband. How they would never steal another treasured piece of family regalia.

Chapter 30

He didn't tell Markleson what he was doing when he gave Claire the access code. There was no way he would have received permission and if he was discovered he would probably lose his job. He might even go to jail. But if it meant he could figure out who was behind all these murders and thefts, who had threatened Claire and therefore threatened him, then he was willing to risk it. The RCMP computer system allowed access to far more information than any public system. With it he could search everything from immigration records to land titles and from airline movements and passenger manifests to customs and excise. Of course that was only for Canada, but he still thought the answers would be found here and if he solved the Canadian end of things, the Australian crimes would be solved too.

He left Claire in the salon going through a list of the websites and codes and went forward to the wheelhouse to call Markleson.

"I'm going to head back north. If I'm going to be able to sort this out, that's where I need to be."

"In November? And what about Claire? She going to stay here? I can probably find her a good place to stay."

"She's coming with me, and I might try to pick up Walker on the way. He's doing pretty well and Annie will probably be glad to get rid of him."

Markleson gave a brief laugh. "So you're telling me you're not following standard police procedure with this one."

"Have I ever?"

"No, but at least you kept close enough that I could pretend."

Dan laughed. "Well, just keep on pretending. I only told you because it may be Claire calling you instead of me. If I'm out in the Zodiac, I might need her to relay information and questions. That going to work for you?"

Markleson sighed. "I guess it will have to, but make sure you keep her safe. Seems kind of risky taking her with you and I'm fond of that girl."

"Not as fond of her as I am, and she'll be safer with me than on her own, even down here. Whoever this is, they've got a long reach."

***

He spent the rest of the afternoon provisioning the boat, filling the water tanks and taking on fuel, and by the time a watery sun struggled up over the ridges of the coast mountains he and Claire were already halfway across Queen Charlotte Sound with Calvert Island looming ahead. By that evening they were sitting around the table in Annie's boat with an open box of chocolate chip cookies in front of them, taken from a carton Dan had purchased the previous day and given to Annie on their arrival.

"Still maintaining those good eating habits of yours I see." Walker had been cleaning a salmon down on the shore when they had first arrived but had come up to join them. Dan was amazed at the relative ease with which the man managed to make his way up the old plank leading to the deck. He still had a limp, and a kind of rolling gait, but the twisted body had straightened considerably and his legs were stronger, the muscles more developed than they had been for years.

"Don't have a choice," Dan answered. "You haven't taught me how to fish yet. Kinda hoping you can do that on the way up north."

Walker looked at him from under raised eyebrows. "On the way up north," he repeated. "Can't say I was planning to head north." He glanced at Annie and grinned. "Pretty comfortable here with winter coming on—and I figure Annie could do with my help."

"What the fuck you talking about? I don't need no help." The look of affront on Annie's face made them all smile.

"Pain in the ass, the lot of you," she muttered as she reached for the kettle and poured them all another cup of tea, but the corner of her mouth had lifted in a smile.

"So what's up north that makes you think I'd want to come with you?" Walker was leaning back, looking totally relaxed as he sipped his tea and nibbled on a cookie.

"Maybe nothing, but if I'm right, then maybe a murderer and a whole bunch of stolen regalia—is that a chocolate chip cookie you're eating? Weren't you just giving me shit for my bad eating habits?"

Walker's grin was unrepentant. "Guess Annie must be leading me astray." He glanced at the woman whose hospitality had allowed him to recuperate from his surgery on his own terms, then became serious. "So you figure the answers are up there in Rupert?"

"Close. On Porcher Island," Dan replied. "There's a woman there whose tied into Voudou and it was a Voudou symbol on that helicopter Annie saw. The woman calls herself by a Voudou name, and there's a man who does the same over in Australia where the same stuff is happening."

"Voudou? Can't say I know anything about that."

"Neither do I, but Claire's researching it. Seems it has a lot of spirits—they're called loas—and you know more about spirits than I do."

"You back to _Bak'wus_ again? It was no ghost spirit that stabbed Jimmie to death. Probably couldn't carry off a transformation mask either."

"No," Dan said. "But someone dressing up as one could."

***

There was silence for a while as each of them contemplated what Dan had said. It was Annie who broke it first.

"Well I sure ain't no detective, but it don't seem like a whole lot to go on," she said, helping herself to another cookie.

"There's more," Dan said. "Walker told me someone saw a boat over at Dawson's Landing. Sounds like it had the same Voudou symbol painted on it as the helicopter. And a guy who owns an island near where Claire was working has the same kind of helicopter and it has a symbol too."

"Could just be the paint job they put on the helicopters," Annie said. "Don't mean they committed murder."

"True. But when I've got a guy calling himself Kalfu, which is the name of one of those Voudou loas, asking about how to get his hands on one of the most sacred traditional objects in Australia, and I find out he's a friend of the guy with the helicopter . . ."

***

He still didn't have a logical explanation for what was happening, but Claire's research was starting to pull all the pieces together. While he already knew the symbolism associated with Erzulie, and Kalfu, Claire had found other names he had not heard spoken, but which made him think back to a couple of the descriptions he had either read or heard about. A Loa called *Ti-Jean Petro* was said to be a dwarf like Dahonny, and *Petite Pierrette* was a glutton and enormously fat like the housekeeper. Yet another, *Agassu,* had hands that were crooked and stiffened which matched the description of the woman on the boat at Dawson's Landing.

He still had no proof and it might all be coincidence, simply the product of his imagination, and if it was he was going to feel like an idiot, but it was still the only theory he had and he was going to follow it.

"There's one more thing," he said. "Although I can't be certain. When I was in Darwin I spent some time with the Deputy Commander of the Northern Territory Police and I'm pretty sure I saw the same symbol on a piece of paper on his desk."

Three pairs of eyes stared at him in shock.

"You think it's a cop doing this?" All the humour had left Walker's voice.

"I don't think he's doing it himself, but I think he might be involved. Maybe just doing some cover-up, making sure any investigation goes nowhere, or maybe helping get the stuff out."

"Getting it out to where?" Annie was looking at him like he had grown two heads. "Why wouldn't it just stay there, in Australia?"

"Maybe it does," Dan said. "But I think there's someone organizing it all. And I think he or she is here. In Canada. Maybe even on Porcher Island."

"And you're planning to go there by yourself? When they've already killed three people?" Trust Annie to hone in on the most practical aspect of his problem!

"No, but I am going to go to Rupert. The Bureau has requested satellite surveillance and I can download that onto my computer. That means I can see what's happening there in real time, and if the helicopter takes off, I can check with the airport and if it lands there I'll find out who's in it"

He really shouldn't be telling them all this, but they were already involved, and if they were going to be with him, they had to know.

"Perhaps most importantly, I can contact all the delivery people. Anyone likely to take a parcel or a box or a crate over to Porcher. That way I can intercept it and see what's in it and figure out where it came from. And if it's from a foreign country, I can trace it back to find out not only who sent it, but also which customs agent approved it." He smiled. "And if that happens . . ."

He saw nods all around the table.

"Sounds like a good plan, but you don't need me." Walker stood up and moved to a window. "I'm no good at sitting around waiting for something to happen. Already been sitting here too long. Should be out catching a fish for supper—or is that what you're waiting for?"

Dan laughed. "I hadn't thought of that, but now that you mention it . . ." He turned serious. He might not have been honest with Walker about hauling him down to Vancouver, but he owed him honesty now.

"You've taught me to see things I never saw before, Walker, but I'll never be as good as you. You see things I don't see. Understand things I don't understand. You look at

247

things from a different angle. I think I'm going to need your help with this one."

Walker turned to look at him. The light from the window caught the high planes of his cheekbones and reflected off his black hair and the braid that hung over his shoulder. He looked both regal and remote, and for a moment Dan thought he was going to refuse, but then his mouth twisted into the familiar grin.

"Guess you've got yourself a passenger."

Chapter 31

Prince Rupert was known as the wettest city in Canada, and it was living up to its reputation. The rain seemed endless, falling from low gray cloud that hung like a shroud over both land and water.

For five seemingly endless days Dan, Claire and Walker took turns watching the computer screen and for those five days nothing much happened. They learned there were three other houses scattered among the trees on the Porcher Island property in addition to the house Dan had visited, plus a large building that appeared to serve as a gathering place, and people travelled freely between them. A lot of people. Far more than Dan had thought.

The helicopter came and went twice on apparent grocery runs, both times taking on fuel as confirmed by Joe at the airport. No packages were delivered by delivery companies. No water taxis called.

Then things got interesting.

Walker was away fishing in his canoe when a stranger walked down the float and rapped on *Dreamspeaker*'s hull. The man, whose name was Art, said he was a friend of Walker's and came from Kitkatla, a tiny village located directly across the water from the entrance to the Porcher lagoon. Walker had asked him to keep an eye out for any activity there and early that morning he had seen a boat carrying two people heading towards that entrance. It had been dark blue in colour with a weird pattern on both its hull and canopy that made it very hard to see against the heavily treed shoreline and he had quickly lost sight of it, but he thought it had gone in.

Dan thanked him and immediately called Vancouver. He had been the one watching the satellite stream that morning and he had seen nothing, but after five days he had been starting to give up hope and it had been hard to focus his attention. He might have missed it.

"Any chance you can re-run some of that satellite video?"

"Possible, but it gets very expensive. It's a live feed so they have to get someone to set it up and that takes time. Is it important?"

"I don't know, but it certainly could be."

There was a long silence and Dan could almost hear the wheels turning. Finally there was a sigh.

"Okay. Just don't make this a habit. What do you need?"

He gave them Art's estimate of when he had seen the boat, and they told him it would take at least an hour, probably two, to get the video back to him.

While he waited, Dan went to the wheelhouse where Claire was watching the screen, and peered over her shoulder.

"Our visitor was another of Walker's friends," he told her. "He said a boat went into the lagoon this morning. Can you see any sign of it there now?"

"What kind of boat?" she asked. "There's certainly nothing big—and there's no wharf to tie up to."

"He said it was a powerboat. Blue with some weird pattern that made it hard to see. I'm wondering if it was the same boat that was seen down at Dawson's Landing."

"Well if it was there earlier, it's not there now." She nodded towards the screen.

Dan leaned closer. "There's a lot of overhanging trees all along that shore. Maybe that pattern serves as camouflage. If it hugged the beach . . ."

Perhaps he should have asked to see a wider area, but he had wanted to focus on the lagoon and the land immediately surrounding it. If he included all the possible approaches he would lose detail, and there wasn't much of that now.

He was back in the galley heating some soup for lunch when she called him.

"Dan! Look at this."

He raced back to the wheelhouse and tried to see what it was she was excited about, but couldn't see anything.

"There. See that? I think that's a wake."

He leaned so close to the screen his nose almost touched it. "Where?"

"See that kelp moving? And there's reflection off the ripples."

"So where's the boat?"

He felt her shrug. "Has to be under the overhang, like you said earlier."

He straightened up and looked out the window at the harbour, wishing he was looking the lagoon instead. If there was a boat, where had it come from, and why was the pilot taking such pains to keep it hidden? Surely there was no way the people there could know they were being watched—unless someone had told them. But who? The only people he could think of that might have alerted them would be one of the delivery companies or water taxi operators he had spoken with—although it was possible they had told someone in customs at the airport or the docks. He slammed his fist down on the dash in frustration. There were too many details he couldn't control. Too many possibilities.

He pulled out the chart of the area and studied the island. As he had thought, there was only one entrance to the lagoon, but that entrance and the coast to either side of it was guarded by a mass of small islands. It would certainly be possible for a small boat to slip in and hug the shore all the way to the end of the inlet, but it would take skill and patience.

There was also a short, narrow channel leading into a smaller lagoon above the first. It might be possible for something with a shallow-keel to pass through that, which meant he could have been wrong in thinking they didn't have a boat. But if they did, he doubted it could be big enough to safely make the mainland. That left Oona River, a tiny community of only thirty or so inhabitants on the west side of the island as their base, but that didn't make sense. There was nothing at Oona River except a couple of boat-sheds. Still, he needed to check it out. If he could locate both the boat and the owner . . .

He called the Prince Rupert detachment on their private channel and spoke with the commander.

"Is there anyone at Oona River I can talk to. I need to know if they've got a boat moored there—dark blue with a weird symbol painted all over it."

"This linked to that case you're working on?"

"Yeah. There was a boat in the lagoon earlier on and I want to know where it came from."

"Maybe talk to Sven Halvorsen. His house is right by the float so he would know all the boats there."

Dan thanked him and was about to sign off when the man added: "You might want to talk to Rick Sanders too. He's up at Humpback Bay. He's an odd-ball, lives completely off-grid, but there's a derelict cannery there and an old wharf. I heard he even gets a few visitors in cruising season."

Talking to Sven Halvorsen and Rick Sanders meant another trip in the Zodiac. There was no way to contact either of them by radio without risking being overheard and that meant waiting for Walker to return because he wasn't going to leave Claire alone. As Dan headed back to the salon, the satellite phone shrilled again.

"Connor," he said, expecting to hear either Markleson's gravel voice or the more cultured tones of the Contact Bureau commander. Instead the deep baritone belonging to Joe at the airport boomed into his ear.

"You asked me to let you know when that helicopter came in to refuel."

Dan stared out the window. What the hell was going on? First a boat entering the lagoon without showing up on the satellite feed and now a helicopter he hadn't seen either? It didn't seem possible he could have missed something that obvious.

"Are you talking about a couple of days ago? You already told me about that."

"Nope. Talking about today. Only a few hours ago, but I came on late so I didn't hear about it till just now. And it wasn't that helicopter from Porcher with the girl pilot. This was a different one. Same make and model but blue, not black, and there was a guy at the controls."

Dan squeezed his eyes shut and tried to slow the racing of his heart.

"Did it have that same yellow pattern on it?"

"The guys said there was a pattern but I don't think they'll be able to say for sure it was the same as on the black one."

Surely there couldn't be three of these helicopters. It had to be the chopper Annie saw.

"And it took on fuel?"

"Yep. Forty liters in the tank and another twenty in the auxiliary. Guess they were running low, but they might have left the auxiliary empty to compensate for the weight of the other guy."

For just a moment Dan thought his heart might have come to a complete stop.

"The other guy? He had a passenger aboard?"

"Yeah. The guys said he was a weird looking dude. Tall and skinny. Must have had to fold himself in two to get into that little bird. They said he was wearing these baggy white pants and a long-sleeve shirt that hung halfway to his knees. Looked like some phony Indian guru or something."

Dan took a deep breath and asked the most important question of all.

"Did he have long hair. Black. Maybe some red streaks in it?"

"They didn't mention his hair. I can ask them if you like."

"Yeah. Do that. And ask them if he was carrying anything."

Was it possible Kalfu had come here? If he had, was that who was in that boat this morning? More importantly, why? Surely it had to be something important to bring him all the way up to Porcher Island—or was he simply delivering the masks stolen from Ahas'wit?

***

Less than an hour later Dan was looking at a file of photographs taken at the immigration kiosks at Vancouver Airport and less than an half-an-hour after that, he had a name. According to his passport, the man who called himself Kalfu was in fact Martin de los Santos, citizen of the Dominican Republic, and he had arrived the previous week on a Qantas flight from Sydney.

Chapter 32

Dan was on a video call with the commander of the Contact Bureau. They were both staring at a photo of Martin de los Santos as Dan laid out his case.

"Ernie, the guy I told you about with the aboriginal police in Darwin, has seen him at both the airport and the wharf there. I saw him myself at the Spirit Gallery asking about tjuringas, and I'm pretty sure he crewed on a fishboat owned by the man who was murdered in that village near Bella Bella."

He reached out and picked up a print-out sitting on the table beside him.

"I've got immigration checking on previous arrivals and departures, but last week he flew in from Sydney. Somehow or other he connected with this helicopter—I've got a request into Rupert to track its ownership from the registration number—and he arrived here this morning."

"And you think he went over to Porcher in a boat, but you didn't actually see him?"

"Hell, I didn't even see the goddamn boat, and that's something else that makes me very suspicious. If this is just a friendly visit, why go to all the trouble of sneaking in like that. Why not just motor in like anybody else?"

The commander sighed and ran his hands over his crew cut hair.

"Look, I understand where you're coming from, but you don't have enough to get a search warrant, at least not yet.

Keep working on it from your end. Find out who owns that helicopter and see if you can figure out where he picked this guy up. See if you can track that boat you think you saw and find out where it came from. I'll work on Mr. de los Santos. Maybe we'll get lucky. If he's lied about anything—address, occupation, anything—then perhaps we've got a chance."

It wasn't much, but it was better than nothing. The problem was it would all take time and time was something Dan didn't think they had much of. It was a long way from Darwin to Prince Rupert. If, as Dan suspected, de los Santos was either the thief, or the man who planned the thefts, the reason behind this trip could well be another theft. And as had now been proven on three separate occasions, that also meant the possibility of another murder.

"Maybe I should pay them another visit? Shake them up a bit."

"Absolutely not! That would put everything at risk, including you. It would give them an excuse to claim harassment. Just keep on doing what you're doing and let's talk again tomorrow. I should have some information by then."

And that, thought Dan as he replaced the handset, was exactly why he preferred to work alone. Here he was, already in place, maybe able to prevent another theft or even a murder, maybe able to catch the guy doing it, but unable to do a damn thing because he had to wait for permission! At least when it was Markleson he was working with, he could do what needed to be done and then tell him later—but he knew that was just his frustration speaking. That wasn't the way it worked. He might keep a few details away from Markleson, but he always kept him in the loop. He would never expose his boss to any serious consequences resulting from his actions.

It was too late to take the Zodiac over to either Oona River or Humpback Bay to search for the boat. Darkness fell early at this time of year and with the heavy cloud cover there would be no moon. Besides, people who lived in remote off-grid communities likely went to bed early so even if he managed to make his way over to either place, he probably wouldn't get the information he was looking for. In any case, Claire had been staring at the screen for the last couple of hours and needed a break and Walker had yet to return. The best he could do was to take his own turn at the computer, and while he was watching, follow up with the people in the office at the airport to see if he could track down the owner of the helicopter.

***

"Marcus Guzman?" He repeated the name to make sure he had it correct. "And his address is Whistler?"

"That's what it says here."

"Do you have a record of him coming in before this?"

"Not that I can see. It looks like it was his first time, at least in the last twenty-four months."

It seemed no matter how many questions he asked, every time he got an answer he also got another question. Who was Marcus Guzman and how did he fit into all this? Had he flown to Vancouver to pick de los Santos up or had de los Santos made his way to Whistler? Either way the fact Guzman had never flown into Rupert before probably meant that this trip was the result of some special circumstance. Something urgent. But how did that tiny helicopter get from Whistler to Prince Rupert? It had to have landed somewhere to take on fuel and he needed to speak with air traffic control to find out where that somewhere was.

Early the next morning, the wind blowing cold across the dark water, Dan made his way over to the north end of Porcher Island. It was barely light when he arrived in Humpback Bay and slid in beside a row of rotting stumps. The cannery had disappeared long ago, and the wharf had collapsed, but the broken pilings remained and they served as mooring posts for two boats. One was an old lapstrake runabout, its paint peeling, the motor cowling rusted. The other was a dark blue fiberglass beauty maybe twenty-four feet long with twin Yamaha outboards hanging off the transom and a long canopy covering the center-console cockpit. Both hull and canopy were covered with an intricate pattern: the Vèvè of Ayizan. Finally luck had been on his side. He had found what he was looking for in the first place he visited. As he stared at the sleek lines of the boat he felt adrenaline pour into his system and his nerve-ends started to thrum, the vibrations so strong he thought they must be visible on his skin.

"That your boat?" he asked the man who had come down to the shore to meet him.

"Who the hell are you?" Sanders was covered head to toe in grubby work clothes, his long hair hanging out of an old knitted cap and his feet stuffed into gumboots.

"Dan Connor. Nice boat. I saw it going past Oona River yesterday. I'm looking for something like it myself. Just wondered how you like it."

Sanders turned and spat into the water.

"It ain't mine. No way I want a plastic gas guzzler like that. Belongs to some folks down in the lagoon. They don't have a float there so I let 'em keep it here."

"Long way from the lagoon. How do they get home?"

Sanders stabbed his thumb over his shoulder. "Got an ATV. It ain't far if you go overland."

Dan leaned over and peered into the cockpit. "You think they'd mind if I took a look at it? Just take a minute."

Sanders shrugged. "Guess it can't hurt."

It only took Dan a few seconds to wrap a line around one of the cleats and step aboard. The boat was obviously well-maintained, but it looked as if it had been left in a hurry. Two empty coffee mugs sat in holders on either side of the console and a pair of insulated neoprene gloves sat on top of it. He would have liked to take the cups to have them checked for DNA but Sanders was watching him and he had nowhere to hide them. What he wanted even more was a small, zippered bag that was lying on the floor below the seat.

He leaned down and pretended to scan the controls. "Looks pretty nice," he said. "You think it's got trim tabs? I don't see any switch, but maybe they're automatic."

He watched with satisfaction as Sanders moved back along the shore to get a better look at the stern, and as soon as he was sure the man wasn't looking, Dan slid the bag under his jacket. He would have to make up some excuse as to why he took it, and it was unlikely anything it contained could ever be used as evidence, but if it helped him solve the case, he was okay with that.

"Looks like it," Sanders said. "You can probably see 'em if you look between the engines."

Dan feigned a smile, glanced briefly between the twin white cowlings, and climbed back out of the boat.

"Yeah. Looks good. Guess I'll see if I can find a dealer. Thanks."

He started the engine on the Zodiac, waved, and slid back out to sea, his heart racing. A boat worth a couple of hundred thousand dollars kept hidden in an almost uninhabited cove, and an All-Terrain Vehicle that traversed a path through a forest so dense that even a satellite couldn't pick it up. They'd gone to a lot of work to keep things secret, but they weren't going to be secret for very much longer. He would see to that.

***

Back on board *Dreamspeaker*, a cup of hot coffee in his hand, Dan tried to make sense of the contents of the bag. There was a small plastic bottle containing a clear liquid, a package of push-pins, each with a drop of some kind of paint on the head, and a tiny notebook filled with letters and numbers, presumably some kind of shorthand or code. He set aside everything but the notebook which he opened using the tip of a pencil.

"The sleuth at work?" Walker had finished cleaning the two rockfish he had caught earlier on. "You find that boat you were looking for?"

"Yeah, I did."

"And helped yourself to that stuff?"

Dan grinned. "Finders keepers. They won't let me go in and search the place, so I figure I'm going to have to find another way. I'm hoping this is it."

"Don't recall you ever telling me that." Walker gave his familiar grin as he reminded Dan of how they had met.

"I think the circumstances might be a little different. If I'm right, this guy may have murdered three people. He needs to be stopped."

Walker leaned over and looked at the odd collection. "Looks like a pile of junk."

"I don't think so. I think it's all important. I just don't know how or why, but if I can figure out what all these letters and numbers mean, then maybe I can figure out the rest." Dan nodded towards the notebook.

"Maybe that Latitude and Longitude stuff you use all the time," Walker said. "Never did figure out why you white guys need a bunch of numbers to tell you where you are."

"No, it's not that. There's a bunch of letters mixed in. Might be some kind of code. Looks like most of them are grouped the same way. There's only one that's different."

After an hour of looking at them, Dan finally gave up. Maybe if he sent it all down to Vancouver they could run it through some computer program—but then he would have to explain how he got it.

He stood up, stretched his shoulders and headed for the galley. Perhaps a beer and a sandwich would help clear his mind.

***

"Wow. I haven't seen that for a while."

Walker had replaced Claire at the computer screen and she was now staring down at the notebook on the table. It took a couple of seconds for Dan to register what she had said.

"You know what that is? You can understand it?"

She looked at him and nodded. "I think so, at least part of it, although I'd have to check them out on the computer to tell you where they refer to." She slid onto the bench behind the table. "They're geocodes. I used to use them when I was researching the otters."

Chapter 33

Geocodes, Claire explained, were used to identify exact locations on the earth's surface by assigning geographic coordinates, and it didn't take her long to run each reference through the computer program. There were only eight of them, and once Claire had separated the code from some other letters that appeared at the end of each line, it was easy.

The first four identified pointed to the each of the first four villages that had reported thefts, the fifth was Tsatsquot, where Jimmie Alfred had lost his life, the sixth was Warrimuyanga, off the north coast of Australia and the seventh was Ahas'wit, the village where Leonard had been killed. The eighth was in a labyrinth of islands northwest of Klemtu.

"We've got him!" Dan's yell was loud enough to disturb two kingfishers sitting out on the pilings. "We've got the bastard!"

He thumped the table with his fist, but then he caught himself and checked the list again.

"It looks like they're in chronological order." He ran his finger over the names. "That's the first one, down there off Mussel Inlet, and that's the second up near the end of Seymour. See that? And here's number five, Charlie's village." He looked at Claire. "Maybe those letters at the end of the codes stand for what was stolen?"

After each code there were two or three letters and Dan opened his notebook to confirm what he was seeing.

"RTM. That has to be the Raven transformation mask. And here. BX. Bentwood box." His finger traced down to the fifth line. "And this TM would be the Thunderbird mask from Charlie's village. It all matches —except for this last one. There hasn't been a theft reported from Kla'wis."

"Not yet. But maybe that's why he's here." Walker had been sitting quietly, listening to everything. "That's where the next theft is going to be."

Dan stared at him, his mind racing. Walker had to be right, but Dan wanted to be able to tell him he was wrong. That there was not going to be another theft. That once he had talked to the Contact Bureau and they had seen the notebook it would all be over. They would go in and search the houses on Porcher, question everybody, find Martin de los Santos and arrest him.

But he knew it wasn't going to be that easy. It was going to take too long. By the time the police got there, Kalfu was going to be gone.

Walker read the expression on Dan's face. "You don't think they'll catch him?"

"I wish it was that simple, but that's not the way it works. They have to apply for a search warrant and that takes time. When they've got it, they'll send a team to Porcher. Maybe send in some of the guys from Rupert. But by the time they get there, Kalfu will probably have left."

"But their helicopter's still there." Claire had been listening in as she watched the screen.

"Yeah, but we can't see the other end of the island. They might have already taken the boat. Kalfu—de los Santos—could be anywhere."

"But if the Bureau knows he's heading for Kla'wis surely they'll send a team in there?"

"Maybe." It wasn't likely. There were too many bureaucratic requirements that would slow them down. "But he could be way ahead of them."

***

Dan shoved himself back from the table and went to stand beside Claire in the wheelhouse. The light was already starting to fade, the dark water dotted with small boats heading back to shore, and he could feel a cold, jittery energy taking hold of his body. He was so close. There had to be something he could do. His hands clenched into fists as he stared blindly out into the dusk.

"Even if I left now it would take me more than a day to get there!" He pushed the words out of a throat thickened with frustration and anger. "I might be too late."

There was a long silence and Dan knew they were all thinking of the people in that tiny village identified only by the last geocode in the notebook. They would be gathering round fires, cooking supper, laughing, telling stories, completely unaware of what might be coming their way.

"Your VHF working?" Walker was the first to break the silence.

"Sure, but what good is it? I can't use it to warn them. It would alert the people on Porcher, and anyway it's only line-of-sight. That's sure not going to reach as far as Kla'wis."

"It doesn't have to reach Kla'wis. You remember how the guys at Tsatsquot reached me when they wanted to get you?"

"Yeah. They relayed the message—shit! You think that could work here? It's a lot further away and it's late in the

265

season. Not as many boats out now to pick it up and pass it on."

"Worth a try. Better than sitting here waiting to hear this guy has murdered someone else."

An hour later, fuel and water tanks full, they were underway. Dan had called Charles Eden to ask for his help and before they left, Eden and Walker had worked out a message they thought would alert the villagers in Kla'wis while not alarming either de los Santos or the people on Porcher Island if they heard it. *Dreamspeaker* had barely cleared the outflow from the Skeena River when they heard it repeated several times, but then the VHF fell silent and they had no way of knowing whether it had been passed on or whether the chain had been broken. Dan debated calling Waglisla to ask Matthews to help but he couldn't risk it. While he hadn't actually been ordered to stay in Rupert, he knew that was what the Bureau expected and they weren't likely to be anywhere near as understanding as Markleson.

***

The next twenty-eight hours were a blur. The gray evening merged into dark night and then into yet another gray morning, the diesel engine throbbed unrelentingly under their feet, and the lines on the screen scrolled endlessly down to chart their passage.

Dan stayed at the wheel all night, relying on the information on the screen to guide his course and trusting that this late in the year there would be no logs or other detritus in his way. He turned it over to Claire once it was light, but took it back after he had made a pot of coffee and grabbed a couple of cookies, completely ignoring Walker's snort of disgust.

It wasn't until the evening of the following day when they were approaching Waglisla that Dan passed the microphone to Walker.

"See if you can reach anyone. Ask them if they've heard the message and passed it on. We're too far away from either Porcher or Kla'wis for anyone to hear you so I don't think you need to be careful with what you say." Dan's speech was slurred from lack of sleep.

"Thought you'd never ask." Walker depressed the switch. "Wilf Edgar. Wilf Edgar. Wilf Edgar. Walker calling."

There was no answer.

"Who the hell is Wilf Edgar?" Dan snapped. "Just make an open call. Doesn't matter who answers."

"Patience my friend. Patience. Wilf's getting on in life. Might take time for him to get to the radio."

Walker repeated his call with the same result.

"Patience isn't going to help us this time, Walker, and time is something we don't have."

Dan nudged the revs up yet again as he entered Lama Passage, and watched in frustration as a pod of dolphins raced effortlessly past as if to emphasize his lack of speed.

The air now smelled of ozone and overhead the clouds were an ominous yellowish-grey. Another storm was on the way.

"That you Walker?" A thin, reedy voice filled the wheelhouse.

Walker grinned and looked at Dan as he answered.

"Hi Wilf. You there by yourself?"

"Yeah. Rest of them took off to Kla'wis after they got your message."

Walker's grin got wider. "You hear anything from them since then?"

"Nah. No need. S'pect they'll tell me all about it when they get back."

"Shit! Do they know to keep out of the way?" Dan asked.

He reached for the microphone but Walker moved it away.

"When did they leave?" he asked, holding up a hand to stop Dan from interrupting.

"Before daylight. Too dark to see any damn thing except the wake when they took off."

"How many?"

"I dunno. Five. Six. Maybe seven if they picked Richard up."

***

Walker replaced the microphone and leaned back on his chair. "Guess the message got through. Sounds like they'll have it all sorted by the time we get there."

"How the hell do you figure that?" Dan ran his hand over his face, grimacing as he felt the two-day growth of beard. "We've got six or seven guys running around trying to catch a man with a knife who has no problem using it. We could be running into a blood bath!" He stared out the window into the gloom, wishing for a clairvoyance he knew was impossible. "The best we can hope for is that de los Santos sees them, realizes they knew he was coming, and beats it. It means we'll have lost him, but at least it won't . . ."

He would have said more, but the satellite phone interrupted him.

"Connor." He snarled the word into the microphone, not caring who it was calling.

"Where the hell are you?" It was Markleson.

"Coming up on a small cove north-west of Klemtu. The village is named Kla'wis if that's any help, and I can only talk for a couple of minutes. I've got some tricky navigating to do here."

"Goddamn it Connor. Working with you is like running a friggin' circus. You're supposed to be in Rupert. Now I've got the Bureau on my ass asking what the hell you're up to."

"Why? No one ordered me to stay there, and they didn't need me over on Porcher. They took their own team in. I figured I was better off following up on a lead down here."

"Better be a good one. The Bureau says the knife that was used on that guy over in Australia was the same as the one that killed Jimmie and Leonard."

***

By the time Dan ended the call the radar was showing the entrance to the cove and he slowed the engine. There wasn't much clearance to squeeze *Dreamspeaker*'s wide beam through the opening and once inside there wasn't going to be much room to maneuver. He needed to stay close to a steep cliff on his port side. Anywhere else where the shore was lower might give de los Santos an opportunity to climb on board. As soon as he could he put the engine in neutral and let the boat coast in until the bumpers he had hung on the hull kissed gently against the rock wall.

"Think you can keep her here until I get back?" he asked Claire. "There's not much current so she shouldn't need much fiddling to hold her steady. Walker and I will take the canoe in and see what's happening."

She nodded and took the wheel. "Be careful," was all she said.

Dan and Walker slid the canoe into the water and paddled soundlessly to the opposite shore. No lights showed in any of the houses and only the occasional glint of moonlight on the glass of the windows revealed their presence.

"Where is everyone," Dan whispered. "It's not that late. Should be someone still up."

The bow of the canoe scraped against the shore, and suddenly the air was filled with a cacophony of whistles and rattles that rose and faded then rose again.

"What the hell is that?" Dan snapped.

Walker chuckled. "Better let me out, white man. Take the canoe back offshore. This is a *T'seka*. They're taming Man Eater. You don't want to help him escape."

Chapter 34

Walker pushed the canoe away from the shore and disappeared up into the trees, leaving Dan drifting on the water. The chaotic noise had quieted, replaced by an occasional eerie whistle. As his eyes grew more accustomed to the dark Dan could see shadows moving among the trees, but he couldn't make out who or what was causing them. Sitting there, confused and helpless, was not a feeling he liked, but to even dip a paddle in the water could let de los Santos know someone was out there.

It was more than half-an-hour later when Walker reappeared, a dark shadow on the beach, and called him back in. The whistles now seemed to all come from a single location at the head of the cove.

"What the hell is going on," Dan whispered as the keel of the canoe scraped over the gravel. "And don't give me any of this Man Eater shit. Is de los Santos here? Is everyone okay?"

"Whoa, slow down." Walker climbed in, dug his paddle into the water and turned the canoe back towards *Dreamspeaker*. "It's all looked after. Time to get a little rest. You can pick your man up in the morning."

"Walker . . ."

"No. You need to listen. This is our business now. This man has murdered two of our people and stolen our sacred regalia. He's learning there's a cost."

"Walker, I'm responsible. I brought you here. If anybody gets hurt it's going to be on my head."

The canoe bumped against the swim grid and Walker reached out a hand to steady it. As he was tying the line they heard a quick flurry of rattles and a single, frantic scream. His grin gleamed briefly.

"You worry too much. Get some rest."

***

Dan didn't rest. He couldn't. He spent the rest of the night trying to come up with some way of controlling the situation, but there was nothing he could do. To go back to shore in a place he was unfamiliar with, and with who knew how many people running around in the dark, was a recipe for disaster. Markleson was right. This was a circus, and he was the one who had created it.

Dawn found him sitting out on deck, his face haggard. Although it had been quiet for the last couple of hours, the night had been filled with occasional hoots and whistles followed by what sounded like someone or something running on the rocks or crashing through the trees. Across from him, Walker lay on his mat, quietly watching. He didn't sleep much, and he still refused to use any of the bunks inside, but unlike Dan, he appeared rested.

"Looks like you both could use some coffee," Claire said, carrying two steaming mugs from the galley.

"What I could use is knowing what the hell is going on." Dan snapped as he glared at Walker.

"I told you what was going on," Walker said. "Mr. de los Santos is getting a taste of his own medicine."

"That makes no sense Walker, and you know it."

"It does to me and the people here, and we're the ones he stole from. It's our brothers he killed."

272

Dan sighed. "Do you at least want to tell me if I should be calling for assistance—or for an ambulance."

"I don't think you'll need any help with this one."

Walker's calm grin was infuriating and Dan turned away to stare out over the water.

"So you're saying he'll just walk out and give himself up?"

"Nah. The people here will let us know where he is, but you'll probably have to go in and get him. Don't think he'll be in any condition to walk out by himself."

Dan stared at him in horror. "Are you telling me they hurt him? Those screams I heard weren't just fear? Damn it Walker, if they attacked him they could be charged with assault—and we may lose any case we have against him!"

Walker's answer was drowned by a series of sharp, bird-like whistles coming from a group of three men who had appeared on the shore.

"Time to go," Walker said. "You might want to bring a blanket."

***

"Don't look too dangerous now does he?" Walker was standing on top of a steep bank, surrounded by a group of men wearing elaborate wooden masks. His face was impassive as he looked down at the man cowering in the rocks below.

Dan had seen the photo of Martin de los Santos taken on his arrival at Vancouver airport, and he had seen the man himself at the Spirit Gallery in Darwin. What huddled below him now didn't look anything like either version. More apparition than human, de los Santos lay curled into a ball, his knees drawn up near his chin, his hair braided with strands of green string and strips of fabric threaded with bark and moss hanging from his shoulders. His skin was pale, as if all the blood had leached out of it, and long strands of wet hair straggled across his face.

"What the hell happened here?" Dan asked.

"I already told you. He got a taste of his own medicine," Walker answered.

"You're going to have to explain that to me, Walker. Is this about that weird message you and Charles Eden sent out? All that stuff about the Hamatsa and Baxbak . . . Baxw . . .whoever. I never did understand it."

Walker smiled. "The name is *Baxwbakwalanuxwsiwe*, also known as Cannibal Woman, or Man-Eater at the North End of the World. She has four man-eating birds as her companions and they take possession of a Hamatsa initiate when he's sent out into the forest to fast before he enters the *T'seka* ceremony." He pointed to each of the masked men in turn. "That one is Crooked Beak of Heaven. Next to him is *Huxhugwadsayi*: he's a kind of crane. Over there is *Hamasiwe*, sort of a smaller version of Crooked Beak of Heaven, and this last one with the really long beak is a man-eating Raven. They have to be tamed and controlled. It's all done through dance using whistles and rattles."

Dan stared at him in disbelief. "You mean they tried to catch this guy with whistles and rattles? They could have been killed!"

"Worked, didn't it?" The unrepentant grin was back and Walker gestured to the almost unrecognizable shape that was now on his hands and knees rocking back and forth below them making sounds somewhere between sobbing and keening. "This guy was using our stories to steal from us and murder our people. He was dressing up as one of our spiritual beings, using that to camouflage himself in case he was seen. To be able do that he has to have studied our culture. Got to know it. We just turned it all back on him. Made it real."

Dan looked back at the sight below him, trying to make sense of what Walker had said. Was it possible? Could someone like Martin de los Santos, the man he had spent weeks trying to catch, a man who travelled the globe stealing valuable objects and murdering anyone who got in his way, be reduced to this whimpering shell by a few people dressed up in masks and blowing whistles?

"So you're saying these guys made him believe they were spirits? Man-eating spirits? That's all it took to do this? Seems like it would take more."

Walker shrugged. "Why? He has to have been living in some kind of fantasy world. You said he spent most of his time when he wasn't stealing and killing thinking of himself as some Voudou spirit."

Dan hadn't thought of that, but Walker was right, and the same idea could probably be applied to the people living on Porcher Island. It would certainly help explain why Samantha Chauvet called herself Erzulie. It could even explain why they wanted the things they had stolen, although that was something he needed to think through a little more.

"So you're saying because he believed he was a spirit it made it easy to convince him a bunch of other spirits were after him."

"Something like that."

It was starting to make an odd kind of sense and Dan nodded. "Guess he figured he was sort of invisible, sneaking up on a bunch of unsuspecting people sleeping peacefully in their beds. He wasn't expecting to see all these weird shapes creeping about in the forest looking like the creatures whose masks he had stolen, hooting at him from the shadows." He laughed. "Hell, that would probably freak me out too."

He looked at the men who had now removed their masks and were staring down at the spectacle below. "Guess I'd better go talk to him. See what he has to say."

He started to clamber down, but as soon as he got near, de los Santos began to scream hysterically, calling out to someone or something named Papa Legba, asking him to get Baron Samedi to close the gates to the spirit world. Dan reached out a hand to try and calm him, but that only made it worse. The screams rose in pitch until they sounded like the cries of a wounded animal and when the man started to throw himself against the rocks, Dan backed off.

"I think I'm going to need some help," he said. "I can't let him hurt himself."

Walker held out the blanket he had carried up from the canoe. "Told you to bring a blanket."

Chapter 35

It took Dan and two of the villagers to wrap de los Santos tightly in the blanket and get him back to the beach where they had left the canoe. They sat him down with his back propped against the rocks and Dan left him there under the watchful eyes of the entire village while he and Walker paddled back to get the Zodiac.

Back onboard *Dreamspeaker* they locked the still shaking man in a cabin. He had stopped screaming, and appeared calmer, but continued to mutter under his breath and rock himself side to side as they closed the door. After a few minutes of listening for any sign of increased activity, Dan went to the wheelhouse and set up another VHF relay to notify Matthews in Waglisla and ask him to notify the Contact Bureau. He figured it was probably safe to use the satellite phone now, but without knowing how de los Santos had arrived it was better to be cautious.

After that all they could do was wait, and they sat out on deck drinking coffee and watching a pale sun rise slowly over the tree-tops. The air filled with birdsong and the shore came alive with otters and mink in search of food. Men from the village came out to join them, each bringing a gift of food taken from the ocean or a basket full of camus-root or fresh-cooked bannock, and each stayed a while to chat before returning to shore. It was past noon when an RCMP helicopter arrived, and the noise of its rotors sent animals, birds and humans alike running for shelter. An hour later, long after the man they had called Kalfu had been sedated and taken aboard and they had watched the helicopter disappear, the beach remained empty.

***

They didn't stay long after that, although in the time it took Dan to lift the Zodiac up onto its cradle and with Walker's help wrestle the canoe onto the swim grid, yet more dried salmon arrived along with several large crabs, and a basket of shrimp.

Claire waved the villagers goodbye as Walker helped Dan ease *Dreamspeaker* back out through the narrow entrance and turn her bow towards the east.

"That was delicious," Claire said, licking her fingers after they had eaten a lunch of shrimp and bannock. "But when we get back to Port McNeill I'm going to order the biggest steak on the menu. I think I've had enough seafood for a while."

Dan didn't answer.

"What?" she asked, staring at him. "We *are* heading back to the marina aren't we? You've caught your guy. It's over."

Dan reached for her hand. "We caught *a* guy," he said. "And he's probably the guy who committed all the thefts and murders. But we haven't caught whoever was directing him. Until we do that it's not over."

It took her a minute, but then she stood up and went to the galley.

"Well it's over as far as I'm concerned," she said. "I'm sick and tired of watching a computer screen and I'm not going to do it anymore. In fact, if Walker agrees, I think he and I should go for a paddle as soon as you anchor for the night."

278

He laughed and pulled her close. He had been worried about her. She had been too quiet since she returned from Australia, but the feisty, independent woman he loved was back.

"I won't argue. I think we've taken care of any threat to you. Why don't you fly home from Rupert? I won't be far behind and Tom Markleson says he has a place you can stay."

"You going to fly me down too?" Walker asked. "Long way to paddle."

"If you like, but you might want to stay. I suspect they'll find all the stolen regalia over there on Porcher. Be good to have you there to help with identification."

***

Two days later the three of them were sitting around a table in the meeting room of the Prince Rupert detachment office, talking to Commander Bishop as they waited for the regalia to be brought up from the evidence room. Dan had insisted Claire be allowed to join them until her taxi arrived and Bishop had reluctantly agreed.

"We're holding them all except de los Santos and Chauvet in an old hotel near the police station until we can figure out what to do with them," he said, stirring his coffee. "Fifteen of them, and they have to be the oddest bunch you've ever seen. Looks like every one of them has some kind of physical problem. Maybe some mental problems too. We've got a doctor and a shrink in there trying to sort it all out, but it's not going to be easy."

"So where's de los Santos and the girl?"

"Mr. de los Santos is in the psychiatric ward in the hospital and the docs say there's no telling when he'll be fit to question. The girl's in jail."

279

"In jail?" Dan was surprised. "She was certainly antagonistic when I talked to her, but why jail? And why only her? You figure she's the one behind it all?"

The commander smiled. "I think that's likely, and I don't think *antagonistic* quite covers her behaviour when my men arrived. She came out screaming and swearing, said these were "her" people and we couldn't touch them, then ordered them to kill the aggressors. Followed that up by grabbing a weird-looking knife off the top of a sideboard and trying to show them how to do it. Sent two of my men to emergency."

Dan responded by reaching into the briefcase he had brought with him.

"Does the knife look like this?" he asked as he placed an evidence bag containing a Kris knife on the table..

"Where the hell did you get that!"

"De los Santos had it with him in Kla'wis. He dropped it in his hurry to get away from the 'spirits' he figured were after him and one of the villagers picked it up. It's called a Kris knife and according to forensics it, or one like it, was what was used in both the murders here and in Australia. It's supposed to have magic powers."

"Magic, huh?" The knife glinted in the light as the commander moved the bag around with his finger. "Guess that explains the rest of the stuff we found over there in Porcher. You see it all when you were there?"

"Just the hallway and the front room. I wasn't invited in and I didn't have a search warrant."

"Well, we've got as many people as we can spare over there now checking it all out. I'd like you to join them. You've done the research. You might see something that they could miss."

"But you've found all the stolen regalia?"

Dan was interrupted by two uniformed officers who entered the room, each carrying a mask which they placed on top of a long bureau. They returned a few minutes later with a bentwood box and another mask.

Only Dan heard Walker's whispered, "*Gilikasla*, thank you." as he went to stand in front of them.

Commander Bishop stood and joined Walker. "Can you confirm that these were the items stolen from your people?"

It took several minutes for Walker to answer, but Dan knew it wasn't from doubt or hesitation. Walker was welcoming these treasures back and when he finally spoke his voice was reverent.

"They belong to my people. Yes. They have belonged to them for many generations."

"And they are the items that were stolen? You can attest to that?" Bishop was insistent.

Without taking his gaze from the regalia, Walker answered, "I don't attest to anything except the fact that these belong to my people and they need to be returned to them. You need to ask them."

"Easier said than done," the commander said as he returned to the table. "The rules are straightforward. They can only be returned if ownership can be clearly established and as far as I can tell none of the reports even contain a description." He opened his notebook and started writing. "I'll have them sent down to Vancouver. The court case will undoubtedly be held there and there isn't room here to store everything."

***

The silence that resulted from his statement was broken by a knock on the door and a constable announced Claire's taxi had arrived. She stood up, gave Dan a kiss on the check and started to leave, but then stopped.

"You don't need those," she said, turning back and nodding towards the regalia. "If you have to 'establish ownership' in order to use them as evidence, they won't be of any use—unless you plan on going to every village and asking them of course. But even then that wouldn't be enough would it? Masks and rattles don't come with a serial number, and every village along the coast has something similar."

"Procedure is there for a purpose, and they are part of our investigation, " Bishop replied in a tone so patronizing Dan was surprised Claire controlled her response as well as she did.

"Investigation into what?" she snapped, colour staining her cheeks. "Thefts you can't prove? Or are you saying you can use the regalia as evidence in a theft trial without identification but can't return them to their rightful owners. How convenient!" She pointed to the table. "What you do have is that knife, which forensics says was at least the type used in the murders, and may even be able to identify as the actual weapon. Surely putting a murderer behind bars is more important than catching a thief, and in this case it seems to be the same man. Why not simply charge him with murder, forget the thefts, and return the regalia to the people it belongs to?"

"That's not how it works," the commander said. "Both theft and murder are felony offences and should be treated as such."

He turned away but turned back as he heard her response.

"Well so much for that Truth and Reconciliation story you gave Dan as the reason you were sending him to Australia for two lousy weeks to investigate a crime he had no hope of solving. Sounds like it's still white man's rules, even when they don't make sense."

The door slamming behind her created a vacuum that nobody tried to fill.

***

After a long silence the commander left the room, only to return fifteen minutes later.

"Your lady friend made a good point, but the system does require accurate identification to support a charge of theft. Even to return property not needed for evidence."

"You mean the white man's system needs it. Our people don't. They know what's theirs," Walker said.

"Yes, I know. I understand, and I'll do all I can, but . . ."

"Yeah. But. But the regalia is going to be stolen twice, once by a crazy man and again by the government. Great system that. I'll tell them they can go see it in the museum."

A parade of emotions washed over the commander's face as he stared at Walker. There was anger, resentment, and frustration, but finally, empathy.

"I'll see what I can do," he said. "I've already called a couple of people in Vancouver and I know you spoke with a curator from the Anthropology Museum in Vancouver when you were down there. Maybe if everything is photographed and documented . . ." He ran a hand over his crew cut again. "It's certainly not the way we normally handle things but perhaps the same procedures don't work for two cultures. And it *is* time for Reconciliation."

He went to stand in front of the regalia, which now included a ravenstail cape and a chilkat apron, two rattles, a chief's staff, and a shaped stick which Dan recognized as an Australian aboriginal throwing stick, letting his eyes run over each item. "If the items are returned and we're not able to lay theft charges, do you think your people would be upset?"

He had his back to them so he didn't see the smile that passed Dan and Walker.

"I doubt it," Walker answered. "They don't pay a lot of attention to what happens outside the villages."

They watched the commander's head nod a couple of times, then he spun on his heel, straightened his shoulders, and addressed them formally.

"Well, I have to get back to my office and you need to get over to Porcher Island, Detective Connor. Please keep me informed of anything you find."

Without waiting for an answer he turned and headed towards the door. As he pulled it open he stopped and turned back.

"By the way, you were right about Harbinson. He's been suspended without pay. Looks like he's been on Miss Chauvet's payroll for some time, as has Mr. Dahonney. They both helped facilitate the thefts—and it turns out there's been more than the one on Bathurst Island—as well as the shipments of the goods."

Chapter 36

A week later they were heading back south, Walker sitting beside Dan in the wheelhouse while they watched Dean Channel open up in front of them. It was almost December, the slopes of the mountains covered with snow and the jagged summits brilliant white against a cold blue sky. They had spent three days on Porcher Island and had found not only more traditional regalia but also walls completely covered with paintings of Voudou loa and their vèvès, numerous rattles, drums, fetishes, and incense sticks, plus other paraphernalia they could not identify.

"So you were right all along," Walker said, watching an eagle snatch a fish from the water and carry it, gripped in its talons, towards the shore. "It was all about Voudou."

"Right and wrong," Dan said. "That expert they brought in from the university figures it's only loosely about Voudou. Everybody in Chauvet's group certainly comes from a Voudou culture, and a lot of the things we saw there in those houses were related to the practice of Voudou, but they were perverting it to try and get revenge on people they felt had wronged them. That's why they wanted the regalia. They believed it had some intrinsic power, some kind of magic they could use to punish the people who had bullied or shunned them because of the way they look."

Walker was still watching the eagle. "Seems kinda crazy," he said, his eyes following the flight of the bird. "If they'd really studied our culture they would have known that wasn't what it was about—and all that stuff in those houses was really weird. All those dolls and skulls and cigars. And what about those dark glasses we saw with only one lens, and the bottles of rum?"

They had spent their time on Porcher Island searching the various buildings. The largest had obviously served as a meeting place and every available surface had been covered in candles. There were closets full of elaborate white dresses and long black coats, shelves full of tall black hats, most with skulls painted on the hatbands, and racks stacked with bottles of rum. Drawers were filled with sunglasses, most missing the left lens, or with boxes of herbs and powders, or with stacks of recipes hand-written on parchment, labelled with somewhat unimaginative names such as *UnHexing, Enemy be Gone,* and *Develop Psychic Powers.* Each was sealed with wax and stamped with the vèvè of one of the loas.

Bedrooms in the houses contained shelves of fetishes and crude fabric dolls, many with faces drawn in marker pen. Walls were hung with white-painted skull masks and rows of ebony-handled walking sticks.

"All part of Voudou," Dan answered. "I can't remember all the information I read, but it seems each loa has certain powers and certain things they like. Papa Legba is one of them. He can grant wishes and supposedly is able to make souls suffer and he likes cigars, so I guess those cigars were to keep him happy."

"Which is the one who likes those sunglasses? What's he supposed to do?"

"That's Baron Samedi. He's an interesting fellow. No one can die unless he grants permission, but he's also noted for disruption, obscenity, and debauchery. Like Papa Legba and

Kalfu, he likes tobacco and rum and he always wears dark glasses."

Dan checked the screen and made a course alteration before he continued.

"The missing lens can symbolize one of two things. Either he simultaneously sees the realms of both the living and the dead or—and you'll love this—because a penis has only one eye and the phallus is his symbol. Remember those phallus-like things we saw planted on a mound in front of each of the houses?"

"Yeah." Walker grinned. "I figured maybe they were all into some kind of kinky sex. So those were for him?"

"They were indeed. He's important. He's the power behind the kind of magic that can kill, and my guess is he's the one they called on most to help with their plans for revenge. Him and Kalfu. Kalfu, as you might expect, is the grand master of black magic and sorcery and he controls the evil spirits of the night. He prefers his rum laced with gunpowder."

Walker raised his eyebrows. "Gunpowder? And here I used to think rum and coke was pretty fancy. So how many of these gods are there?"

"Well technically they're not gods," Dan answered. "*Bondeye* is the god. The loa are spirits that have certain powers and there's over a thousand of them."

* * *

They had found Samentha Chauvet's bedroom in the house Dan had come to on his previous visit. It had a closet full of long, flowing dresses in every possible shade of pink and drawers full of expensive jewelry. Mirrors hung on every wall, and there were enough bottles of perfume to completely cover two shelves. Make-up and hairbrushes littered the bathroom. This was the home of a woman obsessed with her looks, and it fitted all the descriptions Dan had read about the loa, Erzulie, from her love of the colour pink to her passion for perfume.

It was all somehow grotesque, and more than a little disturbing, but it wasn't until they entered one of the smallest bedrooms that they found what they were looking for. As they opened the door they saw a long dresser, and sitting on top was a line of Styrofoam wig forms each holding a wig with long hair threaded with strands of grass and moss and twists of string. Behind it, mounted on the wall, was a rack holding a number of Kris knives. One of the slots was empty.

"Certainly a strange group of people," Dan said. "I don't think any of them could be called normal, either mentally or physically. But it's also sad in a way."

They were coming up on the entrance to the channel leading to Tsatsquot and Dan slowed the engine.

"Sad for who?" Walker asked. "For Jimmie and Leonard? For their families? And what the hell is normal anyway? Are you normal? Am I?"

"Good point," Dan answered, nudging *Dreamspeaker* into the same cove he had anchored in before. "And yes, it's certainly sad for Jimmie and Leonard, and for Ngarra over there in Australia, and for their families too, but it's also kind of sad for that group on Porcher. It looks like every one of them has some kind of physical problem. Vitiligo, Melasma, Xeroderma Pigmentosum were a few of the terms I heard. I don't really know what any of those mean, but apparently they involve various skin problems as well as some actual deformities: skin discolouration and patches and blisters. Even red eyes and poor coordination. A couple of them are deaf and then there was one who suffers from dwarfism—and that's in addition to the guy on Snake Island who is apparently Chauvet's uncle. Certainly enough to make them the target of bullies and get them shunned. It's probably why Chauvet was able to recruit them to her cause, and certainly both she and the housekeeper had issues."

He had released the anchor and he looked at the man standing beside him as the boat swung on the chain. The sun's rays streaming in through the window caught Walker's face and lit the lines that led from his eyes. Walker had suffered at least as much pain and prejudice as any of the people on Porcher Island, but unlike them he had found the inner strength to rise above both. What had made the difference? How did one man develop pride and courage while another turned to hate and revenge?

"The Bureau told me the woman who was seen on the boat at Dawson's Landing is albino, which would explain both the clothing and the hairs that were found at Tsatsquot. She also pilots the helicopter her uncle—the guy who lives in Whistler—keeps in Bella Coola for when he wants to go bear hunting although it looks like the uncle probably had no idea what was going on."

Dan checked the sounder. "But you're right about those problems not giving them an excuse," he said. "And they certainly don't explain Martin de los Santos. From what I've been told, he not only created his own problems, he also embraced them. The shrinks have got him talking and it sounds like he's actually proud of what he's done. Told them how clever he was to get in and out of the villages without being caught, how he glued moss and grass over himself, and how the people on Porcher needed his skill to—and I quote—

289

'heal the wounds they had suffered.' Said all he was doing was 'balancing things out' whatever that means."

"Hell of a way to go about it—and how did he get in and out without being caught?"

"You were right there too," Dan replied. "He went in by helicopter a couple of days early—those pushpins with the drop of paint on the head? It was fluorescent. He landed well away and then went in to scout the village. He stuck the pins into trees so he could find his way back to the chopper. He listened to them talk, saw when they went inside for the night. Certainly in Leonard's village he knew exactly where the masks were located because he'd been there before. He wouldn't have had to search for them."

Dan paused as he remembered being told Kalfu had crewed on Leonard's boat. "Come to think of it, that may have been true for Jimmie's village too. Could be working on fishboats was part of his planning process. It's another thing Bishop will have to follow up on—although maybe you and I can ask them when we get there."

He switched off the computer and the engine and a silence he could almost feel filled the wheelhouse. It was broken only by the lapping of water against the hull and the cry of birds and he felt himself relax.

"We're going to take the canoe in, right?" Walker asked. "I'm getting tired of your lousy cooking. Time to get back out there to find some real food."

"Better to take the Zodiac. It's faster and there's more room to stow the mask."

Commander Bishop had been busy during the three days Dan and Walker were on Porcher Island. He had flown in not only the woman from the anthology department at the

University, but also Vivien, from the U'Mista museum in Alert Bay. The two of them had documented the regalia, starting with the masks from both Leonard and Jimmie's village. Photographs had been taken, measurements had been made, styles and shapes and markings identified, and while they couldn't identify the specific artist—even the villagers may not have been able to do that—they had been able to estimate the age and attribute the work to a particular nation or clan. It had been enough to convince the authorities that there was sufficient evidence to support the charges without actually having the items themselves physically present, and they in turn gave permission to return them to the villages.

Dan and Walker had stopped into Ahas'wit to return the two Crooked Beaks of Heaven masks, and had watched them being welcomed home with drums and songs and dancing before they were put back on the walls of Leonard's house. Now Walker carefully lifted Charlie's Thunderbird mask from the bunk where it had been resting, wrapped in blankets and wedged in with pillows, and carried it out to the Zodiac where Dan made a cushion of lifejackets for it to rest on before carefully sliding it under a seat.

"We'll take our time. Don't want to bounce too hard. We have some precious cargo aboard and we're not in any rush."

Walker smiled. "Nice to see you're finally learning patience."

***

They were both quiet as they made their way along the steep shores. The scent of cedar mingled with the salt tang of the ocean, and once in a while there was a flash of silver as a fish leapt out of the water.

"My grandmother came from a village near here." Walker's voice was soft, but it carried above the sound of the motor as the Zodiac nosed its way towards the village.

Dan looked at him in surprise. He had never heard Walker talk about his family before.

"She's long gone now, but she remembered when they took my mother away. She told me about it. She said they came in a boat and she could hear the children screaming. Gran ran along the beach, crying, screaming, calling, trying to reach her daughter. She said she stretched her arms out as wide as she could, hoping to be able to touch her and get her back. Her feet were bare and the rocks were sharp so she kept falling. Cut her hands and knees—she still had the scars—and when she ran out of beach she went into the water, but it was too deep and someone pulled her back so all she could do was stand there and watch her daughter disappear."

It took Dan a long time before he could force words out of a throat closed by emotion. "Did your mother come back?"

"Yeah, but she didn't stay long. She went back to the city. The nuns threw her out of the residential school when she was sixteen. Told her her family didn't want her and dumped her in Edmonton. She married some guy from the same school. Gran said she never met him and my mum was already lost to drugs and alcohol when she came home." He shrugged. "Guess it didn't matter. She'd already lost everything else: her family, her culture, her pride. I guess she stayed just long enough to dump me."

Dan still found it hard to speak. "One of the Stolen Generation," he finally said, closing his eyes against the almost painful surge of sadness. He had lost his own mother

292

when he was young, and that had been hard, but it was nothing like this. This was agony.

"Yeah," Walker said staring out over the water. "One of many."

What did you say to that, Dan asked himself, keeping his eyes fixed on the water ahead. What *could* you say? Sorry?

Time passed. Five minutes. Ten. And still he couldn't speak.

"Kinda puts Samantha Chauvet's problems in a different perspective doesn't it?" Walker's grin was suddenly back. "I'm sure she had a tough time growing up, but I guess that's what money and the easy life does for you. Makes you think you're more important than anyone else."

A sudden surge of anger brought Dan's voice back.

"How the hell can you even put your grandmother and mother in the same sentence as Chauvet and her lot?" he asked. He found Walker's words offensive. It was as if Walker's story had become his. The sorrow and the loss now his own sorrow and loss. "And how can you laugh about it? That has to be the saddest damn story I've ever heard."

Walker laughed. "Ahh, but it has a happy ending. Just look at me!"

Dan couldn't help himself. He had to laugh too, but it was with admiration rather than humour.

"Yeah, right. Just look at you."

***

They arrived at Charlie's village not long after noon. A fishboat and a couple of small powerboats were tied to the float, but everything looked deserted and it wasn't until after they had pulled the Zodiac up onto the shore that two men appeared.

"Walker? Didn't expect to see you back here for a while. Good to see you. You too Mr. . . Detective . . ."

"Just Dan is fine." Dan said, and he smiled and stretched out his hand. "Good to see again too. Any chance Charlie is around? We've got something for him."

***

It was almost dusk by the time they got back to *Dreamspeaker,* the last rays of the sun sliding through the trees and glinting off the waves, turning them into liquid gold. The air was cold and ahead Dan could see a bank of clouds forming in the west. It would be raining again by morning.

"You sure you want to leave tonight?" he asked as he slid Walker's canoe into the water. "You know you're welcome to stay."

"Nah. Thanks anyway, but it's time to get going. Been too long." Walker settled himself in the canoe and released the line. "Thanks for everything."

He lifted a paddle in salute, spun the canoe and headed across the inlet. As if to echo his words, a pod of orcas leapt high out of the ocean beside him, water streaming off their muscular bodies as they arched and twisted in the air, the droplets catching the fading light. Dan watched until it was too dark to see and then went into the wheelhouse and called Claire.

"So all the villages will get their regalia back?" she asked.

"Yes. The Waglisla detachment is handling most of it, but they let me and Walker return the masks from Tsatsquot and Ahas'wit."

"Walker must be happy. Is he there with you now?"

Dan laughed. "No. As soon as we got back here he climbed into his canoe. Last I saw of him was ten minutes ago when he was disappearing down the inlet."

"He left now? But it's dark!" she exclaimed. "Couldn't he have waited until morning?"

"I suggested that, but he refused," Dan answered. "Turns out this is where he grew up, so I guess he's comfortable here. Back where he belongs in a way, although I think Walker belongs anywhere and everywhere on the coast."

"Has he even got anything to eat?"

"Oh yes, he certainly does. The folks in the villages really loaded us up. His canoe is damn near overflowing with salmon and herring roe and kelp and god knows what else. Even got a couple of big chunks of halibut in there. I thought for a while it might sink, but what he couldn't carry he left in my galley. You and I can eat for a week or more on that. And I gave him a can of coffee. Seems he's developed a bit of a coffee habit from being on board with me. I think he'll be fine."

She laughed. "And what about you? When are you going to be back where *you* belong?"

Dan reached for the key. He had been planning on leaving in the morning, but why wait? It was a beautiful night and Claire was waiting for him.

"Should be there by noon tomorrow. I'll be the boat with the fancy carved trail-boards on the bow: Raven on one side and Thunderbird on the other. They're gifts from Charlie's village and they look pretty amazing. *Dreamspeaker* might have to get a new name—although that's supposed to be unlucky, so maybe not."

Twenty minutes later he stowed the anchor and left the cove. A three-quarter moon dodged between the scudding clouds and laid a path of silver along the water to lead him home.

***

ACKNOWLEDGEMENTS

This book could not have been written without the help of some wonderful people. Roberta Rich, Keira Morgan, Emerson Nagel, Sandra Baird, Armando Garcia and Antonio Passarello. Thank you all.

Thanks also to Bruce Manual, Trevor Isaac, Aay Aay Hans, Jags Brown and James Cowpar who, knowingly or unknowingly, have contributed their knowledge to every book in the series.

And finally, a huge thank you to the people of the west coast, and of northern Australia, for your grace and generosity.

About the Author

R.J. McMillen is the author of five books and has published numerous stories, poems, and articles in anthologies, magazines and newspapers.

She was born in England, educated in Australia and has spent more than thirty years sailing the Pacific northwest coast. She splits her time between Canada and Mexico.

Find out more about the Dan Connor mystery series and sign up for my newsletter at:

www.rjmcmillen.com